DATE DUE

Becoming Maren

Other Five Star Titles
by Africa Fine:

Katrina

Becoming Maren

Africa Fine

Five Star • Waterville, Maine

NEWFIELD

First Edition
First Printing: November 2003

Set in 11 pt. Plantin by Myrna S. Raven.

Printed in the United States on permanent paper.

Library of Congress Cataloging-in-Publication Data

Fine, Africa, 1972–
    Becoming Maren / Africa Fine.—1st ed.
        p. cm.
    ISBN 1-59414-081-2 (hc : alk. paper)
    1. Teenage girls—Fiction.   2. Mothers—Death—Fiction.
3. Motherless families—Fiction.   4. Brothers and sisters—
Fiction.   5. Traffic accident victims—Family relationships
—Fiction.   6. Durham (N.C.)—Fiction.   I. Title.
PS3556.I4633B43 2003
    813'.6—dc22   2003049283

For Owen, with love

Chapter 1

When my mother was killed, no one really had much to say to me. If she had died from, say, cancer or in a freak construction accident, well, there's plenty to say about that, although I can imagine none of it is especially comforting. You never know about these things. It's God's will. She'll always be with you in spirit. But when people found out my mother was killed by a drunk driver, a man who'd injured others and himself before only to sit behind the wheel once again the day my mother died, their faces froze into grotesque masks of sympathy while their brains shuffled through the old stock phrases. Death is always "God's will," assuming you believe in God, and it's true, you never can predict when death is on its way. But somehow, when faced with a death like this, these sentiments seemed just a little off, because they didn't address the fact that the whole thing was someone's fault, a direct cause and effect that was neither random nor inevitable. So when I told people how my mother was killed, they just stood there and looked at me, trying not to show their pity.

Add the fact that the man, an engineer from Waukegan, only got a few years in some minimum security prison that looked on television reports like a slightly ominous public school, and the horror of the situation began to repel friends and even family. The injustice of trading a few years of his life for the rest of my mother's was unfathomable, and eventually, the well-wishers and sympathizers stopped calling and visiting, determined to avoid the sadness I could not escape. For a long time afterwards, I told people my mother had died in her sleep of a terrible aneurysm that could not have been predicted. It made them, and me, feel better.

Lots of times, when people tell about a devastating event in their lives, something that took them totally by surprise, they talk about how they'd been having a great day, then boom—everything changed. But that seems too convenient, maybe the result of a mixture of grief, hindsight and fear of the uncontrollable. Because I was having a terrible day when my mother died, and while I can't say that I had a premonition, a strange feeling or a sharp pain at the moment of her death, I was embroiled in the all-consuming trivialities of being fifteen.

She died on Thursday, September 15th, 1994, at 3:30 p.m. She was thirty-seven years old. The police said she died immediately on impact as his car came careening down the wrong side of State Street. Her car erupted in flames, and she must have died within seconds. They seemed to think this precision would be comforting, but the more specifically I thought about her death, the more horrible it seemed.

It was cool and windy in Chicago that day, with more than a hint of the winter that would bring ice and wool. This was my favorite time of year, when the world was a rainbow of russet, gold and magenta. Even though the falling leaves and cooling temperatures meant the end to summer, for me these things signaled a beginning. The beginning of a new school year, the start of a new season—I felt like my opportunities opened in the fall, rather than closed. The coming months seemed filled with promise. This was the time I would find out who I was and start becoming the Maren I was meant to be.

My mother was still asleep when I got up that morning, just like every day, because she didn't have to be at work until later. Just like every day, I rushed into her bedroom to kiss her before I left.

"Sleep tight," I said and pressed my lips against her warm cheek.

"Don't let the bedbugs bite," she mumbled with a sleepy smile. It was our joke, a twist on our bedtime ritual from when I was a little kid. She was promoted to anchor the six o'clock news on my ninth birthday, then moved on to the nation's number three gossip show, *The Daily Dish*, just before I turned twelve. Since then, I'd been the one tucking her in before I left in the morning.

It made me feel grown up in a way, being the one to get the household going, wake up my older brother Ellison, make sure the timer on the coffee pot was set. And when that was all done and I was dressed, I always tiptoed into my mother's room because she looked so peaceful when she was asleep. It was the only time she was ever really still—whether she was working or at home, Mom always operated on 10. Except when she was asleep.

I was walking out of the room when she added something to the routine.

"Maren."

I turned back to look at her. Her eyes were still half-closed and the way her short hair stood up at all angles made me smile.

"Yeah?"

"Good luck honey."

"Thanks, Mom."

They were the last words we said to each other.

I made sure I had a T-shirt, shorts and sneakers in my backpack before I ran out to Ellison's car to catch a ride to school. It was the last day of varsity cheerleading tryouts at

school. Only a couple of sophomores would be let on the
squad, and even though it was supposed to be a big honor
to even be asked back for the final cut, I didn't even really
care about cheerleading. I didn't care about the short, red
and white pleated skirt. I didn't care about riding to games
with the bulky football players and the long, stringy basketball players. What I cared about was the fact that at St.
Francis High School, you had to do *something*. If you didn't
have an extracurricular activity (and most people had more
than one), you got lumped in with this loser group that
didn't even have a name like the Sportos, the Brains or the
Weedies. The losers just dragged around school alone or in
pathetic couples, and I did not want to be one of those
people. So I tried out for cheerleading. It was the one activity where being five feet tall was an advantage.

"You've got cheerleading today," Ellison said, turning
on the heater so that the pine-scented air freshener reeked
like a damp Christmas tree. "You'll never make it."

Usually, Ellison didn't say a word to me during the
thirty-minute drive from our house to school. I generally
spent the time either finishing my geometry homework or
watching the spindly branches of the molting trees and the
growing piles of leaves as they flew by my side of the car.
He was seventeen, a senior, and it interfered with his cool-
guy persona to drag his little sister to school every day.
He'd even tried to convince me to go to public school last
year, and I was ready to do it because he annoyed me as
much as I annoyed him, but Mom said no way.

"It's not cold enough for the heater yet." I flicked off the
heater.

"They'll probably let that Melinda girl in your class on,
and maybe Adrienne. Adding them would make three black
girls on the squad, so what do they need you for?" Ellison

switched the heat back on and slapped my hand away when I made a move toward the dashboard.

"You can be such an asshole sometimes."

We were stopped at a light, and he'd been looking in the mirror while I talked. He took after Mom, and he was the best-looking person in our family. He would have been the best-looking in most families, really. And he knew it. We were getting close to school, so he wanted to make sure his close-cropped curly hair was perfectly tousled, his goatee was smoothed down, his pale, butterscotch-colored skin was free of any bits of toothpaste or breakfast. All the pretty girls in school had tried to befriend me when I was a freshman, figuring they could get to the tall, handsome Ellison through his short, not-so-glamorous sister. They'd all dropped me as soon as they realized that I wouldn't be his pimp even if he would let me.

Once he finished admiring himself, he glanced at me. "I'm just being realistic. You know how St. Francis is. There's not that many of us, and that's how they like it," he said.

I rolled my eyes. "Everyone's not racist, Ellison. How about all those white girls you go out with?"

He laughed. "Sex and cheerleading are two different things."

I made a face. "Gross. I do not want to hear about your sex life."

"Why, 'cause you don't have one?"

"Shut up, Ellison."

We pulled into the school parking lot and he trolled the lanes looking for a spot. "I just don't want you to get your hopes up, that's all. You're not like those cheerleader types."

I glared at him. "What's that supposed to mean? I can

11

do all those routines backwards and forward—I did take gymnastics as a kid, remember?"

He parked and turned off the car. When he looked at me, I thought I saw a hint of real concern in his hazel eyes.

"Look, you'd make a great cheerleader if it was about athleticism or talent. But it's not. It's about wearing makeup and having the right haircut and who you hang out with—stupid shit like that. I've dated some of those girls, so believe me, I know."

I looked down at my backpack. He was right. I never wore makeup, I wore my hair pulled back all the time and my closest friend was Jordan, who was red-haired and pretty but just as desperate to find a place at St. Francis as I was. But this wasn't about my deep-seated love for cheerleading—it was about surviving two more years of high school. I couldn't tell Ellison that, though. He'd never had any trouble navigating the social scene.

"Maren. You're just more down to earth and real than those girls. And being black doesn't help. That's all I'm saying."

I was surprised. This was the nicest thing Ellison had said to me in months. Maybe he was softening up in his old age, I thought.

"Thanks, El."

"For what?"

"Saying that stuff. It was nice."

"Whatever. Get out so I can lock the doors." I shook my head and walked toward the main building while Ellison went to join his friends near the edge of the parking lot.

Jordan and I didn't have any classes together, but we had arranged to meet just before tryouts in the third-floor bathroom at Darien Hall. The school, a campus, really, was pretty nice as schools go. It was spread out over 70 acres, with two gyms, a chapel, all kinds of sports fields and anything else a bunch of rich Catholic kids could want. And the administration at St. Francis worked hard to keep up appearances, so they'd recently started renovating the bathrooms in the older buildings, starting with Marian Hall, the main classroom building. But they hadn't gotten to the basement yet. No one ever went in there because it smelled like mold with an undertone of something slightly fetid, so it was the place Jordan and I met when we needed privacy. I got there first and waited, as usual, because she was always late.

"I brought the makeup, like you asked," Jordan said as she rushed in the door. We'd known each other since fifth grade so she didn't apologize for being late and I didn't get angry about it. She dumped a pile of lipsticks, eyeliners and blushes on the counter.

"Do you think the colors will work? You and I don't exactly have the same skin tone, you know," I said.

Jordan pushed her wire-rimmed glasses up the bridge of her nose. "Ha ha. I brought some that I thought would match your skin color, dork. Try them on."

I just stood there, looking at the pile. All those little vials and sponge-tipped applicators were confusing. My mother was always trying to get me to wear makeup, to shop in stores that reeked of perfume, to be more of a *girl,* but it never felt quite right to me and so I'd avoided these types of feminine rituals altogether.

"What's wrong?"

"I don't really know to put it on."

Jordan smiled, efficiently organizing the makeup into mysterious categories. She took over, prying open my eyelids with her fingers and swiping different lipsticks on my hand until she found one that didn't make her turn up her nose in distaste.

"There," she said finally. "What do you think?"

I turned to the mirror and started. I felt like I was looking at a stranger, an older girl whose dark brown skin didn't shine, whose eyes were wide and ringed with long lashes, whose mouth looked rosy and full.

"You look so good," Jordan laughed. "I can't believe it."

I raised an eyebrow at her. "I know I'm not that glam, but do you have to be so shocked?"

Jordan tossed her shoulder-length red hair back. "I just never knew you were so beautiful, that's all. You're going to knock them out at tryouts."

One of the great things about Jordan was that she always knew the right thing to say. I could feel my shoulders relax, and even though I knew she was exaggerating, it made me feel like I had a chance.

"I just hope it works. I can't work on the school paper like you."

Jordan nodded. "It'll work, don't worry. And you're just a sophomore, so you'll be set for a while."

I took my clothes out of my backpack and started to change. "Ellison thinks they'll cut me."

Jordan frowned. "Ellison's a jerk. Cute, but a jerk."

"He says they won't take me because I'm black, and they already have two black girls. Plus, I'm not into all that girly stuff, like those other cheerleading girls."

"Yeah, I've heard other people say that about you being black. But everyone's not like that."

I bent over to tie my shoes. "That's what I told Ellison."

"He does have a point about your image, though. You're so cute, but you walk around wearing baggy jeans and no

14

makeup. But hey, we're taking care of that part of it," she said, looking me up and down and nodding approvingly at my snug shorts and tank top.

But I felt weird, like I wasn't myself. "I don't want to change who I am because of this. I just don't want to be an outcast, you know?" I looked at my watch. "I better go."

Jordan hugged me and kissed the top of my head while fluffing my ponytail. "Break a leg, kid. And call me tonight to tell me what happened."

I waved and jogged the entire way across the school lawn to the east gym.

Things started to go wrong as soon as I got there. For one thing, practice had already started. I tried to ignore the glares I got from the seniors as I slunk into the gym and sat down on the floor next to the other wannabes who were waiting for their turns.

"I thought practice didn't start until four," I whispered to the girl next to me. She glanced at me like she wished I would disappear, or at least stop talking to her. It was Adrienne, the other sophomore who Ellison thought had a great chance of making the team. He *would* think that—she was the same type as El, tall, slim and fair-skinned, almost white-looking. All the girls he paid any attention to at all fit this bill. I didn't know if anything had gone on between him and Adrienne, but I wouldn't be surprised if it had.

"It started at three," she said in a low voice, looking around to make sure no one saw us talking. She rolled her eyes at me and scooted away as if proximity to me might taint her in some way.

"Shit. Do you think they noticed I wasn't here?"

She sighed heavily and adjusted the straps of her push-up bra, making sure her small breasts were sufficiently perky.

15

"Mary, how should I know if they noticed?" Her tone was patronizing, as if I was a little kid who just didn't get it. I felt my jaw tighten, and I briefly fantasized about how it would feel to punch her right in front of everyone.

"It's Maren," I hissed.

"What?" The other girls waiting for their turn looked over at me, then Adrienne. She shrugged at them and shook her head.

"My name is . . ."

"Whatever." She turned away with a flip of her long, brown hair, slapping me in the face with more than a few strands in the process. I was glaring at her tight-T-shirt-clad back when they called my name. I plastered a grin on my face and pretended like I didn't see Adrienne's smirk or hear the other girls' giggles as I stumbled getting up from the floor.

My first routine, a basketball cheer, got off to a great start. My arm motions were crisp, my voice was clear and loud, my smile was brilliant. I was better than anyone else, better than the other sophomores and juniors who'd tried out. It was the first time I'd ever really been the best at something, and I felt invincible.

But when I got to the second routine I faltered. I couldn't remember the words, so I made them up as I went along, and stuttered when I realized my ad-libs didn't always rhyme. I mixed up the choreography, and a twitch in my knee made me hesitate at the wrong moments. Maybe it was Adrienne's sneering contempt that got me off track, or maybe it was just nerves, but whatever, it guaranteed me a spot in the stands for the first home game. And now I'd have to find some other activity to do at St. Francis to avoid being labeled a loser.

I didn't even wait to see the posted names after practice.

I left the gym early to avoid the other girls and find a ride home.

I was dismayed to see Ellison waiting for me in front of the gym after tryouts. I had assumed he would go home at the normal time. But he was hanging out near the front steps of the gym, straightening his dark blue sweater vest and immaculate jeans while he looked out into the darkening sky.

"So?" he demanded when he saw me.

The worst part about floundering at tryouts was the irony of it all. My ideal extracurricular activity would have been to sit in a dimly-lit room somewhere eating Snickers and writing dark short stories, but there wasn't a Solitary Snickers Fiction Society at St. Francis, so cheerleading had seemed like the least of the remaining evils. Failure hurt, but to be rejected by cheerleaders, of all people, truly stung.

Standing there with Ellison, I tried not to let my disappointment show. He could smell weakness like a batch of warm chocolate chip cookies, and once he sniffed your soft spot, he pounced and devoured. The next thing you knew, you were trying not to crumble right there in front of him.

I considered lying to him, telling him I'd decided he was right, cheerleading was stupid, and I'd decided to forget about tryouts and join the debate club or something. But I knew two things: he'd never believe that I thought he was right about something, and he'd find out tomorrow at school anyway.

I sighed. "I didn't make it."

We walked toward the parking lot. I became increasingly annoyed as I replayed the tryouts in my mind. I should have been nastier to Adrienne. I shouldn't have let her treat me like I was some peon who didn't even register on her social radar. I shouldn't have let her get to me.

17

I was so immersed in my thoughts that I didn't realize that a few minutes went by before Ellison said anything.

"You're better off."

He jerked me out of my reverie, and I could feel my cheeks heating.

"Whatever happened to 'better luck next time, Maren' or 'I'm sorry you didn't make it, Sis?' "

We stopped at his car. He pulled out a pack of Newports and stuck one in his mouth before he pushed the button to unlock the doors. I climbed in.

"Why can't you just be realistic about things for once?" he mumbled, feeling around his seat for a lighter.

"You shouldn't smoke that. Mom is going to flip."

He lit his cigarette. "Cheerleading is dumb. You're smarter than that."

He always acted like he knew everything and I was an idiot. Everything came so easy for him—good grades, friends, clothes, looks. He couldn't see it wasn't so easy for other people. It wasn't so easy for me. I turned and snatched the cigarette out of his mouth and tossed it out the window quickly.

"Hey!" He screeched to a stop at a red light and looked at me. "What's your problem?"

I looked out the window at the trees. It was after five o'clock, and it was already getting dark. In this light, you couldn't see the warm hues of the falling leaves. They looked oily and black, hugging the branches tightly, as if they knew their eventual fall was inevitable.

"Mom doesn't want you to smoke," I said to the window.

He snorted. "Like she would even know. She's never there."

"She works. You know that." I looked at him. His hands

were gripping the steering wheel tightly. I could see his hands trembling with the effort.

"She's always working. Always." He said this through gritted teeth. The traffic signal changed and he didn't move.

In a way, he was right about Mom. When my parents first got divorced, I was six years old, and by that time they'd spent so little time actually living together that it wasn't much of a change when my father moved to North Carolina to be near his family. At first, things were okay with just the three of us—Mom had a job at a cable access station and she was there when we got home from school.

But after she moved up into the local news, then national television, things changed. During the past year, she'd spent most of her time consumed by her work, putting us second, or sometimes third or fourth, depending on what she had going on. We saw her plenty, but seeing her on the big screen TV in our family room didn't count. Even when she wasn't anchoring *The Daily Dish*, she seemed more like an occasional visitor in our house than our mother. Perhaps she'd been slowly easing her way out of our daily lives for years, and her death just made things more permanent. Ellison says he noticed it, and maybe he did—he and Mom always fought about dumb things like curfews and smoking, but what it always came down to was the fact that she wasn't really around to stop him from doing whatever he wanted.

I spent most of my time trying to diffuse the arguments between them, playing the peacemaker for two people who couldn't help but rub each other the wrong way. I loved them both, and I hated when they fought. It made me feel uncertain, like I was standing on a shaky old bridge that was about to break. So I tried and I tried, but I was never able to show them the middle ground between their strong personalities.

"The light's green," I said. We just sat there. There were no cars on the dark street behind us. "She loves us."

He turned and looked at me. "She loves being on TV." He pulled into the intersection and continued home.

I could feel tears welling in my eyes and I turned away from him. I hated him for making things worse than they already were. I tried not to let him hear my crying.

"Hey, look on the bright side—maybe you can try out again next year. Or the year after that. And there's always college." His voice was heavy with sarcasm.

"Fuck you, Ellison." I could feel the tears wetting the front of my jacket but I didn't want to give him the satisfaction of seeing me wipe them. We rode the rest of the way home in silence.

When we pulled up to the house, all the lights were out. It was just about six o'clock, time for Mom's broadcast. I usually got home much earlier, and when our mother wasn't there, which was most of the time, I tried to make us dinner in the kitchen, something quick and filling that we would eat in front of the television. Hamburger Helper was my specialty (I preferred the ground beef versions), but I wasn't that great a cook so sometimes I even messed that up and we ended up ordering pizza or barbecue. Ellison always said we should get a housekeeper, someone who does more than clean each week. We lived in Evanston, where not everyone had a housekeeper but lots of people did. Ellison periodically put on a big push, saying that Mom worked hard to get one of the top-rated entertainment shows in the country, and she shouldn't have to feel bad about hiring help. But Mom refused. She was our mother, she said. We didn't need a replacement to take care of us.

That day, we were home so late that I decided to skip the attempt at culinary greatness.

"Want wings tonight?"

We were walking up the front steps and I couldn't help talking to Ellison, although I could still taste the tears on my lips.

He shrugged and stuck his key in the door.

"I thought you'd whip up us some Tuna Helper or something," he said with mock enthusiasm. I grimaced and made a face at him.

"I don't see you cooking. Ever."

He laughed. "Cooking is woman's work."

I rolled my eyes at his back as he walked through the entryway ahead of me and tossed his coat onto a chair. I stopped and listened to the silent house, a bad feeling growing suddenly in my stomach. We came home to an empty house more often than not, but that day, it didn't feel quite right. Ellison's steps echoed on the plank wood floors as he went from room to room, turning on lamps and flipping light switches. He went into the family room and turned on the television but left the lights off.

"Come on, Mare. Mom's going to be on in a minute."

I walked slowly into the room and sat down next to Ellison on the sofa. He turned up the volume on the big-screen television as *The Daily Dish* jingle should have tinkled though the speakers.

Usually at this time, Mom came on, her eyes perfectly lined in black, her lips perfectly red. She would smile and talk about John Travolta's big comeback movie, the O.J. Simpson trial, Burt Reynolds' money troubles. She usually made playful banter with her co-anchor Jonathan Macy, a fifty-year-old man who died his hair blonde to try to look thirty-five. He came to our mother's Christmas party every year and drank too much eggnog, then went on and on about how my mom was the only person who was allowed to call him "Jon."

But tonight, Mom wasn't there. They were showing a rerun instead. We listened to the opening song, and when the commercial came on I pushed mute and glanced at Ellison, who looked like he was trying to pretend nothing was wrong.

"Where's Mom?" The funny feeling in my stomach just wouldn't go away.

"How should I know?"

"I just have this feeling something's wrong," I insisted.

He laughed. "I knew you'd be sorry for going out for cheerleading, but I figured it would take a while before the regret set in."

I hit him on the shoulder as hard as I could. "El, I'm being serious."

He rubbed his shoulder, his lips curved into this nasty smile that wasn't a smile at all. "Me, too."

I've heard people talk about how things seemed as if they were going in slow motion when they got the bad news. But for me, time sped up until it felt like voices were rushing by me at a nauseating speed. First there was the knock at the door, then the jaundiced brown of the deputy's uniform, then the roughness of his surprisingly nasal voice. He sounded like a kid, and the whole time he was talking all I could think of was that no kid could come to my house and tell me my mother was dead.

I don't remember what Ellison was doing, although I assume it was something more than trying to block out the disconnected voices in his head that babbled on and on about what could not be true. That's what I was doing. The policeman's voice sounded far away, as if he was talking to me from another room, and all I could think about was the fact that I hadn't had the chance to be the daughter she wanted. I hadn't had the chance to say goodbye.

I couldn't stay in that room another moment; it was as if there wasn't enough oxygen in the air. I ran to the downstairs bathroom, sat down on my mother's hand-woven Indian rug, and cried.

I felt as if I had been there for hours, and every time the tears began to dry I started crying all over again. My mother, gone forever.

I needed to feel close to her, if only to make her death feel less real, less permanent. I wanted to think about times when we'd been close, when we'd been like a normal mother and daughter, doing normal things like shopping or watching chick flicks. But there weren't many times like that, not only because Mom worked so hard, but because I hated the mall and romantic comedies depressed me. I knew that my mother had wanted us to share those things, but I felt inadequate around things feminine; I thought I'd never know enough about makeup and clothes and finding Prince Charming. So I had avoided it all, and in some ways, avoided my mother as well.

Sitting there on the bathroom floor, the only good memory that kept returning to my mind was from last Christmas. We always had a tree and gifts, the usual Christmas trappings, but our true holiday tradition was our annual trip. Each year, the three of us made a list of the places we'd like to go on vacation, always warm, of course. Then we put them all in a red felt stocking and Mom would pick. The first year, we went to Jamaica. The second year had been Los Angeles. But last year had been the best vacation yet—Maui.

We arrived at the Hyatt Resort in the morning. None of us felt the effects of jet lag yet, so we went to change for the beach. Ellison and I shared a suite next door to Mom's, and once we were ready, Ellison couldn't wait to see the beach and agreed to meet me and my mother outside. I dug my feet into the thick white carpet and munched on complimentary chocolates while I waited for my mother.

When my mother walked into the suite, I was stunned by how beautiful she was. Usually, she was just Mom, certainly not a typical mother, but Mom all the same. But that day, I saw her as if she were a stranger. She wore an orange sari decorated with large blue and white flowers, the bottom edge of the fabric just scraping the tops of her white sandals. She wore a white halter top and her usual gold jewelry shone at her neck and ears.

But it was something else that struck me, something almost intangible. Maybe it was the way her honey-colored skin glowed, or the way she held her shoulders back, confident in her petite prettiness. Or maybe it was that she simply looked relaxed. And happy. She wasn't running around between assignments, she wasn't thinking about ratings or the latest gossip or making public appearances. She was in Hawaii with her kids, ready to go to the beach. And she was happy.

It was the first time I was aware that my mother didn't always look this way. It was the first time I'd stopped to think about Vanessa Emory the woman, not the mother.

"What?" She looked down at her clothes, picking at imaginary lint. "Is something wrong? Don't I look okay?"

I shook my head. "You look great. Really nice, Mom." I paused, then continued. "I wish I looked like you."

She grabbed my arm and pulled me in front of the

mirror, where she stood next to me. "You do, honey. You do look like me."

But when I looked in the mirror, all I saw was the same plain old Maren. She was gorgeous, the kind of woman who got stares from men of all ages when she walked down the street. No one ever noticed me, and it felt like no one ever would.

"You don't have to say that, Mom. I'm nothing like you."

She smiled gently. "It's true, we're different in a lot of ways. But you're beautiful in your own way. You just haven't figured that out yet."

She hugged me, then went to pick up her beach bag. "Now, let's go find your brother."

It seemed impossible that my mother who had been so happy and vibrant just a short time ago was now dead. It seemed impossible that I would never see her again. It seemed impossible that I would ever stop crying.

Chapter 2

The night they found out their mother was killed, Ellison took it upon himself to talk to the policeman, while Maren watched, looking frightened as he talked with the cop in this calm voice, like it was perfectly normal to be discussing your mother's death on a Thursday night. Yes, he'd go down to the hospital to identify the body. No, he hadn't talked to any other family members. Yes, there was an adult available to stay with them temporarily. The policeman had wanted to argue about who that adult would be, but Ellison refused to give a name, mostly because he didn't have one to give. He stared at the detective's name-tag pointedly, as if he were making a mental note that Mulgatto was not performing to the best of his ability. When Mulgatto tried to insist that they go into state custody that night, since he and Maren were minors, Ellison thought his thin veneer of cool might crack. But he calmly repeated himself, saying that his Aunt Miriam would come as soon as he had a chance to call. Aunt Miriam didn't exist as far as Ellison knew, but he had to think of something so the cop would leave him alone to think. Ellison knew who he should call, of course, but he wasn't ready to dial his father's number. Not quite yet. For some reason the policeman backed off and agreed. Ellison supposed that the cop figured that they'd been through enough, and there was also the way he looked at Ellison, his eyes dripping with pity, that didn't hide the fact that he couldn't stand to be in the room one moment longer than he had to. Funny, this was the policeman's job; Ellison would have thought he'd be used to this type of thing by now. He frowned at Mulgatto's back as he walked out the door, and there was something like rage bubbling just beneath the surface of his calm. He felt like following the cop and ripping at his tan polyester shirt, just to slap that sympathetic look off his face, but Maren's hand on his arm stopped him.

"El."

As he looked at her dark brown eyes, puffed from crying, he wondered if he would ever feel normal again.

"Okay. Okay," Ellison said mechanically as he turned to the kitchen window and watched the cruiser pull away from the curb.

"I need to get out."

Maren frowned. "Now?" She peered outside as if there were dangers lurking among the bushes and trees surrounding the Colonial-style house. "It's getting late."

"I don't want to be alone," she added.

Ellison nodded. "I'm supposed to go to the hospital. To see the body." His voice cracked on the last word. How was it possible that this morning his mother had been "Mom," and tonight she was a "body?"

Maren held out her hand as if to stop him, her eyes telling him that it could wait, wait until tomorrow, or never.

He shook his head. It couldn't wait. If your mother was dead, you had to find out for sure right then. There was no tomorrow until you knew for sure. He picked up a set of keys lying on the breakfast table and walked toward the back door.

"I'm going with you."

He shook his head. "Maren, you shouldn't see something like that."

She frowned. "And you should?"

"I'm older than you."

"She's my mother, too."

He noticed that she used the present tense. Neither of them could think of their mother as part of the past. He looked at her arms, folded tightly across her chest, saw the tear stains on her cheeks and nodded.

"Let's go."

He supposed it was the dishonesty of the family that he had always hated. It looked good on paper—Chicago native and single mother Vanessa Garnett Emory works her way up in the broadcast business. But the press bio skirted a lot of the truth. Like, the fact that his father had moved away when they were just kids and they had only seen him twice in nine years—the last time being five years ago. He wrote letters that Maren cried over and Ellison ignored, talking about his writing and never asking to see his kids. He lived with his mother, Ellison's grandmother, in Durham, and he'd been "working" on the same novel for as long as anyone could remember even though no one had ever seen more than an incomplete chapter. When he allowed himself to think about his father, he considered the novel-in-progress to be a convenient excuse for not getting a real job.

Maybe his father would come up with an excuse not to come live with them, Ellison thought as he drove along Lake Shore Drive looking at the homes of the people richer than his mother, the people she envied and emulated. But then what would they do? Ellison was probably old enough to fall through the cracks, but not Maren. Fifteen years old wasn't quite old enough to be on your own.

He glanced over at her. She was looking out the window, taking slow deep breaths as if she were trying not to cry.

"Are you okay?" he asked.

She rubbed her hands over her face.

"Yeah."

It was a lie, of course, but they had an unspoken agreement to pretend that this was just an ordinary crisis, like not making the cheerleading team or getting grounded for smoking. It was imperative, if they were to get through the next couple of hours, that they not acknowledge the sheer horror of losing their mother.

"What do you think it'll be like?" she asked, still looking out the window.

"What?"

"Seeing mom . . . seeing the body." She choked out these last words, her voice a whisper.

Ellison wished he had insisted that she stay home. She was too fragile for something like this, too young. Just hours ago she'd been crushed over not making some stupid cheerleading squad, and now she expected to go to a morgue to identify her dead mother?

"I'm taking you home," he sighed, slowing the car to turn around.

"No."

"You can't handle this."

She whipped her head around and glared at him.

"Stop treating me like a baby. I'm going to see her." Her voice softened. "I *need* to see her."

Ellison shook his head and made a U-turn, fumbling in his pocket for a cigarette and pushing in the car lighter.

"I said no, Mare."

Her face contorted. "So now you think you can tell me what to do? Who made you the boss?" she screamed, punching him in the shoulders with both hands. He veered off the road and put the car in park.

Grabbing her pummeling hands, he held her small fists to his chest.

"I am in charge, at least for now. It's just us, Mare," he

said quietly, watching her face crumble.

She sagged against him and he hugged her, wiping tears away as fast as they came.

"I'm taking you home. Okay?"

She sniffed and nodded, and he headed back toward their house.

After he dropped off Maren, promising to be home soon, he finally lit his cigarette and took a deep drag. This was what he always did when he needed to think—he went for long drives, chain smoking and blaring old Temptations songs on the CD player. The melancholy of "Just My Imagination" or the anger of "Papa Was a Rolling Stone" were usually just what he needed to leave his problems behind. On this night, he'd left his sister standing in the darkened kitchen, trying to absorb the shock of their mother's death. Ellison had wanted to say something to her, some big-brotherly thing that would make her feel safe and protected. But he didn't have the words to fit this particular occasion, so he just drove, taking the long way to Cook County Hospital to see their mother.

He thought maybe driving around would clear his head, maybe the sweet and salty smell of the lake would make his teeth unclench. He drove recklessly, passing the few other cars on the road and swerving in and out of lanes, daring fate or God or whoever to kill him in the new BMW his mother had bought him only two months ago.

He pulled over onto a side street and turned off his lights, shivering as the October air coursed through the car. He was old enough—in lots of places, being seventeen years old meant being a man, although he didn't feel much like an adult—to know that he had to figure out some way to get through this without breaking down or becoming some stereotypical statistic, one of those people whose entire life becomes a horror story. He thought of Maren standing in the kitchen, looking like a child, and hoped she was old enough to know this, too.

Ellison pushed his seat back a little more and wished he had a joint instead of this stupid pack of Newports. He sighed and lit another from the bud of the first, tossing the old filter into the ashtray and holding the fresh cigarette tightly between his lips while he turned the ignition just long enough to roll up the windows, leaving his open just a crack. It was cold. Ellison closed his eyes and flicked the cigarette out the window, then rolled it up completely. He'd started smoking years ago when his mother anchored a special Channel Six report on the evils of the tobacco industry. Back then, he didn't really like the taste of cigarettes but to stop would have been like admitting she was right about something, and that wasn't fair. It wasn't fair that she got to tell him what to do but she never had to do it in person. It wasn't fair that she was always, always gone, and his sister acted like it was okay, always pointing out the good things their mother did as if they cancelled out the bad. He felt tears seeping out from beneath his lashes and he got angry. It wasn't fair that she was gone and now he couldn't get mad at her anymore. Of course, he knew life wasn't fair— who didn't know that? But knowing didn't make it hurt any less.

Ellison looked at his watch, surprised that two hours had passed. Maren was probably ready to send out a search party. He shook his head, took a deep breath and started the car.

On television, the identifying of a body is always melodramatic and filled with conflict. The loved one who has been so abruptly left behind staggers into the morgue as attendants in bloodied lab coats hustle around matter-of-factly, driving home the utter horror of the situation. There is always music playing, some soft, mournful tune that held all the sadness and loss in its melancholy melody. The right opening song or underscore could make a masterpiece out of the mediocre, his mother had always said. On television, people take one glance at the body and sag back into the arms of some protector, often a friend but sometimes a benevolent police officer or medical professional.

But Ellison's visit to the hospital began with the filling out of what seemed like hundreds of forms. Forms asking about himself, his mother, next of kin. Who counted as next of kin, he wondered as he sat in the dingy waiting room, scratching his pen against the papers trying to fill in as much as he could. His father? Maren? His mother's parents were dead, and she'd been an only child. He decided to put himself down since he was the oldest. Ellison hoped that being the next of kin didn't involve any other responsibility beyond this, because he wasn't sure he could handle anything else.

After he shoved the clipboard back at the receptionist, she glanced at it and did a double take, peering at him as if she were looking for some kind of sign.

"You're Vanessa Emory's son?"

He took a deep breath and willed himself not to get upset.

"Yes."

The receptionist ran her fingers through her short, spiky hair and opened her mouth to say something, but no words escaped.

"I need to see my mother," he said, hoping she would just let it go. He didn't feel like hearing about how she loved *The Daily Dish* and watched it every day, how she'd heard his mother speak at last year's Urban League banquet, how she'd been a fan since Vanessa was the morning weekend anchor on the local station. All he wanted was to do what he had to and leave.

The receptionist nodded as if he had spoken his thoughts aloud. She glanced back at a nearby orderly and mouthed something to him. The orderly nodded and came out to lead Ellison to the morgue.

It never bothered Maren, but he had always hated being recognized as "Vanessa Emory's son." When she had moved from cable access to the local networks, her good looks and intelligent demeanor had made her an instant local celebrity. And when *The Daily Dish* came along, things had only gotten worse. Whenever they went anywhere—even the grocery store—people asked for his mother's autograph and tried to tell her about gossip they'd heard.

A couple of years ago, his mother had latched on to the idea that he and Maren should meet her for lunch so they could spend more time together. She'd ignored him when he said that they could spend more time together if she spent more time at home, and their first lunch outing had been a disaster. Even though it was December and snowing, they had arrived at Marcelli's early, earlier than their mother, at least, although when Ellison checked his watch he noted that she was already 10 minutes late.

The waiters at Marcelli's knew Ellison and Maren—they ate there all the time because it was right downtown near *The Daily Dish* studio. Sitting at the table rearranging his silverware while Maren went to the ladies room, Ellison wondered how many other teenagers met their own mother for lunch because if they didn't, they'd hardly ever see her.

He looked around the restaurant, at the high ceilings and the white tablecloths accented with bouquets of wildflowers and real silverware. They served eggplant parmesan, Ellison's favorite, even though the version they had at Marcelli's was considerably fancier than he preferred. The staff was always courteous, often obsequious. His family never had to pay for their dinner because Vanessa Garnett Emory was the chef's favorite TV personality. Ellison hated Marcelli's.

He looked at his watch again, shaking his head, and when he looked up his mother was standing next to the table.

Actually, he should have known she was in the room, since the gasps and chattering had begun a few seconds before he saw her. This was how it always was with his mother, people fawning all over her while he and Maren sat ignored. In Chicago, she was the second-favorite television personality next to Oprah, and she got a lot of airtime because she did endorsements that afforded her luxuries that her generous anchor's salary did not.

"Hi, honey," his mother said tentatively. It wasn't like her to be timid, and he knew she was more uncomfortable about this than she would let on.

"Maren's in the bathroom."

She looked at him for a moment, then nodded shrugging off her short fur jacket and motioning to the maitre d' who came immediately to take it from her heavily-ringed fingers. When she was on air, she always dressed in the same conservative style as all the rest of the anchors, maybe adding a Hermes scarf or an extra bracelet. But when she wasn't working, she dressed like she was going to a trendy cocktail party—no matter what the time of day. He watched her arrange herself in the booth across from him, adjusting the low neckline of her tight black jersey dress and smoothing down her stylishly short hair. She hadn't always been like this. He had vague memories of her in jeans and a halter-top, when he was nearly a baby and Maren was newborn. He couldn't remember when she'd become this woman with diamond earrings and twice-weekly manicures, but he missed the way things had been when he was a child.

"So," she said finally, watching Ellison's face closely. She was trying to read him, and he didn't want to make it easy on her, so he composed his face into a look of bland in-difference. He looked at her and waited for her to make the next move. She cleared her throat and played with the corner of the menu. He could tell she was rattled by the way she blinked too often and kept brushing at her immaculate sleeve, and he felt bad because seeing her rattled made him feel happy. Or, at least, a little less angry.

She looked toward the bathroom. "Actually, I'm glad Maren's in the bathroom. It gives me a chance to talk to you alone for a minute."

He hated this, the way her words were so stilted, the way he felt compelled to maintain this posture of unconcern so she couldn't see how upset he was by the whole thing. It wasn't the lunch—he wouldn't have minded accommo-dating her schedule if she ever did the same for him and Maren. But she didn't. It was either lunch at Marcelli's or they wouldn't see her at all. He wasn't sure why it had mat-tered so much—he was almost fifteen then, and in a few more years he'd be far away at college, too far away to worry about any of that. But it bothered him all the same.

"Talk about what?" he asked quietly.

His mother sighed. "I just want you to know that I miss you and Maren. I'm just trying to make time for us."

He rolled his eyes. "Most mothers don't have to squeeze

in their kids between work. For normal people, it's the other way around," he'd said.

She sighed and looked at him. "I can't be the perfect 'Stepford Mom' that you want, Ellison."

He frowned. "It's always all about you, isn't it? What about me? What about Maren? She needs a mother, you know."

It was easier for him to talk about Maren than himself.

"Maren has a mother. So do you," she said in a low, angry voice.

"Do we? I hadn't noticed. Tell me more about this 'mother' person," he said sarcastically. "Actually, why don't you wait for Maren? She'll want to hear this." He rose halfway out of his seat, as if to go fetch Maren from the women's bathroom, but just then he saw her walking back toward the table. He slowly sat back in the booth and looked around the restaurant filled with diners in suits, briefcases at their feet.

"Hi Mom," Maren said cheerfully. She noticed their angry expressions and rolled her eyes. "Please tell me you two aren't arguing already."

"We were just talking about how Mom's career is more important to her than us, and how these lunches are supposed to make it all better," he spat.

"Shut up, El." Maren had always hated it when they argued, although Ellison figured she should have been used to it.

"You're not being fair, you know," Vanessa said.

He wanted to laugh but couldn't. "I'm not fair? Is it too much to ask that you act like our mother?"

"Please stop it," Maren interjected.

Their mother leaned forward, angry. "I'm working to feed you, to keep you in that fancy private school, to buy your expensive clothes, to keep you living in Evanston with a big yard, a view and a maid. That's why I have to work hard. So don't make it seem like I don't love you," she'd hissed, quietly enough so none of the hovering waiters could hear.

He closed his eyes for a long moment then watched her face. "Don't try and make this my fault. Our fault."

She sighed and looked away. "It might be hard for you to understand, but—"

"I said stop it!"

They looked at Maren, surprised. She rarely raised her voice, and now she looked startled at hearing herself get angry.

"You two are always arguing, over the same stupid things. Can't we just have a nice lunch together?"

Their mother held up her hands. "Okay, okay. Let's just order." She glanced at her watch. "I have to be back at the studio soon."

Ellison let out a sarcastic chuckle. "Oh, sorry to take up your time."

Maren looked like she was ready to cry. "El . . ."

"Ellison, that's not what I meant."

"Yeah, well, whatever. I'm not going to be responsible for any important gossip being late," he spat as he got up and walked out of the restaurant. It was snowing when he left Marcelli's, with fat, wet flakes covering his hair and coat as he walked to the corner, where he just managed to catch a bus. The methodical sound of the windshield wipers punctuated the relief he felt to be out of the restaurant, away from his mother, who couldn't say anything that would make him understand the way she acted.

He thought about that day as he followed the orderly

down the long, shabby corridor to an unmarked door, duplicate forms clutched in his hand. The orderly nodded to Ellison and walked quickly away. He wondered if there shouldn't be some kind of official guy or someone to supervise him, but then he figured there wasn't much to risk in the morgue.

He pushed the door open slowly, and he walked up to a small desk where a sleepy-looking clerk with long dreads sat. He handed the clerk his forms.

"I need to see Vanessa Emory. The body, I mean. I need to identify the body."

He felt nervous, but the clerk just walked over to a metal table and paused.

"You ready?"

Ellison nodded. He didn't trust his voice not to crack. The clerk nodded back, and pulled back the sheet.

He stood completely still, looking at his mother. He wished he hadn't come. He couldn't look farther than her face, which was surprisingly untouched. Besides the fact that her hair was mussed, she looked normal. Except her ears. She always wore earrings, whether she was sitting around the house, going to the grocery store or even sleeping. Today, she'd worn her favorite pearls. But one of them was gone, and somehow, it made her look naked. While the clerk wasn't looking, Ellison reached over and took out the remaining pearl. He knew she wouldn't have wanted to be seen with just one earring.

This was real. This wasn't just a cop standing in his kitchen saying the words. This wasn't some terrible joke being played on his family. It was true, and no one could take it back. Their mother was dead. He and Maren were alone. He felt his chest tighten, and he signaled to the clerk that he was ready to go.

★ ★ ★ ★ ★

He wasn't sure what time it was when Maren tiptoed into his bedroom. He was lying quietly, concentrating on the way the moonlight peeked through his blinds to create monstrous shadows on the walls. As she drew closer and leaned over to look at him, he smelled the peach-scented shampoo she always used.

"Are you asleep?" she whispered, standing next to his bed. Their breathing was the only sound in the room. Ellison thought about pretending to be asleep until she slipped away as stealthily as she'd arrived.

"Nope." He scooted over in bed and made room for her. She rustled the bed covers around, making a barrier between them before she assumed a position identical to his on the other side of the queen-sized bed. He smiled slightly. When they were small, they would always build this boundary between them with the explicit agreement that the pile of sheets and comforter was impenetrable, no matter what. He couldn't remember why they'd started this, probably just normal childhood modesty. It had been a long time since they had been in the same bed, years and years, he would bet, but the old tradition had stuck. Ellison figured they'd be visiting each other in nursing homes and hospitals when they were eighty, asking for extra blankets to get the barrier just right.

"You okay?" he asked. Maren sniffed, and he wondered why he had bothered to ask.

"How was the hospital?" He took his time answering, trying to decide whether to tell her the truth.

"It was . . . weird." Weird was the most benign way he could think of to describe the unnatural stillness, the way he felt like he was seven instead of seventeen when he stood in that ice-cold room full of death.

39

He knew she hated his tendency toward sullen under-statement when he was put on the spot, but she sounded grateful this time.

"What do you think is going to happen now?"

He could see the top of her head over the barrier, but he couldn't see her eyes.

"Our father will come here, I guess. Or something."

"Our father? Something like what?" She was still whispering, even though they were alone in the house. There was fear and longing in her voice, as if she were wishing that he would say something to make it all better.

He sighed again and took a deep breath. He wasn't going to let himself cry. Ellison couldn't remember the last time he cried—not when their father moved away, not when he broke his arm in the seventh grade, not earlier that night when they'd found out about their mother. And this was no time to start. Maren needed him to be strong, and he was going to do it. So there would be no crying.

"Remember when we were little, how Mom used to buy us penny candy and let us eat it all at once?" She blurted this out, startling him. Her voice quavered.

He sat up and looked over at her. "Maren, don't."

"What?"

But he knew she understood. Don't start talking about the things Mom used to do. Don't start thinking of her as a memory. Not yet.

"I'm scared," Maren said, and now she was crying. He sniffed and figured it would be okay, just this once, to breech the barrier. He burrowed under the bedding until he found her hand. Ellison held it as her tears became full-fledged sobs, and he didn't pull away. He just rubbed her hand until her breath gradually became more regular.

He didn't remember falling asleep, but when he woke up the sun was streaming through his bedroom windows. Maren was curled up a ball facing him, a frown on her sleeping face, and their hands were still clasped.

Chapter 3

It was dark when we left Evanston for good, ten days after our mother died. I didn't even have a chance to really say goodbye. My loose ends were tied up. Or at least, as much as I could manage. I'd written Jordan a letter, too chicken to face her, too afraid to see the look of pity on her face. I'd packed all my most important stuff. I'd made sure my room contained no remnants of me—I couldn't bear the thought of some person I didn't even know finding an old photo or a note I'd written, catching a glimpse inside my soul.

But I thought there should be some kind of moment of official farewell, something where I stood on our front lawn and took one last look at the house, but the white stucco exterior was barely distinguishable in the pre-dawn blackness. I shut the front door behind me and breathed deeply, trying to imprint the smell of home on my memory forever.

Ellison had his car packed full of as much stuff as we could carry, and he was anxious to get on the road. He wasn't anxious to move, or to see our father, but once something was decided, he liked to get on with it, get where he was going as quickly and effortlessly as possible. I liked to linger and putter, sometimes wasting entire days on nothing much at all, and Ellison hated that. His days seemed to be divided into discrete sections, the logic of which only he was privy to. He never offered to explain what was so wrong with, say, eating waffles for dinner or taking a nap during the day, but over the years it became clear to me that in his mind, there were specifically acceptable times for eating breakfast foods and sleeping, and he couldn't tolerate any deviation.

He was the reason we'd gotten up at three in the morning to take quick showers, gather up the few things we hadn't packed in the week since the funeral, and get on I-90 East in his BMW. I might have liked to sleep in, get breakfast somewhere and then start driving, but Ellison wouldn't even entertain the notion. He was also the one who decided that we wouldn't stop, we'd just drive as many hours as necessary to make sure we made it to Durham in the allotted 14 hours the auto club claimed was needed for the trip.

I was in charge of the map, and I put it carefully in the glove compartment to make sure I knew where it was when Ellison started barking requests for navigation later in the trip. We hadn't taken many road trips together, and from what I saw when we did, that was a good thing. There was something about being virtually trapped in a small metal box with wheels that brought out the worst in my brother.

We were silent as he drove quickly through the residential streets of our neighborhood. The streetlights were still glowing, although it was almost five o'clock, and I could see the first hints of daylight in the sky. During the afternoon, our streets were usually filled with kids playing games of hide-and-seek and the sound of basketballs slapping against the concrete on backyard courts. But at this time of day, it was like a ghost town, the minivans and luxury sedans standing hulking and silent in driveways. Would anyone miss us? This wasn't the kind of neighborhood where people baked cookies for each other and gossiped on the sidewalks while holding the hands of squirming children, but we were all cordial and friendly in a distant way. The television trucks and reporters had finally stopped coming around—after a week, they were on to bigger and better things, like what shoes O.J. was wearing the night of the murder—so maybe our neighbors would forget us in the same way. Maybe, someday, something they saw on television might remind them of a semi-famous neighbor they once had, but they wouldn't remember the names, and the dates would be fuzzy. Ellison and I would become a footnote in their lives and it would almost be as if we were never here.

I adjusted myself against the seat, playing with the knobs on the side until I was comfortably reclined, and checked my backpack to make sure I had my snacks, magazines and books ready, as well as headphones in case Ellison turned the radio to one of those hip hop stations he liked and I hated. I made sure my magazines were facing away from the front of the backpack so Ellison couldn't see that I was reading *Cosmopolitan* and *Seventeen*. I wasn't in the mood to hear him tell me how stupid those magazines were or ask me why I even bothered to read them since I hated hair rollers and makeup so much. I could never tell him that it wasn't the beauty tips I was looking for in those magazines. I was looking for the answers, the keys to being a woman that seemed to be second-nature to everyone but me.

As we neared the interstate, Ellison spoke, his voice still raspy with fatigue. I looked at the dark circles under his eyes, and wondered why he was so stubborn as to deny even himself a good night's sleep for the sake of travel time to a place where neither of us really wanted to go.

"Want to get something to eat before we get on the highway?"

I shook my head. "I can wait."

As we pulled onto the road to our new life, I leaned my head back against the seat and closed my eyes as Ellison turned on the CD player to let the Beastie Boys shout "Sure Shot" in our ears.

★ ★ ★ ★ ★

I didn't go to my mother's funeral. It was incongruously sunny that Wednesday, and warm, the kind of day that invites you to sit outside on the back porch with a book, your bare feet cool against the soft grass. We had a flash of Indian summer that day, driving the temperature up near sixty-five and reminding me of Frisbee games and pool parties. It even smelled of summer, the air crisp and clean with no hint of moisture or chill. Even though the leaves had already begun to change, what I noticed the day of my mother's funeral was the green that was still left in the grass and on the trees that were late to shed their healthy foliage.

I had a dress all picked out, this long black thing that fit me loosely. Ellison said I was drowning in the dress, but that was what I liked about it. I could hide in that dress, and it flowed so voluminously around me that it was like I almost wasn't there. That's all I wanted on the day of the funeral—to pretend I wasn't there.

I even walked out to the limousine with Ellison. It was parked in our long, cobblestone driveway as if it was prom night, and Ellison and I were just a couple of normal teens preparing to negotiate the sexual politics and temptations of an all-night party. Except there were no adults taking pictures with pocket-sized Nikons and telling us how grown-up we looked. The only adult we really had at this point was our father, but we hadn't talked to him at all. Ellison hadn't even called him as far as I knew.

He climbed into the limousine first and looked up at me, waiting.

"Are you getting in?" He wore a dark blue suit, specially purchased for the occasion, and he adjusted his gray striped necktie as he talked. "Come on, Maren."

It was the first time in a long time that I'd seen him

dressed up. He liked to wear jeans and sweaters, although they had to be Ralph Lauren or Tommy Hilfiger. In my mind, the way he meticulously ironed every pair of pants he owned and threw out shirts with just a hint of wear indicated an unnatural attention to appearances, but for some reason he drew the line at wearing a tie and jacket.

I stepped back from the car quickly. If I got in, it would be admitting that it was over, that the part of my life that included a mother was as dead as her body lying in the coffin Ellison picked out. I couldn't do it. I couldn't go to the funeral and cry at all the right times and pretend that some stupid minister from a church we never went to could understand how much my mother meant to me.

And there would be lots of people there, hundreds or maybe thousands of my mother's fans standing around the church, grieving a stranger they thought they knew. I didn't think I could watch that without getting angry, without feeling like their tears should be mine, without hating them for being able to go back to their nice little lives after the funeral. After the initial shock wore off, they'd probably forget about her. She'd be a faint memory, a woman whose face and voice would be eclipsed by the new co-anchor of *The Daily Dish*.

"No." I looked away from Ellison as I said it, hoping that he would understand. I hated the idea of funerals, people staring at a coffin filled with what was left of the person you loved. Funerals always seemed to me like the honoring of a body, not a person, not a life. I didn't want to think of my mother buried deep underneath the grass in some well-manicured cemetery. I wanted to think of her alive and smiling, talking about the latest Hollywood release or putting on her makeup in front of her vanity table.

"What do you mean, 'no?' " Ellison frowned. "How can

you skip your own mother's funeral?"

I cleared my throat, but my voice still came out raspy and weak. "I don't want to go."

"Maren, people will wonder where you are."

Why can't you just let it go? I thought silently.

"So? Let them wonder."

He moved closer to the door, as if he planned to grab me by the arm and pull me into the long black car. I flinched involuntarily and he rolled his eyes.

"Fine." He slammed the limousine door and the driver pulled away from the curb. I sighed and walked slowly back into the house.

As I changed out of my funeral dress into jeans and a sweatshirt, I realized that this was the first time I'd been alone in the house in the three days since my mother died. Ellison and I hadn't been to school at all, operating according to some silent pact that we'd go back once we figured out what we were going to do. The problem was, no one seemed to be doing much figuring. *The Daily Dish* executive producers arranged the funeral (and proceeded to brag about it on air, I found out later), so weren't forced to do much of anything.

We'd spent the time sleeping late and avoiding certain television programs, lest we see one of the many special news stories devoted to false sympathy for our mother. Generally, the syndicated stations were safe as long as you turned quickly to HBO or Showtime when it was time for the news or *Entertainment Tonight*.

I thought we should call our father right away, to tell him the news if he hadn't already heard, but Ellison refused.

"Not yet," he told me. I'd barged into his room late one night, and he pretended that I'd awakened him from a deep sleep. His curly hair was fuzzy and mussed, but I knew he was faking. He couldn't sleep anymore than I could and had probably messed up his hair tossing and turning.

"When, then?"

He turned over in bed so his back was to me.

"I'm trying to sleep Maren."

I felt panic rising in my throat. Who was going to take care of us?

"Please, El, I'm scared."

He ignored me, waiting until I left the room. It was hard to know what my brother was thinking most of the time, but I thought I understood. Calling our father was just another one of those steps that meant this was all real. Every time we did something we wouldn't normally do, it brought home the point that our mother was gone.

Ellison wouldn't talk about it, so I tried not to think about my father as I wasted the hours in a haze of reruns and Lifetime women-in-peril movies.

But it turned out not to matter whether Ellison called our father. He called us the morning of the funeral. Neither of us was too anxious to get dressed, so we were sitting in the family room, still wearing our pajamas and watching Kiana Tom lift five-pound barbells and talk about nutrition on ESPN 2. I answered the phone, but I stiffened when I heard the "hello" in my ear.

It had been many months since I heard my father's voice, but I knew it was him right away. His voice had always been smooth and bottomless, and he talked slowly, drawing out his words as if he'd carefully chosen each one. Panic rose in my chest and as I sat up on the edge of the leather sofa, I struggled to find the right words. What could I say? Hi, Dad, how's it going? The word "dad" felt unnatural on my tongue. "Dad" was someone who lived with you, who knew that you hated spinach, who read over your English homework to make sure you didn't leave any participles dangling. "Dad" wasn't a near-stranger who lived thousands of miles away and never visited. But I didn't know what else to call him. "Father" seemed too melodramatic, and he definitely wasn't a "Pop" or a "Pa."

I'd been so young when things began to go wrong for my parents, and they were separated a number of times before my father left for good, so my memories of him were hazy and unformed. I remembered him as sweet and mild-mannered, always willing to make mud pies with me or do the voice of Skipper while we played with Barbies. But those types of memories didn't tell me what kind of person he was now; they didn't tell me how he would react to the news that he was now our only parent.

Instead of speaking, I handed the phone to Ellison, who had just come into the room. I couldn't tell much from his side of the conversation. Two "yes's", a "maybe" and an "I don't know." There was also a non-committal grunt, none of which told me anything, so I tried to read the expression on his face as he listened to our father. But he was inscrutable as ever, besides the usual anger that was never too far from the surface with my brother.

He hung up and took a deep breath, staring at the television.

"So?" I couldn't wait for him to end the silence.

He looked at me. "He wants us to come down there."

I nibbled on my fingernails, a bad habit that I hadn't had since I was ten.

"And then he'll come here to live with us?"

Ellison shook his head slowly. "Nope. He wants us to come to Durham. To live."

I frowned. "But what about all our stuff? What about

Mom's stuff? Her will and all that?"

Ellison looked at me briefly, then looked past me out the big picture window. "I don't know, Mare. I guess he'll handle it all."

We sat for a while without talking, listening to the tinny aerobics music coming from the TV. Finally, I said what was on both of our minds.

"Do we have to? He hasn't even been around for years. Why should we have to go with him?"

Ellison looked at me, his eyebrows raised. "You were the one bugging me to call him."

I shrugged. "I thought he might come here. Or something. I don't know what I thought."

I didn't feel the relief I'd expected to feel once we talked to our father. I thought he'd have some kind of answer, some way to help our lives get back to normal. But normal did not include me living in Durham, North Carolina. I'd never been there, but our father used to talk about it once in a while, how small it was and how everyone in certain neighborhoods knew just about everyone else. It seemed claustrophobic and outmoded. Even the name sounded ugly to me.

Ellison picked up the remote and turned off the television. "I've thought about it, and I don't think we have much choice."

I fought the tears that came to my eyes at the sound of the words. It hadn't even occurred to me that we would have to move. But then again, I never thought our mother would die, either.

"So what do we do now?" It was funny how just a few days ago, Ellison was the last person I'd look to for advice. We hardly even talked unless it was to insult or hassle each other.

He closed his eyes for a long moment. "I guess we pack."

All this was on my mind the day after the funeral. Ellison had gone for another one of his long drives. He'd been in a funk ever since our father called, and I knew enough to leave him alone when he got that permanent crease in his forehead. When things went wrong, Ellison became more withdrawn than ever. He tended to be a loner anyway, but he clammed up completely when he was troubled. I was different—I liked to talk about things and ask questions, questions that never had easy answers. It drove Ellison insane.

We hadn't packed much. I had made a half-hearted gesture toward the project by throwing out some old magazines, but that was about it. It was still sinking in, the reality of moving to live with our father, but I couldn't drive off to think things out like Ellison, so I figured I'd start packing.

Without much thought, I walked straight to the door of my mother's room. It was closed and no one had been in there since she died. I opened the door and peeked in. The room was a mess, with clothes strewn around the floor and colored plastic hangers hanging from anything that could serve as a hook. My mother cared a lot about what people thought, how things looked on the surface, but she was a slob when no one but us was around. She must have left that last morning in a hurry, just like every morning; there never seemed to be quite enough time for her to fix her hair, makeup and pick out the right outfit before she was late for taping. Once, I asked her why she put on makeup, when the makeup artists at the studio redid everything anyway, and she just looked at me like I was crazy if I didn't understand that she couldn't possibly allow people to see her naked face.

At first it was disconcerting to see her room like that, as if she was coming back any minute. But it was comforting, too, and I walked in, making sure not to step on any of her expensive outfits. I don't know why it mattered whether I wrinkled a silk blouse or creased a wool blazer, but it did. I smoothed the fitted sheet down on the unmade bed and sat on the edge, looking around. I considered getting some boxes, folding her clothes, but the thought of moving her things made me tired. After a few minutes I laid my head down on her pillow and I could still smell the scent of Chanel No. 5 that she'd worn ever since I could remember.

I didn't realize I'd fallen asleep until the bedside table phone sounded like an alarm in my ear. I couldn't think of anyone I wanted to talk to, so I let the machine pick up, and I walked out to the hall to listen to the machine pick up the long dial tone, then cut off. I was still bleary-eyed from the nap as I walked back into my mother's room. It had been one of those uncomfortable rests where you fall asleep thinking, and the thoughts continue to tumble through your head even when sleep is supposed to shut off your mind. I sat on the bed, but the room began to feel unbearably small and stuffy, and suddenly I felt like an intruder. I stood up and looked at my watch. Ellison was probably on his way home by now, so I hurried out of my mother's room and shut the door behind me. I felt as if I had been doing something wrong by being in her room. He would think I was wallowing in sadness, making things worse by being so close to her things. I went into my room and closed the door. Maybe he'd think I was sleeping or crying and leave me alone.

I needed a distraction, so I looked on my shelves for a book to read, something that would take me to another world and help me forget about everything for a few hours.

I squatted down to look at the bottom shelf, where I kept all my old favorites and the ones I was embarrassed to let people see. I knew the difference between good writing and bad, but sometimes there was nothing that could make me feel better than the saccharine language and improbable horrors of *Flowers in the Attic, or the overblown trashiness of Hollywood Wives.* I kept these paperbacks almost hidden, squashed between *To Kill a Mockingbird* and old family photo albums that I'd once stopped my mother from throwing out. It was one of these albums that I pulled out and took over to the bed, where I flopped down on my stomach and opened it.

It was filled with dog-eared pictures of my parents from the 1970s and 80s. They looked so young in the first pictures, my mother with a short reddish Afro and my father wearing a baseball cap pulled down low over his eyes. She looked happy and lighthearted, as if she didn't have any worries or fears. Then there was a picture of some kind of a dance, maybe the prom, where my mother wore a gauzy sky-blue dress and clung to his arm like she was afraid to let go. They were both very thin, and for the first time I could see that Ellison looked a lot like our father, too.

The next series of photos showed my mother with an increasingly large belly. She must have been about eight months pregnant when she took the one near Lake Michigan, her now-straightened hair flowing behind her, her egg-shaped body outlined by her thin, sleeveless dress. I guessed my father took the picture, because she was standing alone, looking out at the lake, her eyebrows knit together. I wondered what she was thinking—was she sad? Wondering about the baby she was carrying? Did she suspect the baby would turn out to be Ellison, difficult and stubborn?

There was a separate album of Ellison's baby pictures

sitting on the shelf in our dining room, but I guess they'd given up on that idea by the time I came along, because my baby photos were right there in the main family album. There was my father holding me, wearing a Members Only jacket and tight jeans, his hair already beginning to thin even though he couldn't have been more than 23 or 24 years old.

There was a family portrait that I didn't remember taking. I must have been about three years old, and I had this brilliant smile on my face while the rest of the family looked as if they were about to have root canals. Smoothing my fingers over the photo's matte surface, I could see how similar they all looked. The same exasperated set to their lips, the same pale skin and wavy hair. I was like a brown-skinned stranger they were using as a prop in the portrait. I brought the photo closer to my eyes. Who did I resemble? Not my mother and Ellison, with their vanilla skin and gentle beauty. Not my father, with his slightly goofy good looks and heavy eyebrows. Why was I smiling while they looked so unhappy?

"Maren?" Ellison called in through the closed door. I shut the album quickly and slid it under my bed. He would think it was stupid to be looking at all those old photos. Or he might try to take the album for himself. I didn't want to take the chance.

"It's open."

He came in and sat on the edge of my bed. "Why are you up so late?"

I shrugged. "Why are you up?"

He smiled slightly. "I've got to keep tabs on my little sister." He knew I hated it when he called me "little," even though it was true both chronologically and physically.

"I'm not that little." I scooted back on the bed until my

back was against the headboard. He glanced at me appraisingly.

"You're pretty little."

"What do you want?"

He sighed and played with the hem of the shorts he always wore to bed. "I just want to make sure you understand about North Carolina."

"What do you mean?"

"When we go stay with Dad. Just don't expect a miracle."

I frowned. I had my doubts, but I couldn't let them have free reign. I had to believe it was all going to work out, somehow. "What's that supposed to mean? He called, he wants us there, that should count for something, right?"

"He's been gone for a long time, Maren. Just don't think he's going to be Super Dad all of the sudden."

It reminded me of the whole cheerleading thing. But Ellison had been wrong—it wasn't racism that kept me off the team, it was me. Maybe this time I wouldn't mess up. I looked at him.

"Don't you ever think anything's going to turn out right?"

He got up abruptly and walked to the door. "Sleep well. I'll see you in the morning."

"El?"

"Goodnight, Maren."

I must have slept for hours, through a couple of states and several CD changes. Now, Janet Jackson was cooing through the speakers, offering herself anytime and anyplace to some fictional man. I sat up and looked out the window, trying to figure out where we were from the green signs.

"We're almost to Toledo," Ellison said.

"Already?"

"You slept for three hours." He was great at making me feel guilty for nothing in particular.

"Sorry."

He grunted. His eyes looked more alert, the shadows less pronounced now that the sun was high in the sky. I grabbed the map from the glove compartment to chart our progress. Once we got to Cleveland, we'd turn due south on I-77, which would take us through the rest of Ohio, West Virginia and a tiny bit of Virginia before we got to North Carolina. At Winston-Salem, which sounded like a brand of cigarettes to me, we'd turn east again onto I-85 and head straight into Durham.

Seeing the route on the colored map made it seem more real, and yet, it was still just a place on the map, without a real face or identity for me.

"What do you think it'll be like?" I asked.

He shrugged and looked back toward the window. "I'm looking forward to seeing the mountains. I've never really seen a mountain before."

He was being deliberately obtuse, but I refused to give up. "What about our grandmother?"

He smiled. "You think our grandmother lives in the mountains?"

I shoved him and leaned back in my seat. "I'm being serious."

I tried to make it seem like I didn't really care that much, like I was just passing the time by talking about it all. But I was scared, and in a way, I wanted my brother to admit he was scared, too.

"She's probably some little old lady with lint-covered mints in her pockets and a dry cough. Don't worry so much," he said, flashing me his Mr. Charming smile.

I nodded and relaxed my shoulders. "Yeah, you're probably right." I wished I could just let it go, but I couldn't.

"What about Dad? What do you think he'll look like?"

Ellison rolled his eyes. "Hopefully better than he used to."

Disapproving of my father's appearance had always been one of the few areas where Mom and Ellison were in total agreement.

"Remember, whenever I had friends over after school, he was always there, barefoot, wearing some random T-shirt and ripped jeans," Ellison groused.

I thought for a moment. "I can remember him telling jokes that you hated."

Ellison smiled slightly. "He loved riddles, especially the ones that rhymed."

I laughed. "I liked them."

He rolled his eyes. "Not to mention that his hair was always messy and he wore those dorky glasses. God, what a slob."

"You're so worried about how people look. You're a snob," I laughed.

Ellison shrugged. "Is it too much to ask that the man clean himself up once in a while?"

I shook my head. I would never convince Ellison that everyone shouldn't spend hours ironing their designer clothes to starched perfection.

My stomach growled. "Let's get something to eat."

Ellison glanced at the clock. "It's a little after nine now. Can you wait until Cleveland?"

I shrugged and rummaged through my backpack to find a Butterfinger. I loved the way the fake orange stuff splintered in my mouth. When I was a kid, I used to eat Butterfingers and pretend I was eating wood. Tearing off the wrapper, I crunched into the bar, oblivious to anything but the sweet peanut flavor. I liked to eat chocolate in tiny bites and chew slowly to make it last.

Ellison cleared his throat. "Where'd you get a Butterfinger?"

I rolled my eyes at him. "I brought snacks. Of course."

"Of course."

I took another bite and watched the wheat-color fields fly by our window.

He cleared his throat again, and when I looked at him, his eyes were widened in his best imitation of a six-year-old boy. "Can I have a bite?"

I wanted to tell him to forget it, since he was the one who wanted to wait to eat until Cleveland, but he pooched out his bottom lip and looked so pitiful that I relented. I handed him the bar and he proceeded to put as much of the candy in his mouth as possible, leaving me the last inch.

He grinned at me, his cheeks full, with orange crumbs in his goatee, and I had to smile.

"You asshole," I said, trying to pretend I was mad. But when he said "Thwonk Woo," and spit Butterfinger all over the windshield, I couldn't help laughing.

The first thing I noticed about Durham was the smell. The sickly sweet fragrance wafted in through the open windows of the car as Ellison followed the careful directions our father had provided, navigating the winding streets that didn't seem to follow any sort of pattern. The smell was heaviest as we passed cavernous warehouses on their way through what passed for downtown in Durham, and the odor was familiar, although I was fairly certain I'd never smelled this particular scent before.

"Tobacco," Ellison said.

"What?"

"The smell. Tobacco."

I nodded and smiled slightly. That was why it smelled so familiar, and yet not.

"He used to talk about how tobacco was manufactured in Durham for years and years," Ellison said. "Even though the warehouses are now stores, you can still smell it."

"You remember that?" I said.

Ellison shrugged. The smell was much thicker and more oppressive than the smoke that wafted from the end of my brother's cigarettes; it was as if someone had crushed thousands of cigarettes and pushed them into my face.

"It makes me crave a Newport," Ellison said.

"Please—the smoke bothers me. Plus, smoking is gross."

He smiled. "I know, I know. I'll quit—just for you."

I looked at him, knowing he wouldn't admit the real reason he hadn't smoked during our whole trip. Mom was gone—he didn't need to use cigarettes as another way to aggravate her anymore.

Ellison slowed the car as we passed part of Duke's campus. I strained to look at the Gothic buildings surrounded by happy-looking young people with backpacks full of books.

"Must be nice," Ellison grumbled.

"What?"

"Being in college, only worrying about the next chemistry exam and keg parties."

I nodded. Not so long ago, he had been just like those young students, with classes, girls and parties among his chief concerns, and not necessarily in that order. But now we were here in Durham, far away from the "L" and deep dish pizza and the comforts of home. All of that was gone. We had left behind our lives like an old rattlesnake skin, emerging as different people in a different town, starting all over again. And who was I outside of my old skin? We wouldn't be going to a St. Francis, with its sprawling grounds and pampered students. There wasn't any lake in Durham, no water at all unless you counted pools and bathtubs. I knew money wasn't the most important thing, but it made a difference. And it was more than the money anyway—it was what it signified. No mother, no stability, no familiarity. None of the things that were truly important.

There was hardly anyone walking around the streets in Durham; it was late, almost nine o'clock. Those who were out walked slowly, ambling about as if they were headed no where in particular, and I was struck by how different their bodies seemed from the people I was used to seeing in Chicago. Their limbs had a fluid quality, their joints loose and loping, and their movement was unlike the straight, quick walk of Chicagoans, who tended to hurry as if whomever they were meeting might not be there when they arrived. At a stoplight, I watched as two people, a man and a woman, passed each other on the sidewalk, exchanging brief pleasantries before continuing on their way. They didn't know each other, that much was clear, but I was struck by the fact that they spoke, said hi and smiled. In Chicago, people didn't talk to each other randomly on the street. The stark difference made me uncomfortable.

"Are you going to sit here forever?" I grouched from the passenger seat. I was tired, and it was late. Ellison was stalling, trying to put off the inevitable.

"Sorry."

As we wove through the residential streets, the houses grew shabbier, their front porches sagging, the paint peeling. Many of the wood-frame homes were large but di-lapidated, the kind of places listed in real estate listings under "Has Potential," which really means "Money Pit with Dirt Lawn and Leaky Basement." I hated the sinking feeling in my stomach as I read from the directions and Ellison said we were almost there. I wished I didn't care what kind of house I lived in, but I did.

"This neighborhood is kind of grubby," Ellison said.

"Yeah."

We pulled up to a two-story house that had at one time been painted cream but had now darkened with dirt and time to a brownish-gray. There was a set of concrete stairs leading up to the front porch, where an empty lawn chair sat next to the screen door. The grass was browning but neatly cut, and he could hear what sounded like a large dog barking somewhere nearby. Ellison pulled up to the curb and turned off the car. We sat there, looking at the homes surrounding our grandmother's house, which were in varying stages of disrepair.

I sighed. "So this is it."

I wondered if he felt as out-of-place in this world as I did.

"Let's go in," I added.

He nodded. "Just give me a minute."

I put my hand over his, noticing how tightly he clenched the steering wheel. He let go of the wheel but held my hand as we walked toward our future.

Chapter 4

Ellison heard his father's voice through the open door of the house. The words were indistinct and mumbled, but the tone was familiar. Deep and booming with bass notes, there was a drawling rhythm to the words that hinted at the Southern roots. It was the kind of voice that comforted even when the words were mundane. It was the voice of a protector, a provider.

"He's singing," Maren whispered. Ellison tried to make out the melody of the song—maybe a hymn? Something that rang from within his deepest memories. They hadn't spent much time in church. Their mother was raised Catholic but evolved into an agnostic and their father was raised a Southern Baptist, so there wasn't much middle ground. But there had been a couple of times, when he and Maren were really small, when they'd all gone to church together, and Ellison held his father's hand while they sat in hard wooden pews. During those times, Ellison had felt the closest to his father, his mother, even Maren. During those times, he was at peace.

Ellison breathed deeply and thought about his father. It seemed important to collect himself before going to the door, to be calm and sharp, prepared for anything. Maren was wrong, he thought. He did have hopes that things would turn out okay, that his father would somehow be different, more reliable, a constant in their lives again. But he kept his hopes small and hidden, unavailable for dashing. That was the difference between him and Maren, he thought—she let herself get hurt over and over again, while Ellison's shield of detached disdain protected him. But now that their mother was gone, there was no room for Maren's softness, her willingness to give away her emotions as if they had no value. He would have to help her grow up, he thought, help her develop a toughness that would protect her when things went wrong. It was a heavy burden, and Ellison wished it were not sitting squarely on his shoulders.

He looked out the car window, past the houses to the sky. It was overcast and dark, and there was a fierce wind scattering leaves around the yard like scraps of discarded paper, although it was many degrees warmer here than in Illinois. At home, this would have been a perfect day to go to the lake, Ellison thought. He didn't like the lake during the summer when it was crowded and hot. This was his favorite time of year to sit under a tree near the water and listen to the waves fight each other for position, watching the way the dark sky met the edge of the lake like old friends greeting.

Watching the fat clouds move through the dusky skies, he tried to remember important things about his father. What kinds of books did he read? Did he like basketball? Had he loved Ellison's mother? How had he acted with Maren? Had they been close? Ellison was old enough to remember these things about his father but couldn't. The years had erased whatever memories he'd once had.

He closed his eyes and concentrated, but all he could remember was the sound of his father's electric toothbrush whirring in the mornings and at night, and the way he liked his toast what Ellison considered burnt, although his father called it "well-done."

He turned to Maren, who was staring at him, worried. She looked like she was waiting for him to say something helpful and comforting. He didn't know what that something might be.

"Let's go."

They got out of the car and walked up the sidewalk to the front stairs. He put his hand on her shoulder.

"Hey, Mare?"

She turned and looked at him.

"It's going to be okay. No matter what happens with Dad, we're going to be okay." He watched her eyes tear, and she looked down.

"What if he hates us? What if we hate him?" she whispered.

He moved closer and put his arm around her and kissed her forehead, ignoring the surprised look on her face.

As they walked up the stairs, the words to the baritone song became clearer as they slowly approached the front door.

> "What child is this, who, laid to rest
> "On Mary's lap, is sleeping . . ."

Ellison knocked on the aluminum screen door, wincing a little at the loud, tinny sound. He felt Maren edge closer to him so that their arms and shoulders were touching. The singing inside stopped, and he heard the sound of bare feet slapping against the wood floor.

He wasn't sure what he expected when his father appeared in the doorway. It was hard to set expectations for someone you hadn't seen in so long. But still, he felt unnerved by the fact that his father looked the same as he had when Ellison and Maren were kids. He had a little less hair and a little more belly, but other than that, he was the same—right down to the beard, the bare feet and the frayed khaki pants.

Calvin held open the door and waved them in with a smile on his face that was a little too perfect for Ellison's tastes. They stepped in, looking around the surprisingly large living room. There wasn't much furniture, just a tan sofa and loveseat covered with a rose design, a glass-topped coffee table and an antique maple china cabinet. The rest of the wall space was taken up by rows of bookshelves filled with paperbacks and hardcovers that weren't arranged in any particular order.

With Maren still glued to his side, Ellison felt flustered, although he was determined not to show it.

"You made it. Look at you. You're both so grown-up. Your grandmother's on a church trip, she'll be back tomorrow," Calvin babbled nervously. Ellison was glad he wasn't the only one who was uneasy. He noticed that his father was holding a spatula in his hand, and he sniffed the air to try to place the fragrance of whatever was cooking in the kitchen. Something fried, he thought. Maybe chicken.

"Christmas carols?" Ellison said. It was the first thing that popped out of his mouth, and he was instantly sorry for it. "Hi," he added and looked at Maren, who frowned at him before echoing his greeting. She wanted him to be nice, to get things started on the right foot. He wanted that too, if not for himself then for her.

Their father's smile widened slightly. " 'What Child is This' has always been one of my favorite songs."

Me too, Ellison thought. They all stood there as if they were waiting for someone else to come in and show them all how to move, where to sit, what to say. He wondered at this formality. It was like they were three strangers who just happened to be meeting for a late dinner. But then his father walked closer and hugged Maren tightly, then moved toward Ellison, who backed away a step. Calvin nodded and settled for quickly patting Ellison's shoulder.

Calvin ran his hands over the top of his head. "I'm glad to see you. It's been so long." He clamped his mouth shut, and Ellison watched him as he seemed to search for that welcoming smile to gloss over his words. Ellison could see how much his father regretted bringing up the fact that they hadn't seen each other in years. It made them all think about how they had only talked on the phone occasionally, strained conversations where nothing important was said.

"Are you hungry? I'm making dinner."

"Sure," Maren piped in. Ellison frowned. He hated the way Maren was always so quick to pretend that everything was alright. If it were up to her, their father would just step back into their lives with no explanation, no hesitation. But burned toast and a smile wasn't going to be enough for Ellison.

But he stopped himself from challenging his father's pleasantries, the unconvincing smile, the false cheer. He was suspicious, but right then, he decided to make an effort for Maren's sake, even though it bothered him that his father hadn't even mentioned their mother, not since they'd talked on the phone that first time. It was like he thought he could smile and pretend like this was a normal family gathering, not a hasty reunion thrown together by death.

And then, it was like he read Ellison's mind.

"I'm sorry about your mother. So sorry."

Now, Calvin's face was shaped into a mask of sympathy with just the right amount of sorrow. But somehow, Ellison wasn't convinced, and it took every inch of his will not to say so.

"I don't want to talk about this right now. Can't we just have dinner?" Maren said.

Ellison glared at her. "It's the only thing that got us together in five years—how can we not talk about it?" The mention of his mother opened the floodgates.

Maren narrowed her eyes. "You're such a jerk."

"You're such a baby."

Calvin held up a hand to stop them. "Please. Let's just eat first." His calm voice annoyed Ellison.

"We don't need you to cook for us. We've been fine without you," he snapped.

"El, I'm hungry," Maren pleaded, turning to their father. "I'll have something to eat."

But both of them ignored her. They stared into each other's eyes, and although Ellison expected Calvin to back down out of guilt or sympathy, he didn't.

"Ellison, why didn't you call me? You know I could have helped with the arrangements or something."

"I don't *know* anything about you."

An injured look fleeted across his face before it was replaced with a mild anger. "I'm your father."

"Some father."

"God, Ellison. Why are you always like this?" Maren groaned.

"Like what? Honest? Is that a bad thing?"

At some point, he and Calvin had walked closer to each other so they were standing face to face. Ellison could see the hairs in his father's beard quivering, his hands clenched at his sides.

"Forget it." Ellison made a move to leave the house, immediately realizing that storming out wasn't going to work the same way it had back in Evanston. For one thing, he didn't know where he was going. But his father stepped into his path. He hated the way his father's eyebrows were knitted together, resented the fact that Calvin had suddenly been granted some authority over their lives. Ellison hated that he was scared of what would happen next.

"Sit down." His father pointed toward the flowered

sofa. Ellison's gaze followed the unfamiliar finger and he opened his mouth to object.

"Now," his father added severely. Ellison walked over to the couch and sat.

"Maren, you sit too, okay?"

Ellison stared at the wall, focusing on a large, black and white photograph of a stern-faced woman and a tiny, pale baby, and he noted that Maren was asked to sit, not ordered.

She shrugged. "Sure. I'm not the one with an attitude problem."

Ellison snorted. "Yeah, whatever, cheerleader."

"Asshole."

"Bit—"

"Ellison. You will not call your sister out of her name. Just sit there and shut up for a second."

Ellison wiped his hand over his face. He hadn't meant to call Maren a bitch, not really. But it was like she wanted to provoke him, make a bad situation even worse. He stole a glance at her and was slightly surprised at the venom in her glare.

Their father cleared his throat and looked at Maren for a long beat, then Ellison. "Look, I know this is a bad situation. But we're family." He paused for a moment. "I'm going to give you a chance to relax for a minute, and whenever you're ready, come in to the kitchen and we'll eat." He walked out of the room.

His father didn't say it, but Ellison finished the thought in his mind. He's all we have left. That's what he means. And it's true. He sighed and looked at Maren.

"I'm sorry. You're not a bitch."

She smiled a little. " 'Don't you call your sister out of her name,' " she said in a quiet, deep voice, mimicking their father. Ellison couldn't help but laugh, and after a while, Maren joined him.

Dinner was quiet, with their father trying to make stilted conversation and Ellison making sure his mouth was full of food at all times. He couldn't think of a way to beg out of dinner without making things even more uncomfortable than they were, and in any case, he was hungry. While they ate fried chicken, mashed potatoes and a slimy okra dish that Ellison shoved to one side of his plate uneaten, he quietly tried to size up his father, tried to read his eyes to see how he really felt about Ellison and Maren dropping into his life from nowhere.

Well, he had some idea about the kind of man his father was, Ellison thought as he scooped more potatoes from the serving dish. He was the kind of man who would move a thousand miles away from his kids and visit only a couple of times before letting five years go by with just phone calls and birthday cards. But did that mean he was a bad person? Ellison thought about how he and his mother had argued all the time, how he'd judged her time and again. And now she was gone. Ellison wasn't sure he should come to any conclusions about his father. Not yet.

When they'd finished eating and Maren couldn't control her yawns, Ellison excused himself to what was suddenly his room, and Maren followed him. When they stopped in front of the scratched door of the room Maren would occupy, he looked into her sleepy eyes.

"Goodnight, Mare."

She took a deep breath. "If I get scared . . ."

"You know where to find me," he said, squeezing her hand before turning into his room.

He laid down on a twin bed that was lumpy and soft, lis-

tening to the unfamiliar sounds of the neighborhood outside his open window, and allowed himself to think about
his mother. He suspected that in the coming days, there
would be a lot of practical things to worry about, and there
wouldn't be a chance to think much about her. But he
didn't want her to become distant from him, detached because she wasn't a part of his new life. If he thought about
her while he lived in this new place, she would stay a part of
his life, a part of his heart.

What he thought about was the last time he'd spoken to
her, the last words they'd said before she was snatched
away. It wasn't much, because she'd still been lying in bed
when he peeked into her room to say goodbye while Maren
waited for him in the car. He didn't usually go into her
room in the mornings—that was Maren's thing—but for
some reason, that day he'd gently opened her door and
stepped inside. She was lying curled in a ball, her back to
the door.

"Mom," he whispered. "Are you asleep?"

She turned over languidly and smiled. "Nope, Maren
was in here. Woke me up a little."

He shifted his weight from foot to foot, feeling uncertain. He was never sure what to say to her, always wanting
to have a conversation that didn't involve accusations and
anger but powerless to make it happen.

"I'm glad you came in. I wanted to talk to you," she
said. "About Maren."

"What about her?"

His mother had sat up, her silk nightgown slipping off
her shoulder, embarrassing him. He couldn't see anything,
just the bare skin of her shoulder, but it was more than
enough to make him feel like he'd done something wrong.
He looked away quickly.

"You know she's trying out for cheerleading."

He shrugged, keeping his eyes focused on the window. "So?"

"Just watch out for her, okay? I know how those high school girls can be."

Ellison looked back at her, surprised. "Maren can take care of herself."

She smiled, and Ellison was struck by how beautiful she was, even in the morning with no makeup or expensive clothing. "Please? For me?"

He nodded. "I gotta go." As he ran down the steps two at a time, he'd realized that was the most pleasant conversation they'd had in weeks.

It was these last moments together that he wanted to imprint on his mind as he spent his first night in Durham. It hadn't always been bad between them, he thought. Not always. He put his hands behind his head and drifted off into an exhausted sleep, dreaming of the smell of his mother's perfume.

Chapter 5

My grandmother hated me. Or maybe hate is too strong a word. Disdain, dislike, disgust—any of the "D" words would help describe the curl of her lip when she looked at me.

The morning after we arrived in Durham, Ellison and I woke up early, nearly bumping into each other in the hall as we both made a beeline for the small bathroom we would share. Our father was still asleep.

Ellison yawned and made a sweeping motion toward the bathroom. "After you," he whispered.

The house was nearly silent; the only sounds were the soft pat of our feet and the ticking of the grandfather clock in the dining room. The house was two stories, but compact, and as I gently shut the bathroom door behind me, it seemed as if every noise I made echoed though the walls. I turned the water on low, not much more than a trickle, and splashed my face.

Ellison was leaning against the wall when I came out, his eyes closed. He barely opened them to shuffle into the bathroom.

I went to my room and opened the blinds. It was sunny and blue, not a cloud in the sky. I could hear kids shouting to each other, running to catch honking school buses and giggling. Some of them wore plaid uniform skirts or neckties, and it reminded me that I hadn't been to school in weeks. St. Francis seemed a million miles away, and it was hard to believe that Jordan and everybody else were going on as if nothing had changed.

This was something that I thought about a lot, the fact

that so many people led simultaneous lives without ever being aware of each other. I had been so absorbed in my own life back in Evanston that I never thought about the types of experiences people were having in other places. But since my mother died, I was hyperaware of each experience; each new situation was magnified in importance and impact. The weather, a look from Ellison, my grandmother's feelings toward me—all these things meant more to me without Mom.

"How'd you sleep?" Ellison was standing in the doorway, watching me.

"Barely." I looked around the room. The walls were white and there was nothing on them—not a family photo, not a cheap print, nothing. The squeaky twin bed occupied one corner of the room, a rag rug lay on the floor and a battered oak dresser was shoved against a wall. The room looked deserted, as if someone had hastily removed all signs of him or herself just moments before I arrived. I felt like an interloper, as if I didn't belong here. Or was it more that I wasn't expected to stay long, so no effort needed to be made to make me feel at home?

Ellison nodded and sat on the bed, which whined in reply. "My room's not exactly great, either."

I sat next to him. "So, what do you think of Dad?" I was anxious to hear Ellison's opinion before I formed mine. I didn't trust my own instincts.

"He looks the same as always."

I frowned. "I'm not talking about how he looks."

"What, then?" He leaned back on the bed, scrunching up my pillow under his head. He closed his eyes.

"You know what I mean. Do you think he really wants us here? Do you think we can be a family?"

He raised himself halfway, leaning on his elbows and

squinting up at me. "If he really wanted us here, he could have called us three months ago. Or five years ago."

My chest tightened. This was the answer I expected, not the one I wanted. "But maybe he didn't ask because he knew we'd say no."

He sighed. "Maybe." Then, as if something had been decided, he sat up next to me and put his arm around me. "Mare, let's try to make the best of it, okay? No more deep questions—let's just get through it."

I was surprised. Ellison wasn't the type to make the best of things. But then, a lot of things had changed over the last few weeks. I was happy to have a better relationship with Ellison but I wished it hadn't come at such a steep price.

I reached over to hug him, but he moved quickly and shoved me facedown, tickling me until I begged him to stop, which he did only after I declared him king of the world.

I lay on my back, catching my breath between leftover giggles, and Ellison smiled down at me.

"Hungry? I think I saw some cereal downstairs." He held out his hand to help me up, but I looked at it warily.

"Come on—I'm not going to tickle you again."

I narrowed my eyes. "I don't believe you."

He stopped smiling. "Trust me," he said, wiggling his fingers. I looked at him for another moment then grabbed his hand. He pulled me to my feet and we went downstairs.

We made ourselves comfortable in the living room, turning the television down low and trying not to slurp the milk and cereal from our spoons. Ellison managed to balance the remote control, his spoon and the bowl all at once while he flipped through the channels.

"Want to watch?" he mumbled through a mouthful of cereal.

"Ricki? What time is it?"

"Eleven."

"Dad sleeps late, huh?"

He shrugged and took another bite. "Is that a yes or a no to Ricki?"

"Yes."

Finished eating, I set my bowl on the coffee table and put my feet up beside it. I mashed one of the throw pillows behind my head, and Ellison did the same.

"How much do you want to bet the blonde guy has a same-sex crush?" Ellison said.

"No bet. Look at him."

"Remember the one about paternity tests? 'You my baby daddy!' "

"The *one?* Isn't that the topic of Jerry, like, every other day?"

Our laughter was cut off by the slamming of the front door. Loud, heavy footsteps echoed, and our grandmother appeared in the doorway. She was tall and full-bodied, her breasts and hips jutting out from her torso. Her face had an angular shape with sharp cheekbones and a square jaw. Her skin was pale and smooth, and despite the severe frown and the tensed lips, she looked much younger than I expected. Grandma Esther wore a dark green wool suit with black velvet buttons on the jacket and a wide brimmed hat to match. Even so, she looked almost exactly like our father.

Ellison and I sat frozen as if we had been caught in the act, although we didn't know Grandma Esther well enough to realize what, exactly, we were guilty of. There was a long moment where no one said a word and the only sound in the room was the hooting of Ricki's audience.

Our grandmother walked resolutely to the television and turned it off with an emphatic click. She stood in front of the box, and I thought, now we're watching the Esther Emory Show.

"Well," she said. "You made it." She glanced disapprovingly at my feet, and I snatched them off the table and stood, nearly getting tangled with Ellison as he did the same.

I braced myself for a lecture, and as her eyes took me in slowly, I could feel the disapproval coming at me in waves. But Grandma Esther didn't say anything about the bowls of cereal, the loud television or my feet on her coffee table.

She just frowned at me and turned to Ellison. "You are the spitting image of your father. Come give Grandma a hug."

I felt as if I'd been left out of something, something important. This wasn't the welcome I'd expected, and it was even less satisfying because my brother seemed exempt from her cool gaze. His feet on the table couldn't have been any less offensive than mine, and yet, it was me she seemed to blame.

After hugging Ellison while I stood uncomfortably near the couch, she motioned to me. "You too, sugar. You know you're supposed to greet family with a hug."

I walked over and she embraced me briefly, patting me on the back like I was a friendly acquaintance from church rather than her granddaughter. Even though she smiled at me before rustling into her bedroom with her overnight bag, there was something off about the whole thing. She didn't care for me, and I got the feeling she'd felt that way before she walked in the door. And I had no idea why.

We hadn't seen Grandma Esther since we were little kids, and even then, she was a rare presence, someone referred to occasionally but seldom seen. When I was in kindergarten we used to make cards for our families, and any occasion would do. Mother's Day, Valentine's Day, Halloween, even St. Patrick's Day—we always made craft projects out of colored construction paper and thick rubber cement. The other kids had many relatives to choose from, cousins, aunts, grandparents. But all I had was Mom, Dad and Ellison, and El was never interested in the cards I made.

So I pestered my mother. "Don't I have any cousins?" I asked on the Thanksgiving day when I was five years old. I was sitting at the kitchen table coloring my turkey-shaped place mats. It was still early, but my mother was already up mixing batter for cakes and cornbread stuffing for the turkey. She was standing at the sink rinsing celery, her back to me.

"Not really, sweetie. I don't have any brothers or sisters, but your father has a younger brother. In North Carolina."

"Can I send him a place mat?"

She sighed and turned to me, drying her hands on a paper towel. She wore her hair short and natural then, and she looked very thin in her red and white apron. "I don't think it's a good idea."

"How about a granny?"

"My mother went to heaven. Remember I told you that? And your father's mother, well . . ."

I waited patiently. Arts and crafts were big business in kindergarten and I needed to expand my market. I was willing to wait to learn about other family members who needed turkey placemats and pictures of crooked Christmas trees.

But Mom just walked over to the cabinets, where she took out a bowl and began snapping green beans into it. Finally, she said, "Esther isn't the kind of granny who likes arts and crafts."

Even at age five, I knew that there were things my mother wasn't telling me, that the words she did say were a code for something more.

"Doesn't everybody like arts and crafts?" I couldn't imagine that someone, particularly a granny, wouldn't like something that I made. My mother kept every school project I ever did, including the lumpy yellow ashtray I made in ceramics. I was still young enough to think everyone would love me like my mother.

She looked at me, her lips held tightly together. "No hon. Not everyone." Then she shook her head and smiled. "But I love your artwork. Will you make me a special place mat for dinner tonight?"

I nodded and bent over my coloring, but I never forgot that feeling that there was much more my mom wasn't saying.

My earliest memory of Grandma Esther was during that same year, before I turned six and just before my father left for good. She came to Chicago in January. Mom was away on an assignment, and Dad said Grandma Esther was coming to help him take care of us.

The day she arrived was frigid. I'd had my first trip to the beauty salon a few days before, and I'd been sleeping with my forehead on my arm so I wouldn't mess up the pretty curls. I didn't want to wear a hat, but Dad said it was too cold and pulled the hat firmly around my ears. I pouted in my room until Ellison came to the door and called me a stupid crybaby.

Once we piled into our old brown Impala to pick Grandma Esther up from the Greyhound station, my spirits were up. Dad had let me ride in the front seat even though it was supposed to be Ellison's turn, and I took every opportunity to look back at him smugly from my perch up front. More importantly, I was looking forward to finally having what all of my friends had: a granny.

I had seen grannies on television and on the street. They had gray hair and wore knitted shawls, and they always seemed to have some sort of treat—candy, usually. I was hoping my granny wouldn't be any different.

But when we arrived at the bus station, the woman our father waved to frantically, then hugged, wasn't like any granny I'd ever seen. She didn't have gray hair, and she was wearing a cream-colored pantsuit instead of a shawl. There was sharpness to her eyes, and when she looked at us, I knew she didn't have any Butterfingers stashed in her purse.

My father was all smiles as he dragged Ellison and I over to her. Ellison was still angry over getting the backseat and punched me in the shoulder when Dad wasn't looking.

"Kids, say hi to your grandmother," he said, coaxing Ellison forward.

"Oh, Calvin, he looks just like you! You used to do the same thing when you got mad." She smiled at Ellison's frown and patted him on the head.

"And this must be Maren." She looked at me without smiling, and it made me nervous. The grannies on television always smiled, especially when they saw their little granddaughters with curled hair. My shoulder still hurt from where Ellison punched me, but I wanted to be nice. It seemed important to get off on the right foot with your one and only grandmother.

"Hi Granny," I said in my most proper voice. She frowned, and I scooted closer to my father's side, grasping his hand tightly.

"Granny?" She looked at Dad. "Who told them to call me Granny?"

Dad cleared his throat. "She thinks all grandmothers are called Granny."

Grandma Esther rolled her eyes and bent down so that her face was inches from mine. I could see the faint outline of a mustache over her lip and I smelled something bitter on her breath.

"You're to call me Grandma Esther. Not granny, grammy or anything else. Grandma Esther," she breathed.

I looked up at my father and burst into tears, making Ellison laugh. My father sighed.

"Mama, please . . ."

Grandma Esther shook her head. "She needs to learn to respect her elders," she said loudly.

Dad grabbed Ellison's hand and shook him to make him stop laughing. "Let's go."

I spent the rest of the weekend avoiding Grandma Esther as much as possible, keeping quiet when I had to be around her so she wouldn't look at me with those mean, narrowed eyes. She fawned over Ellison, reading Hardy Boys mysteries with him and laughing at his stupid jokes. She didn't seem the least bit concerned that I wasn't around, and I watched them from my hiding places with growing envy. Ellison hadn't even cared that she was coming. He didn't care about having a granny. But I did, and it turned out she didn't like me.

On her last night at our apartment, I waited up past my bedtime to talk to my father. I wanted to ask him what I'd done wrong, why Grandma Esther didn't like me. When I heard him washing the dishes, I sneaked out of my room. But as I approached the kitchen, her voice rang out.

"The least she could have done was be here when I visited," she said.

"She had an assignment. She's trying to build a career in

journalism. She can't just turn down assignments," Dad said.

"A woman shouldn't let a job come before family," Grandma Esther grumbled.

My father was quiet for a long time. Finally, he said, "Mama, Vanessa has invited you to visit a million times and you never came. Then you picked this weekend, when I told you she had to go to Milwaukee."

"Oh, so it's my fault? I couldn't miss church next week. I told you that."

"What about the week after that?"

I heard the sound of a chair being pushed back from the table.

"Calvin, you didn't used to talk to me like this. You used to be a good boy. Until you married her."

"She has a name, Mother. Vanessa."

"I know her name, believe me. I also know she's a spoiled girl who only thinks of herself. And she's raising that girl to be just like her." Grandma Esther's voice raised, and I could hear her walking toward the door where I was standing. I quickly hid behind a tall rubber plant.

"Maren is my child, too. And she's not spoiled!" My father called after Grandma Esther as she stormed out of the room. She walked right past me, and I held my breath so she wouldn't know I was there.

But none of that really explained why she hated me now, I thought as I sat on the squeaky bed unpacking one of my suitcases. Why blame me for some problem she had with my mother? Why blame me and not Ellison? I hated to admit it to myself, but I had been hoping that my grandmother might be someone I could talk to, someone who would understand the girl stuff that frustrated Ellison. But so far, she didn't seem interested in being that person for me. I couldn't imagine us even getting past the reprimands and stares to have a normal conversation.

Grandma Esther had said she was tired after her trip and needed a nap, and Ellison had retreated into his room before I had a chance to talk to him about her. So I sat there unfolding sweaters, trying to think of a reason why Grandma Esther didn't open her arms to me like she did with Ellison. Maybe I reminded her of my mother, but even that was hard to believe, since my mother was beautiful and glamorous and I'd always been plain and quiet. Still, it was no reason to dislike a person you hardly knew—especially if that person was your granddaughter.

I was lost in thought so I didn't hear the door open.

"Hey."

I whirled around, startled. A guy stood at the entrance to my room, filling the doorway and then some. He must have been 6'3" or 6'4", his hands stuffed into the pockets of his baggy, faded jeans. He had curly black hair that must have been quite long when it was set free, but I couldn't tell for sure because it was twisted into baby dreads all over his head.

He had the darkest skin I had ever seen. Deeper than the darkest chocolate, his skin was ebony, emphasizing his intense brown eyes. He wasn't smiling, but I could see in his eyes that he wasn't far from it, as if he'd enjoyed surprising me. His shoulders were broad underneath his gray Carolina sweatshirt, and when he did finally smile, I realized he was beautiful.

"Hey," I croaked, clearing my throat.

"Can I come in?"

I nodded. At first I'd thought he was young, maybe Ellison's age, but his voice had the deep, self-assured tones of someone older. I wondered who he was and why he was in my room. Some family friend? As he stepped closer, he looked familiar, as if he resembled someone I'd seen on television or in the movies.

He sat next to me on the bed, still smiling.

I cleared my throat again. "Umm. I don't want to be rude, but who are you and why are you in my room?" He was sitting close enough so that I could smell his cologne, a sweet, clean smell that reminded me of springtime. His eyes never left my face, and I felt uncomfortably warm.

"Wait a minute, I should be asking you that question. This is my room," he laughed.

I stared at him. "What?"

"Don't look so nervous." He leaned even closer, so our shoulders were touching side to side. "I don't bite."

My cheeks flushed, and I scooted back an inch. He flustered me, and I wasn't sure why.

He raised his eyebrows. "Too close?"

I looked away toward the window. I could hear an old car chugging by on the street. "Yeah, too close for someone who hasn't even told me his name or who he is," I said, still looking away.

He stood up, and I turned back to him. He looked down at me with that almost-smiling look again. "You're right. I shouldn't have messed with you like that. I'm Chris."

I stood up, but he still towered over me. "I'm Maren." I stuck out my hand. He took it and held it still, a disconcerting move.

"I know," he said cryptically.

His hand felt warm against mine, and slightly rough. I felt odd, standing there holding hands with a stranger, but I liked the way his skin felt against mine.

"How do you know my name? And you still haven't told

83

me who you are, other than your name."

He shrugged and opened his mouth to speak, but Ellison walked into the room before Chris could get the words out. Ellison stood near us, looking from our still-clasped hands to my face, frowning.

"Mare?"

I snatched my hand away from Chris's and took a deep breath. For the second time that day, I felt like I'd been caught doing something wrong. First Grandma Esther, now Ellison. But at least Ellison's disapproval was born of concern. I wasn't sure what Grandma Esther's motivation was.

"Hey, El. This is Chris, and he was just about to tell me what he's doing in my room."

Ellison made a face at me, then looked at Chris.

"This is my room," Chris repeated.

Ellison and I just looked at him, waiting for him to continue. He looked as though he might wait us out, then thought better of it.

"I'm Chris Emory. Your dad's brother. I was living here with Mama while I went to school, but when you guys came, well, I had to find other arrangements."

He was my uncle. Our father had never really talked much about his only brother, who was actually just his half-brother, since they didn't have the same father. Chris was much younger than Dad, so they didn't really have a close relationship when we were kids. But now that I knew who he was, I could see the resemblance. My father was fair-skinned, true, but they were both tall and lanky, with that curly black hair and intense brown eyes.

Ellison looked relieved, and they started making small talk like I wasn't even there. I sat back down on the bed and listened. Chris was older than I'd thought, twenty-one years old. He went to North Carolina Central University, a school I'd never heard of before.

Watching him joke with Ellison, I noticed that even his smile was familiar. He smiled just like Dad, just like Ellison.

Suddenly, Chris looked at his watch. "Damn, I'm late for class." He looked at Ellison and they clasped hands warmly. "It'll be good to have another young guy in the house, you know what I mean?"

Ellison nodded as if he knew exactly what he meant. Then Chris turned to me. "Hey, Maren, see you later, right?" he said as if we'd made arrangements to see each other.

I nodded and smiled. "Why, are you coming to take your room back?"

He laughed and walked to the door. "Nah. I don't mind sharing," he said over his shoulder.

After Chris was gone, Ellison looked at me. "Are you okay?"

I ran my hands through my hair. "Why? What do you mean?" I was nervous for some reason. I hadn't done anything wrong, I was sure of it, and yet, I felt guilty.

Ellison narrowed his eyes. "I didn't know what was going on. I came in here, you were holding hands with some strange guy."

I rolled my eyes. "We weren't holding hands. We were shaking hands," I said.

"I didn't see any shaking. Just holding."

I laughed. "What, you think I was holding hands with my own uncle, like we're dating or something?"

He shrugged. "Whatever." He plopped down on the bed next to me.

I changed the subject. "So what was all that with Grandma Esther?"

Ellison laid back and closed his eyes. "She was pissed because we had our feet all over her coffee table. I can't blame her. I would have been mad, too."

I lay down next to him, leaning on one elbow. "Yeah, but she was way more pissed at me than you."

"Why would she be?"

I sighed. "I don't know. That's why I'm bringing it up."

He turned to look at me. "Mare, don't look for things to worry about, okay? It was just an awkward situation, that's all. Don't read more into it than it is."

I nodded silently. I decided not to tell him about my memories of the time she'd come to visit in Chicago. He'd think I was being melodramatic or imagining things.

Just then, our father called to us from downstairs. "Kids, come down here for a minute."

Ellison and I looked at each other. There was something surreal about being called "kids" by a father we hardly knew. I could tell Ellison wanted to say something, make a snide remark. But he held his tongue. It was all part of Making the Best of Things.

He stood up and walked to the doorway. "Coming?"

I nodded. "Yep. In a minute." He loped off and I lay there for another minute, looking at the stucco ceiling, wondering how many times Chris had laid here doing the same thing.

The next morning, I resolved not to worry about Grandma Esther or living in Chris's bedroom, since I had so many other things to worry about. That included trying to build some kind of relationship with my father.

I wandered downstairs to the kitchen. It was Tuesday, but my father sat in his robe at the table, drinking coffee and reading the paper as Ellison sat across from him.

I could hear him slurping from his cup before I reached the kitchen doorway, and I knew from the expression on my brother's face that it was driving him crazy. He'd always hated the noises people made while eating and drinking. He frowned upon chewing with mouths open, and he preferred not to hear the audible crunch of potato chips. But nothing annoyed Ellison more than slurping.

My father looked up and smiled, rising quickly when he saw me. "Good morning. Want some breakfast? Eggs? How about you, Ellison?"

Ellison shook his head. "No thanks. Coffee will be fine."

He raised his eyebrows. "Aren't you a little young for coffee?"

"I'm seventeen, not seven," Ellison snapped, then looked at me guiltily. I knew he was making an effort, but going with the flow didn't come easily for my brother.

"I'm sure he didn't mean it like that, El. I'll have eggs," I said quickly. I wasn't hungry, but I wanted to diffuse the situation if I could.

Our father nodded and held up his hand as if to request a truce. "Sorry. You're right." He moved to the counter and filled a mug with coffee. He smiled again as he set it on the table.

Ellison poured cream and sugar into the cup until the liquid was taupe and tasted as sweet as he could stand it. I was glad for the distraction of watching him stir and sip. The sound of his spoon clinking against the mug filled the room.

My father watched Ellison but my brother took his time in looking up.

Dad cleared his throat. "I know you're not a little kid, either of you," he said, glancing at me. He paused, seeming to consider his words carefully. "I guess it's just that the last time we were together, you were children. It'll just take me some time, that's all."

From the way he fidgeted and played with his napkin while he spoke, I knew he was sincere. I looked at Ellison and he met my eyes and smiled slightly. I needed him to get along with Dad; I needed peace.

My brother must have read my eyes. "I guess it's going to take us all some time," he said.

I reached across the table and grabbed my brother's hand, and he held on.

Calvin cleared his throat again—a nervous habit, I thought. It was a small thing to notice, but it was intimate, the kind of thing normal kids know about their fathers. It had been a long time since I knew much at all about my father.

"Fried or scrambled?" Ellison asked.

Dad looked confused. "What?"

Ellison laughed. "You said you were making eggs. Fried or scrambled?"

Calvin chuckled. "Scrambled. I only eat scrambled."

"That's funny—I only like scrambled eggs, too." It felt good to have something in common with my father.

Ellison nodded. "Me, too." It was a lie; he loved fried eggs. I squeezed his hand and he squeezed back.

After we ate, the three of us moved to the living room. Dad settled into a chair to finish reading the newspaper and Ellison sat on the sofa, reading a magazine. I stood in front of the bookshelves, searching for something to read. I picked out a Stephen King book I hadn't read. I'd seen the movie, though, and that's why the book was a perfect choice. I already knew how it ended, so the book wouldn't require too much from me. It was enough to distract me, and what I needed was a simple distraction.

We all tried to get a conversation going, but our phrases were stilted, our ideas unfinished, punctuated by uncomfortable silences. We weren't quite sure what to say to each other, so we focused on our reading, pretending this was just a normal day for the Emory family. I had just read the first page of the novel when my father spoke.

"I was thinking, maybe you two want to go to the Carolina-Duke game this Saturday. It could be sort of a family outing."

Ellison hated football and he knew I did too, but he smiled anyway. "Sure. You've already got tickets?"

"I've got a friend who can get me a few if I need them."

I followed Ellison's lead, choosing not to say anything about the football. "I think it'll be great for us to do something together."

I hoped this would be the thing that made the difference for us, that helped us begin to feel like a real family.

The silence that followed was punctuated by the rustle of newsprint, the flapping of pages. I looked down at my book, pretending to read while I listened to the sound of Ellison's breathing.

I was the first to speak into the quiet. "So . . . I thought you'd be gone by the time I got up," I said to Dad.

I could see my father tense up at my words, and I wondered why.

"Gone?"

"To work. I heard Grandma Esther say that you guys get up early for work every day."

Until that moment, I hadn't really thought about the fact that my father was still in his robe at eleven o'clock on a weekday. I noticed that Ellison watched our father carefully, waiting for his response.

"Oh, she must have been talking about herself. She

goes to work fairly early."

I glanced at Ellison, confused. He kept his expression neutral and waited.

"Oh, what time do you leave for work?" I asked, looking at my watch.

Calvin cleared his throat. "It depends. If I'm subbing at a school, I leave early. But if not, I usually start writing around noon or so," he said, averting his eyes to look at the newspaper.

Mom hadn't talked much about Calvin, especially in recent years, and I'd never thought to ask what, exactly, Dad did for a living. I had assumed it was—wasn't that part of being an adult, having a job? I looked at Ellison.

"No job?" I mouthed silently, glancing at my father to make sure he wasn't looking.

Ellison shrugged. "Later," he mouthed back.

I cleared my throat and changed the subject. "I met Chris last night."

Dad looked up sharply. "Chris? Was he here?"

I was disconcerted by his sharp tone. "Yeah. He said I was in his room."

He frowned. "He should have been living in the dorms all along anyway. With his coming and going, he was too much for Mama to handle."

He said this almost to himself, and I was intrigued. This wasn't the brotherly sentiment I'd expected.

"He seemed nice," I said cautiously. "I never realized we had an uncle so close to our age."

He shook his head. "You should make friends at school, Maren. Chris is in college."

I could feel Ellison tense up next to me. "He's your brother, what's the big deal?" he said impatiently.

I tried to laugh it off. "We're not becoming best friends.

I just met him once, okay?"

Ellison and I exchanged glances, wondering why our father had gotten so weird at the mention of Chris's name.

Dad frowned. "Never mind. Just forget it."

His mood had soured, and he now turned the pages of the newspaper with an aggressive flicking motion.

Ellison sighed and glanced at me. We'd had just about enough family bonding for that morning.

"Want to go for a ride?" he asked.

I nodded gratefully. Dad grunted our way when we said goodbye. Ellison looked like he wanted to say more, but I grabbed his hand and dragged him out the front door.

Chapter 6

The streets were quiet as they left their neighborhood; most people were inside writing memos or taking calls or lifting boxes to make their livings. It was warm and sunny, and the air still smelled like summer even though it was late September, autumn in other parts of the world.

Maren didn't say much as they sped through the streets, making turns indiscriminately until he had absolutely no idea where they were. When he saw a sign for Duke's campus, he decided to turn in and park. He and Maren got out of the car silently, walking to a grassy quad, where they sat near a library and buildings that looked like they might be dorms.

Sitting here, Ellison was in awe of the campus. He'd never seen a school where the buildings looked like castles, complete with stone gargoyles peeking out here and there. The gothic buildings surrounded generous stretches of grass, and he liked the hum of activity that was everywhere he looked. Professors carrying worn leather briefcases, students lounging on benches, periodically punctuating their murmurs with loud laughter. They sat facing an enormous chapel that rose above the quad like a benevolent overseer, and from the constant movement, Ellison could see that this was a main artery of campus.

There were only a few students lying on the grass, some studying, others appearing to sleep. Ellison lit a cigarette and closed his eyes, liking the feel of the sun on his face, letting the smoke cleanse thoughts of his father from his mind.

Maren was the first to speak. "You said you were going to quit."

He nodded. "I am. I will. I just got all tense after that whole thing back at the house."

She sighed. "Yeah. Why do you think he doesn't work?"

Ellison shrugged and tapped ashes from his cigarette onto the ground. He thought Calvin should be embarrassed about not having a job, not a real one, anyway. As far as Ellison could tell, his father was spending most of his time writing and living off his mother. But he didn't feel like getting into it with Maren right then so he said nothing.

His sister stretched out her legs, and leaned back on her arms. "I think it'll be good to go to the football game. Maybe we can all get to know each other a little better."

After Calvin's outburst, telling Maren what kind of friends she should have and acting weird about his own brother, Ellison wasn't sure how well the three of them could get along, but he'd promised himself he wouldn't say anything negative about their father today.

"Are you freaked out about him telling you to stay away from Chris?" he asked carefully, taking one last drag of his Newport before stubbing it out in the grass.

He looked at Maren but the sun blinded him, making him squint.

She played with a blade of grass while she considered his question. "Not really. It was weird more than anything. What do you think he was talking about?"

Ellison shrugged again and changed the subject. "You look different today."

He'd noticed it right away when she came down for breakfast. Her hair was still wet and hung down around her shoulders instead of being pulled back into her customary ponytail. She wore jeans and a lightweight sweater, but there were pearls on her ears, reminding Ellison of the night he'd seen his mother's body in the hospital. Her eyes were lined, and her lips had a reddish coloring that he knew must have come from a tube. When had she started wearing makeup? When Maren smiled, Ellison was taken aback—he'd never really noticed how pretty his sister was. The realization made him feel even more protective of her.

Now it was Maren's turn to shrug. "So?"

"So, you never used to wear makeup back home. We get to Durham, suddenly you're changing your image?" he joked.

"I'm not 'changing my image.' So I put on a little makeup, big deal."

Ellison could tell she was trying to sound casual, like it really wasn't a big deal, but he knew better. Maren had been so against girly stuff like makeup and skirts and high heels. She wasn't a tomboy, exactly, but she liked to wear baggy jeans and T-shirts that hid her from the world. He'd always thought she felt self-conscious about her growing curves.

But then, she'd tried out for cheerleading, and that was totally unlike her. And now she was wearing makeup and wearing her hair down.

"But why are you wearing it?" he pressed.

She sighed, exasperated. "It reminds me of Mom, okay? She was always trying to get me to wear makeup and stuff but I never would. So now, this is something I could do for her."

She looked away. Ellison wanted to tell her that their mother had only been trying to get closer to Maren by sharing makeup secrets. He wanted to tell her that she didn't have to be someone she wasn't. He wanted to tell her that she didn't need to make anything up to their mother, not now.

But he didn't say any of that. "Hey, want to walk around campus? If we can find the bookstore, maybe I'll even buy you a T-shirt," he teased, poking her shoulder.

She swatted his hand away, laughing. "I can buy my own T-shirt," she grouched. But when he got to his feet, she did the same. They walked toward one of the studying students to ask for directions.

What they found was the Bryan Center, which not only housed the bookstore, but a series of darkened rooms where students munched on breakfasts of doughnuts and orange juice while they watched *The Price Is Right*, *Ricki Lake*, and various soap operas. Ricki brought back unpleasant memories of their first encounter with Grandma Esther, so Ellison and Maren settled down on a long sofa to watch *All My Children*. They sat mesmerized by the doings of Erica Kane and company, and for Ellison, it was a welcome escape from everything that was going on in his life. He'd much rather find out who was the father of Erica's secret love child than go back home to deal with his father. Once the show was over, they whiled away the afternoon, wandering into a nearby restaurant called The Rat to buy french fries and fried chicken strips and then planting themselves back on the couch. Ellison liked the fact that no one even looked twice at them, and even the guy who had left after the noon news but returned for *Oprah* at three o'clock didn't blink an eye at finding Maren and Ellison still sitting there.

They didn't talk much at all beyond comments about whatever show they were watching at the time. But when four o'clock rolled around, Ellison turned to Maren.

"I guess we should head back."

She nodded. "He's probably wondering where we are."

Ellison took her hand as they walked back across campus to his car.

Ellison and Maren woke up early Saturday to get ready

for the football game. Calvin had said that they needed to get there early because traffic would be terrible in the hour leading up to the game at noon. Ellison showered after Maren, making the water as hot as he could stand it. He wasn't really looking forward to the game, but he was looking forward to an opportunity to spend at least a few hours feeling like a real family again.

When he emerged from the bathroom, he found Maren standing in his room looking in the mirror.

"What's wrong with the mirror in your room?"

She wore a short black skirt he had no idea she owned and a tight T-shirt. Her face was fully painted and her hair was fluffed out into curls around her face. "Do you think I should wear a denim skirt instead?" She held up an equally short skirt.

He frowned. "I think you're way too dressed up for a football game," he said.

Her face fell. "I wasn't sure what to wear. I know it's just a game, but well, it's sort of a special occasion, too. This will be the first time the three of us have done anything together."

He could see the amount of thought and effort she had put into getting dressed, and it made him sad. "I think it'll be special no matter what you wear. Why don't you just put on jeans?" he said gently.

She nodded and rushed off to her bedroom, returning wearing more casual clothes. But her hair and makeup were still intact. Ellison decided not to press the issue; she seemed nervous enough as it was.

They went downstairs, nearly running into Grandma Esther at the foot of the stairs.

"Where are you-all off to?" she said briskly, eyeing Maren suspiciously.

"We're going to the game," Ellison said. "Is he ready?"

Grandma Esther frowned. "Your father? He left hours ago."

Ellison felt a sense of foreboding, then dismissed it.

Maybe their father had needed to run some errands or something. "Did he say when he'd be back?"

Grandma Esther shook her head. "I'm busy—I can't keep track of everyone's comings and goings," she grumbled, moving past them up the stairs. Soon the vacuum roared to life and they could hear her moving from room to room, cleaning.

They went to the living room to wait, where Ellison picked up a magazine to keep from fidgeting. Maren sat stiff-backed in a chair, staring out the window.

Ellison knew exactly how long they waited: two hours and twenty-one minutes. Grandma Esther finished cleaning and went over to the church. At one point Maren looked at him and began to speak, but her words trailed off before the question formed.

The magazine Ellison held grew crumpled and damp under his fingers. The game had begun, Ellison saw when he turned on the television. It was then that Maren burst into tears and ran upstairs. Ellison thought about following her, but really, what could he say? Their father had stood them up.

He took off his shoes and propped his feet on the coffee table, not caring if Grandma Esther came in and caught him. He watched the Duke–Carolina game without really seeing it, thinking about his father. Ellison was angry. He supposed there could have been an accident, or some sort of emergency, but something told him that wasn't it. Maybe Calvin was scared, or maybe he had simply forgotten, but there wasn't really any good reason to leave your kids at home waiting for you without so much as a call.

As Carolina's score rose and rose, Ellison remembered another time when his father had stood him up.

It was something small, really. An incident that had gotten lost in the upheaval that followed, something that only had meaning in retrospect. But now, Ellison could remember it clearly, just a few days before his father had packed his bags and left their apartment for good, when Ellison was just eight years old.

Calvin had promised to take Ellison, and Ellison alone, out for ice cream. He'd taken his first real test in school. It was math, and the teacher had written on his paper: "Excellent job, Ellison—97%." He had been so proud of that paper. He was smarter than the other second graders, at least when it came to subtraction, and he even knew some multiplication already. This paper was proof of his ability, proof that he was nothing like Billy, who farted in class and got a fifty-four on the test, or Elaine, who sucked her thumb raw and got an eighty-three. Nope, Ellison was special, and this proved it.

After school that day, Ellison practically ran the two blocks home from the school bus stop, hoping his mother would be home so he could show her. But when he burst into the living room of their small apartment, he stopped short. His mother was there, that was normal—she picked his sister up from her kindergarten every day because Maren was still too little to ride the bus. But his father was home, too, and that was unusual. He never came home before dinnertime.

"Where's Maren?" Ellison asked, shutting the door behind him. He stood uncertainly in the doorway, unsure whether to sit with his parents or run to his room. He didn't actually care where Maren was—whenever she was around she followed him and repeated everything Ellison said until he was ready to punch her. But he couldn't think of anything else to say as he looked into his mother's red-rimmed eyes.

"In her room coloring. Maybe you want to go help her," his mother said sweetly, wiping her cheeks to get rid of the signs of tears.

Ellison frowned. He most certainly did not want to help Maren. Plus, he was old enough to know when adults wanted to get rid of him.

Ellison walked into the room and sat down between his parents, pulling his test paper out of his backpack.

"Look, I got an 'A' on my math test."

His mother smiled weakly. "That's great, honey."

He looked at his father for additional praise.

"Maybe we'll go out for ice cream to celebrate." Calvin looked at Vanessa for a moment, but Ellison didn't know what the look meant. "Just us boys."

Ellison jumped up, excited. "When? Now?"

"Soon, I promise. Now, El, I really think you should help Maren. Your mother and I need to talk." His father made a "go away" motion with his hands.

Ellison frowned and considered sitting down again. He had a bad feeling about whatever it was they were talking about.

"Ellison," his father warned.

"Honey, just go, okay? I'll be up in a minute to hear more about your test," his mother added. Her voice soothed his anger and fear, and he went to his room without another word. Later, she fawned over his test and made cookies that were burned. But he ate them anyway because he wanted to see her smile.

Without much fanfare, his father moved out later that

week while Ellison and Maren were at school. He wasn't exactly surprised to see his father's suits and shoes gone from the closet. He knew something was wrong; he'd known it for some time.

But his father hadn't even mentioned the test, hadn't taken Ellison out for ice cream, hadn't even said goodbye.

Sitting there watching the end of the game, Ellison couldn't believe he'd forgotten this. True, it was a small thing. Maybe a man shouldn't be expected to remember a promise to a child in the midst of a breakup. Or maybe a better man would. He knew it wasn't fair to hold a grudge about a missed ice cream cone so many years ago. But today, well, that was inexcusable. Maren had spent so much time getting ready, looking forward to the game. She thought of the outing as a new beginning for the three of them. Ellison could admit to himself that he'd been looking forward to it, too. He wanted his father to prove himself fit, to prove Ellison wrong, but so far he seemed dead-set on doing just the opposite. He flicked off the television and vowed never to trust his father again.

Chapter 7

I had a knot in my stomach the entire morning on my first day of school. It seemed like years since I last sat in class, decades since I tried out for cheerleading, forever since I laughed. But I was glad to be going back. I was glad to regain a bit of normalcy in my life, even though things were anything but normal and seemed as if they never would be again. I needed to spend my days thinking about something other than my family. I needed to be a teenaged girl again.

It was supposed to be Ellison's first day, too. But he was still in bed, suffering from a cold he'd had for a few days. I was suspicious of his convenient illness when he'd begun coughing and complaining last week. This morning, I tiptoed into his room and shook him.

"Hey. El. Are you getting up?" I'd whispered.

He moaned and slapped my hand away from his shoulder. "I'm sick."

I sat on the bed. "Are you okay?"

Ellison turned over and looked at me. "You think I'm lying?"

I didn't know what to think. I knew that we both had been avoiding reality for a while, but it was getting to me, watching television all day, Grandma Esther's glares, my loneliness. I had thought he'd be ready to go back to school too, but he didn't seem to be in any hurry.

"I just think we should both go to school," I said tentatively.

He glared at me. "Why, so we can pretend that Mom never existed? So we can pretend to be one big happy family?"

I felt the tears building but I tried not to let him see. "I would never pretend that Mom . . . El, we have to go back to school sometime."

He laid back down, sneezing loudly for good measure. "I'll go tomorrow. Or the next day. When I feel better, I'll go."

"Fine." I walked toward the doorway.

"Mare?"

I sighed. "What?"

I didn't even bother to turn and look at him.

"I didn't mean that. About Mom."

I glanced at him. He really did look ill, although I couldn't be certain that it wasn't an act.

"I know El. Feel better."

My father was substituting at the middle school that morning, so he couldn't take me to school. I thought about asking Grandma Esther but I thought she would make me even more nervous than I already was. So I took the bus to school alone, hoping the cloudy sky and cool temperatures weren't a bad omen for the day. I wished I had someone there to hold my hand and tell me everything was going to be alright.

The air inside the school smelled stale, as if someone had left a bag of half-eaten cheeseburgers and cold fries sitting out too long. The odor assaulted me, making my nostrils flare as other students jostled by me in the halls. McNeil High School was a two-story building that was long and narrow, divided by a hallway down the middle of each floor. Because of this setup, every classroom had windows, but only along one of its walls. There were half-sized lockers along the walls of the hallways, and I was amazed to find out, when I opened mine, that students shared lockers.

I managed to find the office and get my schedule from a pretty woman who was working at the front desk. Wandering through the halls trying to find my homeroom, what was most amazing was how different the atmosphere was from St. Francis back home. At my old school, there had only been several hundred students; here there were thousands. The halls were noisy, filled with kids running, laughing, kissing and arguing. At St. Francis, anyone making too much noise in the hallways was quickly reprimanded by Sister Mary Ellen, who always seemed to materialize just when you least expected her. At McNeil, there was no Sister Mary Ellen, just a series of bored security guards who looked like they might fall asleep on their feet at any moment.

Sitting in my first class, I surreptitiously looked around while the teacher discussed the last reading assignment. I'd already read *Romeo and Juliet* several years ago, so I tuned out and took in my classmates, especially the girls. The more I looked around, the more I realized that fitting in at McNeil was going to be an entirely different prospect than it was at St. Francis.

For one thing, all the girls wore long extensions in their hair or had their hair done up in elaborate styles that seemed to require several cans of hairspray. They wore bright lipstick and long acrylic nails with designs painted on them. Gold was the jewelry of choice, and the more the better, it seemed. When these girls spoke, whether it was to the teacher or to each other, they spoke loudly, boldly, as if they had no idea what it was to be shy or quiet or scared— all of the things I was. They were peacocks, and I was the ugly duckling.

As the day wore on, I eavesdropped and watched, trying to discover what the cliques were and who was most popular. I'd never been in the "in" crowd at St. Francis, but it didn't take a genius to figure out who was in and who was out at McNeil.

There was one girl whose name kept coming up, who always seemed to be in the thick of things, whether it was in the cafeteria or in class: Phyllicia Johnson, or P.J., as everyone except the teachers called her. She was tall and pretty, with enormous eyes, skin the color of honey, pronounced cheekbones and long hair pulled back in a scrunchie. I could tell by looking at her that she was the kind of girl that guys fought over. With girls like P.J. it didn't even matter if the other girls hated her because she always got what she wanted anyway. I'd learned at St. Francis that it was better to be friends with the P.J.s of this world, or if you couldn't be friends, at least stay under their radars.

Back in Chicago, I'd chosen to stay under the radar of the cool kids. The night I was ridiculed after trying out for cheerleading proved that I would never have been one of the elite at St. Francis.

But here at McNeil, everything was different. I wasn't the old Maren who'd known my classmates forever. None of these people knew me, and this was my chance to be someone different, someone better, someone more popular.

The perfect opportunity to be the new me came up in seventh period geometry when the teacher asked P.J. the answer to one of the homework problems. Sitting next to her, I noticed that she averted her eyes, shuffled her papers and tried to stall.

"One hundred and fifty degrees," I whispered, barely moving my lips.

P.J. never even looked at me, but said the answer clearly for the teacher to hear.

After the teacher had moved on to someone else, P.J.

glanced my way quickly but I couldn't read her eyes.

After class, she caught up with me as I made my way to study hall.

"Hey," she called.

I turned, nervous. I hoped she would take my help as a gift rather than as an attempt to make myself look smart.

"Hi," I said, hoping my voice didn't shake. The last thing I wanted was to get off to a bad start at my new school. I just wanted to fit in, and I couldn't do that if I alienated the popular girl on my first day.

P.J. looked me up and down for a long moment before she spoke. I resisted the urge to tug at my clothes and pat down my hair; I didn't want to seem like I was trying too hard.

"That was cool, what you did in there. Thanks."

"Sure."

She smiled, finally, and I relaxed.

"You're new, right? I haven't seen you around."

"Today's my first day. I'm Maren." I almost put out my hand to shake hers but it occurred to me that she would think it was dorky.

"I'm P.J." Just then, a group of girls called out her name. She looked up at them, waved, and turned back to me.

"Well, thanks again, Maren. I'll see you."

"Yeah. See you."

It was warm and the sun had come out, so I took off my jacket and walked to the bus stop, smiling. It wasn't much. But it was a start.

A few days later, it was my turn to clean up the kitchen after dinner. I'd quickly learned that everyone had chores to do around Grandma Esther's house, and when she said it was time to do them, she meant now. Not in an hour, not in five minutes—now.

So I went to work without being asked, taking my time scraping the leftover barbecue sauce off the plates and enjoying the quiet. Everyone had gone their separate ways after dinner, and it was nice to be alone in a room for once—it didn't happen that often.

I still felt out of place in Grandma Esther's kitchen. It was so unlike our old one, which was big and sunny and filled with stainless steel appliances that my mother rarely used. Grandma Esther's kitchen fit a table and the basic appliances, but there wasn't much space left over so you always felt cramped and crowded with more than one person in the room. The refrigerator and stove were old and almond-colored, with no ice maker and gas burners that made the house reek when turned on. And of course, there was no dishwasher.

It reminded me of the Chicago apartment we lived in after my father left, before my mom had money. Even though I was just a little kid then, I remembered the feeling that there hadn't been enough of the things I wanted most, toys, clothes, special cupcakes from the grocery store, lunchboxes with cartoon characters on them. Things were the same way here in Grandma Esther's house. She rarely spoke explicitly about money, but she bought generic and turned out the lights every time she left a room, and my father didn't have steady work. To me, it all added up to the fact that we were poor.

I stacked the last of the dishes in the cabinet and stretched. I thought I would lounge on the sofa for a while, maybe watch television or flip through a magazine.

But when I walked out to the living room, I was surprised to see Grandma Esther sitting in the arm chair knitting. She glanced up at me sharply, and I wished one of us could disappear so we wouldn't have to talk.

"Girl, you startled me, standing in the doorway like that."

I couldn't think of a polite way to run up to my room and slam the door, so I reluctantly sat down on the sofa.

"Sorry."

She resumed her knitting, and I watched, trying to figure out what her nimble fingers were weaving.

"Is it a scarf?"

She shook her head. "It's a sweater for a boy at church. His family doesn't have much, so we try to help them out whenever we can."

I thought that it didn't seem like we had much, either, but I didn't say this aloud.

Her voice softened when she talked about the boy from church. I took it as a good sign.

"What's his name?"

She smiled, a rare occurrence. "His name is Denver. Reminds me so much of Chris when he was little. He always had a charm about him. All his teachers loved him, the church people loved him. That's the kind of boy Denver is."

Grandma Esther looked at me appraisingly. "Did your father ever tell you much about our side of the family?"

I shook my head. I had always wondered about my relatives. Every time we made family trees in elementary school, I never had enough names to fill up the page. After a while, I just made them up, assigning colorful nicknames and imaginary histories to my make-believe family.

My father hadn't told us much, just that his own father had died when he was just a boy and he'd been nearly grown when Chris was born. My mother didn't have much family left; by the time I was born, both her parents were dead, and she was an only child.

So I was eager to hear Grandma Esther's stories, and she talked while she knitted. As she told me all about her parents and siblings, about my father and Chris, about moving to Durham from rural Erwin, North Carolina, I watched her closely. This was the first time I'd seen her face relaxed and happy. She even smiled as she talked about herself as a girl, working on her father's small farm, meeting my grandfather, having my dad right away when she was barely out of her teens.

She had a surprisingly pretty smile. Her mouth was wide and when she was happy, her entire face stretched to show many of her white teeth. She had a loud laugh that seemed to come out of nowhere as she recalled long ago incidents as if they happened yesterday.

When she told the stories it was like I was there, smelling the scent of cut hay and fresh cow's milk. I closed my eyes, and I could see Esther, before she was "Grandma," or even "Mama," saddled with a name that was beyond her years and infected with a carefree spirit that would guide her toward a man her parents didn't approve of.

I pictured Erwin in my mind, houses spaced out between expanses of green, people waving to each other from their porches because everybody knew everybody. I imagined that the tobacco smell was stronger then, not diluted by the smog of progress. I guessed that Esther smiled a lot more then, unfettered by time and responsibility.

And while we sat there, I felt close to her for the first time. I finally felt like maybe we could be a family; I finally thought that maybe I could have the granny I'd always wanted. I quietly asked her questions, not wanting to talk too much lest the spell be broken. What I wanted to hear were the juicy details, like, who was Chris's father? I didn't think she'd been married again. Hadn't she been too old to have a baby? I wanted to know whether she was poor growing up, whether she'd always lived in the South.

But she didn't talk about those things. I was too scared to ask her about Chris, so I asked her about being poor.

"Poor? We didn't have fancy cars or go to private schools, but we made do," she said stiffly.

I wasn't sure what had put the chill in her voice. "I didn't mean anything by that," I said.

She set her knitting aside. "I know you probably looked at this house, at this neighborhood, and thought we're poor, right?"

I averted my eyes and said nothing.

"This may not be Evanston, but it's a nice place to live. This house is old, but there's enough room for all of us. I'm no famous television person, but I put food on the table. So don't turn up your nose at what you've got here."

I felt helpless. "But I never said—"

She stood up before I could finish. "Goodnight."

I watched her back as she stomped out of the room, and I just sat there, trying to understand what happened. It had been so nice between us, and then, without warning, everything went sour again. After a long while, I went upstairs and knocked softly on Ellison's bedroom door.

He didn't answer, so I opened the door and stepped in. The lights were out, but as I neared his bed, I saw his face illuminated by the moonlight. His eyes were closed, but I could tell he was awake.

"El?"

He opened his eyes. "Hey."

I sat on the edge of the bed and started to cry. Ellison sat up. "What is it, Mare?"

I was barely intelligible as I tried to tell him what had

happened with Grandma Esther. But it wasn't just that, it was everything. Mom dying. Our father standing us up for the game. Living in a house that didn't feel like home. Feeling like I didn't have a place in the world anymore.

Ellison wrapped his arms around me and patted me on the back until I could control my sobs. "I wish I could cry like you can, get it all out," he said softly.

I wiped my face. "I'm just being a baby."

"No, you're just being honest. It's a good thing."

I sniffed and took a deep breath. "What do you think the whole 'poor' thing with Grandma Esther was?"

He sighed. "I think she's probably just sensitive about money and stuff."

"But why get so pissed at me?" I complained.

"You brought it up, didn't you?"

I stood up, suddenly furious. "You're taking her side?"

He held up his hands. "What sides? I'm just saying, maybe you should try looking at things from her perspective."

"You say that," I spat. "She doesn't hate you."

"Didn't you just say you guys had a nice talk? She doesn't hate you, either." He was being calm and reasonable, and it infuriated me even more.

"What would you call it? She bitches me out over nothing, she treats me like I'm a second-class grandchild, and all she can talk about is how much you remind her of Dad."

"Mare, come on. You're overreacting."

"Jerk," I said and flounced out of the room. Once in my bed, I laid there, still angry. What I needed was for Ellison to hug me and tell me everything was going to be okay. I needed him to understand how much Grandma Esther's attitude had hurt my feelings. I needed someone to be on my side. Jordan had been that person for me back home, but she was hundreds of miles away, part of my old life that I'd left behind.

I thought I'd never get to sleep, but I was exhausted and it wasn't too long before I fell into a troubled slumber.

The next night, Chris came over for dinner. I was still in my room trying to decide what to wear when I heard him slam the front door closed and call out to Grandma Esther.

My stomach fluttered, and I turned back to the mirror, holding up an outfit in front of me. I had already curled my hair and done my makeup, so now all there was to do was find just the right outfit. There was a small voice inside my head telling me it didn't matter what I wore, that it was only the five of us having a casual dinner, that it was just family. But I ignored that voice, because it was the same voice that questioned the excitement I'd felt when I learned Chris was coming over. It was the same voice that told me that I didn't need makeup or a fancy hairstyle. I hated that voice; it never said anything I wanted to hear.

I could hear Chris laughing with Ellison downstairs, and I desperately wanted to be a part of that, to laugh and joke and forget about everything. I tossed aside the skirt and blouse I held in my hand and quickly pulled on a pair of snug black jeans and a fitted v-neck T-shirt. I bounded down the stairs but slowed a few steps before the end to walk casually into the living room.

Chris was standing in the hallway between the kitchen and the living room being inspected by Grandma Esther.

"I don't know why you'd want to do that to yourself," she grouched, putting her hands on his cheeks and turning his head from side to side.

"It's cool, Mama," Chris said patiently. "Everybody's

got them, and don't give me that old line about jumping off of bridges."

Grandma Esther frowned and shook her head. "Girls pierce their ears Chris. Not men."

He laughed. "Haven't you ever seen a music video? Everyone has pierced ears."

She dropped her hands from his face and sighed. Chris smiled and hugged her. "I still love you, Mama, earrings and all."

Grandma Esther swatted him away playfully. "Stop all this foolishness. It's almost time to eat."

It was odd seeing Grandma Esther so warm, and, well, motherly. I'd doubted that she had it in her. They turned and noticed that I was standing in the shadow of the stairwell, watching.

"Lord! You love to sneak up on folks, don't you?" she said, shaking her head. "I've got to go set the table."

I stood there shyly, not knowing what to say to Chris, who had plopped down on the sofa and was staring at me from a distance. Rather than look into his eyes, I stepped into the room but stood awkwardly, watching the small gold hoops in his ears as they reflected the low lamp light. I didn't think they made him look effeminate, like Grandma Esther had said. I liked the earrings. There was something rebellious and fun about it all.

"You look nice," Chris said, interrupting my reverie. "Different."

My hand flew involuntarily to touch my hair. I still wasn't used to wearing it down, feeling it on the back of my neck. I wasn't used to looking different, inspiring the look Chris gave me. It was an appraising, appreciative glance, and I was much more comfortable flying under the radar. I liked the attention because it made me feel grownup. But it scared me.

"I didn't look nice the last time you saw me?" I teased. I figured that joking might be the only way to get rid of the funny feeling in my throat.

He laughed lightly. "You looked nice. Just different."

On an impulse, I walked over and sat next to him on the sofa, and I immediately wished I had picked a spot farther away. Up close, I could see he was growing a beard, which made him look a little less boyish and a bit more dangerous.

To compensate for the closeness of our bodies, I looked out the window. But it was already dark, and all I could see was my own reflection and part of Chris's.

"Different how," I asked softly, although, of course, I knew.

"You looked younger, I guess. It's not like you look like a completely different person or anything." He paused for a long moment. "One thing is definitely the same."

I turned to him, waiting.

"Your eyes. Sad."

I sighed and looked at the window again, thinking of my mother. This was how she'd always wanted me to look, pretty and girlish. This was the kind of guy she'd always wanted me to meet, someone tall and handsome and nice.

But she hadn't figured on dying, hadn't figured I'd go all the way to Durham, North Carolina before I took my hair down and painted my face.

"I miss her."

Chris put his hand on my shoulder and I looked right into his eyes, wondering if there was anything there besides sympathy and feeling ashamed of my hope that there was. Then, Ellison walked into the room, drying his hands on a dishtowel.

"Dinner's ready," he said, looking closely at me. Chris

stood up quickly and cleared his throat. "I'll go see if Cal and Mama need any help."

Ellison watched him leave the room, then looked at me. "Are you okay, Maren?"

I shrugged. "Yeah. I was just thinking about Mom."

He kneeled down in front of me and turned my head back toward him when I tried to look away. "You sure you're okay, though? Chris didn't say anything or do anything to you?"

I forced out a laugh. "What would he do?"

Ellison looked hard into my eyes, searching in the same way I'd just searched Chris's. I wondered what he found. My brother opened his mouth slightly, as if he wanted to say more, but then he just stood up. "Let's go eat. I made sure they had a salad for you, just how you like it."

I smiled and grabbed his hand as we left the room.

During dinner, my father made lots of silly jokes and told long and involved stories that never seemed to have a point.

"So then, this kid—now, mind you, he's only in the fifth grade, so that makes him about 10 or 11 years old—then he tells me he doesn't have to do his homework and I can't do anything about it. Well, I sent him to the principal, and they called his mother. Now, let me tell you about his mother . . ."

Grandma Esther loved his stories, egging him on. "And then what happened?" she'd prod when he took a rare pause.

Ellison sighed a lot, and I could feel him rolling his eyes impatiently even though I was sitting next to him and I couldn't see his face.

But I didn't mind, because I wasn't really listening. I didn't eat much, just pushed my food around my plate while sneaking peeks at Chris. But every time I tried to steal a glance at him, he was already looking at me and I quickly averted my eyes.

Finally, Ellison couldn't take it anymore and he leaned across the table toward Chris. "You play basketball?" he asked quietly, although it didn't matter; my father didn't even miss a beat of his story as he got up to spoon more food onto his plate.

"Yeah. Sometimes there's a pickup game at the park down the street."

Ellison and Chris got into an animated discussion about basketball. My father and grandmother were giggling about the lack of teeth in some neighbor's mouth. And I was free to look as long and hard at Chris as I wanted. I liked watching his mouth curve when he talked, the way his eyes danced when he laughed. And when dinner was over and Ellison and Chris decided to go shoot around at the basketball court, I tagged along because I liked his absent-minded habit of pulling on his ear when he was thinking.

I still hadn't gotten used to how warm the nights were in Durham. Even in the summer, Evanston was cool at night, reminding you that despite the ninety-degree daytime temps, you were still in the North. I didn't even need a sweater as I followed a few steps behind my brother and Chris, watching them lope in similar rhythm toward the park, where the basketball courts were lit as bright as day.

On Saturday evenings, these courts were full of men, young and old, yelling in staccato bursts, laughing at mumbled comments, smelling of aftershave and hair oil and sweat. But tonight, the courts were empty. It was a week night, and others had to go to school or work the next day. But we were different. Chris was in college and had told us that he'd eliminated morning classes from his schedule altogether. And Ellison and I were still finding our way around the unfamiliar, still trying to figure out how we fit into this new world, still wishing it was six months ago and everything was back to normal.

As we walked the few blocks from Grandma Esther's house to the park, I kept quiet, listening to the sounds of Chris and Ellison's words. They talked about normal guy stuff, the safe topics that don't deal with sadness, fear or inexplicable longing. I wasn't interested in their words so much as the sound of their voices. I knew Ellison well enough to know that talking to Chris was a relief for him. Every time we were alone we ended up talking about Mom, arguing, or crying. With Chris, his tone was so light, his laugh so quick. It was the first opportunity he'd had to just pretend everything was alright.

I was so quiet, maybe they forgot about me. Neither my brother nor Chris looked my way when I slipped over to a bench under a tree where I could think and watch them play. There was a certain grace in the way they stripped off their shirts in unison, both pulling them off in one motion in that way only boys and men do. At first, I didn't think anything of this half-nakedness; I'd seen Ellison's chest a million times, although a few years ago we'd both acquired a sibling modesty that made us loathe to catch each other or be caught uncovered.

I was so blasé about Ellison that I was unprepared for the sight of Chris without his shirt. It wasn't that he was built like a model or anything like that. It was the intimacy of seeing his hipbones just above the low waistband of his jeans, the darkness of his skin that almost seemed a part of the night when he slipped into the shadows for a moment.

My cheeks were hot and I wanted to look away, but I couldn't help watching the way his body stretched out into a jump shot, the way his back muscles moved when he ran. There it was again, that unfamiliar longing that I'd felt earlier, that I felt every time I saw Chris.

Ellison called out that it was game point, and I finally looked away into the dark mass of trees surrounding the court, wondering why a pickup game had elicited these feelings in me. That's when I remembered something about my mother, something I'd either forgotten or repressed. A few years ago, she'd dated a professional basketball player. He played for the Milwaukee Bucks, and my mother had met him at one of the many parties she went to. She always said it was a part of her job, these functions, but I'd wondered how you could meet a basketball player and talk to him long enough to know you wanted him to meet your kids if you were just "working."

His name was Marc. Neither Ellison nor I was all that anxious to meet him, although he was much more outspoken about it.

"I've got a paper due," I'd told her. "I don't think I can go out to dinner."

"We don't want to meet your loser boy toy, Mom," Ellison spat.

But she must have really liked him, because she only rolled her eyes at Ellison and patted my hand.

"He's coming here, so you don't have to go out." She looked at Ellison and smiled at his scowl. "And how can you say he's a loser without at least meeting him?"

"He plays for the Bucks, doesn't he?" Ellison smirked.

Mom ignored him. "Come straight home tonight. Marc will be here around seven."

When meeting a woman's children, timing is everything. And Marc's timing, through no fault of his own, was horrible. It was the summer of 1991, and I was twelve years old, just old enough to realize all the things that I didn't like about my mother. I hated that she was on television and that half the city felt like they knew her personally from watching her show every night. I hated that she sometimes drank too much white wine and was silly and slurry when she came home from one of her parties. I hated that she wasn't like all the other mothers. I was primed to hate Marc, too.

Ellison was fourteen and just beginning to develop the arrogant edge that made his sarcasm that much more biting. He'd grown tall and handsome during the past six months, coinciding with an increasing interest in girls. His hormones were raging, and either he couldn't control them or didn't bother to try.

And he was angry with Mom, much angrier than me. Because in the end, I forgave her for not being perfect; I'm not sure Ellison ever could.

In the month between when Mom met Marc and the night we had dinner, she made sure we were sick of hearing his name. Every conversation, whether it was about laundry or summer camp, came back around to Marc.

"Marc's from Chicago, you know. He went to St. Joseph," she would say cheerily, eliciting an exasperated shrug from Ellison.

"Marc had a great season this year—he was tenth in the league in steals," she informed us. I rolled my eyes. I knew for a fact that my mother knew nothing about basketball and had no interest in it until Marc came along. She used to complain when Ellison and I would monopolize the television to watch the Bulls play, and she was the type of person to mix up sports terminology, calling free throws free kicks and confusing homeruns with touchdowns.

"Marc is really excited to meet you both," she told us.

Ellison had finally resorted to ignoring the constant Marc updates, but I couldn't bring myself to be that rude, so I nodded and smiled and pretended like I was interested in what excited Marc.

The day of the big dinner, I pretended to be sick to get out of going to summer camp, which I hated. It was like school, only smaller, with cliques and popular girls and no English class to distract me from trying unsuccessfully to fit in. Ellison loved his camp, but he was junior counselor, and there were lots of older girls there who thought he was cute.

When I went into her room to tell her I was sick, Mom paused in applying her mascara, peering into my eyes. I knew she knew I wasn't really sick, but she didn't say anything about it. Instead, she asked if I might feel well enough to let the caterers in later this afternoon.

"Caterers?" I couldn't believe she was going to so much trouble.

She raised her eyebrows. "You didn't think I was going to cook, did you? I have to work you know."

I could hear Ellison's voice in my head saying that other mothers managed to work and cook. But I just nodded and left the room.

That evening, Ellison beat my mother home and went up to take a shower. I waited for him in his bedroom, startling him as he came back into the room wearing a shirt and jeans but barefoot.

"Shit, Mare. You scared me." He shook his head at me. "What are you doing in here anyway?"

I played with the edge of his blue bedspread. "I'm trying to figure out how to get out of this stupid dinner with stupid Marc."

"Forget it. I've been trying to think of something all day.

And look on the bright side—I'm sure it'll be interesting," he said.

"That's one word for it."

The doorbell rang and we looked at each other for a long moment. "We better get down there. Marc's really excited to meet us, you know," Ellison said, mimicking Mom's voice. I laughed and followed him down the stairs.

Marc stood waiting patiently, a bouquet of red roses in one hand and an autographed basketball in the other.

"Hi, you must be Maren and Ellison," he said, bobbling all his goodies as we showed him in the door. He had the kind of strong Southern accent that I associated with ignorance rather than region.

"How did you guess?" Ellison said dryly, snatching the flowers from his hands. "Mom's not here yet, but I'm sure she'll love these. Red roses are so . . . original."

Marc sat down on the living room sofa and eyed Ellison suspiciously. He knew Ellison was giving him a hard time, but what do you say when it comes from a fourteen-year-old kid you just met?

Ellison and I sat on the love seat across from Marc, watching him fidget as the silence stretched out. I had only seen Marc on television a couple of times, but he looked different from what I remembered. For one thing, he was much shorter than I thought. He was tall by civilian standards, about six feet, but short by NBA standards. His head was shaved bald, and his looks were, overall, fairly average. As I examined him, I tried to figure out why my mother had even given him a second glance. I looked at Ellison, whose look of disdain told me he was wondering the same thing.

Marc looked down at the basketball he still held. "Oh, Ellison, I brought this for you. Vanessa said you like to play."

Ellison took the ball, examining it carefully before setting it aside. Marc looked disappointed, and I imagined that Mom had told him to butter up Ellison because he was tough to win over.

"So, Marc, what position do you play?" Ellison asked sweetly.

Marc cleared his throat. "Point guard."

Ellison nodded as if he was truly interested. "Now, do you see yourself as an Isaiah Thomas–type? Or are you more like a Magic Johnson?"

Marc squinted at him. "Well, those guys are the best in the league. I'm pretty good, though." He tried to laugh but it came out sounding more like a cough.

Ellison frowned. "So you're not one of the best, then? Maybe that explains why you play for Milwaukee."

Marc opened his mouth to retort, then thought better of it and looked at me. "So. Maren. That's a pretty name. How did you get it?"

I wanted to make some smart-ass comment so he'd realize he was never going to win us over with stupid questions, so he'd realize that Ellison wasn't the only one who was suspicious of someone who'd so completely captured our mother's attention. I tried to think of something biting, something that Ellison would say, but just then, Mom walked in the door, and we were caught up in a whirlwind of unnecessary introductions, appetizers and Mom's cheerful chattering.

Dinner was even more uncomfortable as Ellison made snide comments one after another. Mom had decided early on that if I wasn't going to say anything at all and Ellison only had sarcasm to offer, she was going to ignore us and talk only to Marc.

I shoveled down my food quickly and excused myself,

and Ellison soon followed. I went to my room and stared at the pages of *The Scarlett Letter* without retaining a word. I heard Ellison slam the door of his room down the hall, and I was relieved that we were going our separate ways for the night. We wouldn't have to talk about the way Mom touched Marc's arm while they talked, the way she smiled at him with her eyes half-closed, the way he drawled her name in an overly-familiar way.

I must have fallen asleep. I woke up a few hours later, still in my clothes, with the book lying across my chest. Disoriented, I wandered out of my room and down the stairs to see if my mother was still up. The kitchen was dark and still, so after I grabbed a leftover roll to munch on, I trudged back upstairs. Just as I was turning down the hall to my room, I heard a noise. I wasn't sure what it was, but it came from my mother's room at the end of the hall. I walked quietly and pressed my ear to the door. I waited for what seemed like forever, and I was just about to walk away when I heard it.

"Oh Marc." It was low, almost unintelligible through the thick door, but there was no mistaking my mother's voice. I'd never heard her moan like that, and I felt my face grow warm as I hurried away from the door. I lay in my darkened room, thinking about sex and basketball and my mother and feeling sick to my stomach.

I never told Ellison about hearing Mom and Marc together. I hated thinking of her as someone who wanted sex, which, to my 12-year-old sensibilities, still seemed messy and scary and hardly worth the trouble. But I would have hated it more if Ellison knew, because he wouldn't keep quiet like I did. He would have said something to Mom and reminded me of it over and over again when I just wanted to pretend that it never happened. And I got my wish: after a few weeks, Mom stopped talking about Marc. He never came to our house again, and I forgot all about it until the night I watched Chris and Ellison playing basketball.

I lowered my head and ran upstairs without saying goodbye as soon as we reached Grandma Esther's house. I didn't know what felt worse: my shame over sexual feelings for Chris, my embarrassment at having overheard my mother making love, or the fact that Mom was not there to help me figure it all out.

Chapter 8

As he listened to his footsteps echo in sync with his father's on the speckled tile floor, Ellison was annoyed. It was ten o'clock on an early October Monday, his first day at McNeil High School. He hated to be late, and his father had taken his sweet time over breakfast that morning. He felt his shoulders tensing at every cup of coffee (which his father seemed to be endlessly refilling), every piece of toast, every crackle of the morning paper. It had been like this since Calvin stood them up. He'd apologized, gave them some excuse about errands and car trouble. But Ellison wasn't quick to forgive, and he definitely didn't forget. He was suspicious of everything his father did, skeptical of everything he said. Maren was quicker to accept the apology and move on, but something inside Ellison wouldn't allow him to simply let it go.

"Aren't we leaving soon?" Ellison had said, glancing at his watch as his father slowly rinsed the breakfast dishes and put them in the sink to be washed later.

His father looked at him. "You've missed almost a month of school—getting there late today won't make much difference."

Ellison frowned. It seemed as if every word his father uttered was designed to infuriate Ellison. But he stayed quiet. He thought an argument might delay them even more.

After a while, Calvin finished with the dishes and wiped his hands dry on a paper towel. "Let's go."

Ellison followed his father through the house, forcing himself not to spit out an angry remark. Maybe it shouldn't have mattered what time he got to school. But Ellison still resented the control Calvin now had over his life. His father decided where Ellison lived, what he ate, and now, even something as small as what time he arrived for his first day of school.

Walking through the halls of the school, what Ellison really wished was that his father would have let him drive to school alone. He was old enough to know that parents don't usually mean to embarrass their kids, but he wasn't quite old enough not to be embarrassed. True, his father had spruced up a bit for the occasion, but his appearance wasn't the problem. The problem, Ellison thought as they entered the main office, was that he was seventeen. Almost a man. Old enough to register for school on his own. He didn't need Calvin holding his hand, and he didn't need to have the other kids at school see him being escorted around by his "daddy."

They stood in front of a long counter that separated a small area near the glass-paned door from a larger area filled with a cluster of desks. Only women sat at the old wooden desks, and the hubbub they created sharply contrasted with the silence in the halls. Phones bleated, voices called across the room, and a sharp, cackling laugh periodically punctuated the din.

He looked around the room. All the women were black, unlike St. Francis, where there were just a few black employees and none of them worked in the front office. Ellison felt somehow out of place, even though his skin matched theirs. Some people would feel out of place as the only black face in a crowd of white ones, but not Ellison. He'd used his difference to his advantage at St. Francis, practically daring people to treat him like an outcast. He'd embraced difference, but he made it less about race and more about having a celebrity mom, designer clothes, the prettiest girlfriends. So Ellison was okay with being different—it was this blending in that was unfamiliar. If he was just like everyone else, then who was he, really?

The receptionist was young, with dimples that perforated her cheeks when she talked or smiled. She wore a white oxford shirt with the first two buttons undone and a blue jean skirt that rode up so Ellison could see part of her brown thighs. She was a brown-skinned woman who reminded him of his mother—sassy, confident, pretty.

He was immediately enthralled. All the women in the office at St. Francis had either been nuns or easily nearing eighty years old. And this woman looked young, not too much older than Ellison, he figured.

She smiled up at them. "Hey, honey. How are you?" she drawled toward Calvin. Ellison still hadn't gotten used to the slow Southern drawl everyone in Durham seemed to have. He smiled back and started to greet her.

Instead, his father broke in. "Hey Arnetta. You're looking good today," Calvin said smoothly. Ellison looked at his father, startled.

Arnetta smiled languidly and touched her hands to her long, braided hair. She shifted in her seat, and Ellison could see the tops of her breasts peeking out from underneath her shirt. He wondered just how well she knew his father.

"Did you come down here just to sweet talk me, Cal?"

Calvin grinned and leaned on the counter, looking directly into Arnetta's eyes. "Is it working?"

She raised her eyebrows. "Maybe."

Ellison shifted his weight and cleared his throat. He didn't feel like standing around watching his father flirt. True, his father was pretty young—just thirty-nine years old—but it still made Ellison squirm. And he was disappointed, too. Clearly, Arnetta had been going with his father.

Calvin stood up straight, suddenly looking more official. "This is my son, Ellison. He needs to register for classes," he said quickly, shedding the low, conspiratorial tone he'd adopted with Arnetta.

Ellison wanted to laugh at the way her mouth dropped open. Yeah, he's got a son, he thought. He glanced at his father, who looked miserable, and then it didn't seem funny at all. Calvin seemed to have some kind of relationship with this woman, so you'd think the fact that he had kids might have come up at some point.

"I have a sister, too," Ellison said sweetly.

Arnetta raised an eyebrow at Calvin, who began jingling loose change in his pocket.

She rolled her eyes and turned to Ellison. "Do you have your records, a birth certificate or driver's license and an immunization form?" she said, all business.

He dug into his leather backpack while Arnetta began typing at her computer, her long, red nails clicking double-time with the keys. Even though the room was still noisy, there was a chilly silence at the counter. Ellison smiled to himself and looked up to find Calvin glaring at him. He smiled wider as he handed the papers to Arnetta, unable to resist baiting his father. "Something wrong?" he asked sarcastically.

Calvin grabbed his arm. "Excuse us for a minute," he hissed, dragging Ellison out into the hall.

As the door slammed behind them, Ellison jerked his arm away. "Get off me."

They stood face to face, close enough for Ellison to feel his father's breath hot on his face.

"What the fuck is your problem?" Calvin growled. "Is this about the stupid football game? I said I was sorry for that."

Ellison narrowed his eyes. His father hadn't earned the right to curse at him. "What's the problem? You don't want your little girlfriend to know you have kids? You shouldn't have come to school with me then, smart guy," he spat. "And I hate football."

Calvin shook his head. "You can be a real jerk, you know that?"

Ellison smirked. "You're the one who's lying to his girlfriend, not me."

"She's not my girlfriend."

"Oh, so you're just fucking her, then?"

Calvin stepped into the narrow bit of space between them, his hand raised. Ellison felt a roaring in his head as he braced himself for the blow.

But a loud buzzer sounded, and suddenly the halls were filled with milling students who looked curiously at Ellison and Calvin.

Ellison took a deep breath and stepped away, his anger at his father tasting like steel on his tongue. His father looked around, as if he'd forgotten where they were. He glanced at the office door and back at Ellison. "I'll see you at home," he said sharply and walked off.

Ellison shook his head, incredulous that Calvin had actually intended to hit him. Ignoring the stares of passing students, he stepped back into the office and handed Arnetta the sheaf of papers he still clutched in his hand.

"You okay?" she asked.

He nodded distractedly. "Yeah." But he wasn't okay— he was thinking about his father, who apparently had a temper. Ellison thought about Maren. Would their father threaten to hit her, too? He frowned and vowed to warn her and keep an eye on Calvin.

He wiped a hand over his face and straightened his shirt.

"Yeah, I'm fine," he repeated, giving her his most charming smile. "Just fine."

He'd deal with his father later. Right now, he had to figure out where the cafeteria was and whether he'd have to take calculus.

On his way to the locker that matched the small, tarnished key Arnetta had given him, Ellison realized that it wasn't just the women working in the office who were black—nearly everyone he saw was black. And that was saying something, because McNeil was filled with 2,000 students, twice as many as his old school.

His lockermate had decorated the space with cutout magazine photos of Will Smith and Wesley Snipes, which Ellison thought was pretty unoriginal. There was a small mirror pasted to the inside of the door, and the locker smelled faintly of baby powder and peppermint, fragrant but not overwhelming. He eyed the books stacked neatly in the locker. Geometry. Biology. Some book wrapped in a plain brown paper cover that looked like it might have been made from a grocery store sack. He picked this one up and read the name in the front cover. Phyllicia Johnson.

"That's mine," a high-pitched voice said from behind him. Ellison whirled around to face her. She was pretty in a very dramatic, womanly way, which was in total contrast to her little-girl voice. He smiled.

"What's so funny?" she demanded.

He shrugged. "Sorry. It's just that your voice doesn't match the way you look." As soon as he said it, he wished he could take it back, because her eyes narrowed to slits and her lip curled. He guessed it wasn't the first time she'd heard that.

"Whatever." She pushed him aside and grabbed the geometry book. She busied herself with applying lipstick while puckering at herself in the mirror as if Ellison wasn't there.

"Phyllicia, I didn't mean anything by that. Really." He wished she would turn around so he could apologize properly, but she kept looking at her reflection. After a few moments, he became angry. True, he'd said something stupid, but she didn't have to be mean about it.

Finally, she turned to him. "Are you always this dumb when you meet someone?"

He frowned. "Are you?"

She made a dismissive sound in her throat. "Whatever."

"You said that already."

They stood and glared at each other until the warning bell for class sounded. She took one last look in the mirror and slammed the locker, narrowly missing his hand. She flounced off without another word.

"It was nice meeting you too," he called after her, shaking his head. He trudged toward history class, wishing the day was already over.

Ellison had expected to be harassed a little on his first day. Stuff like that always happened to the new kids at St. Francis. After some initial good-natured hassling, most new kids were then enfolded into the fabric of the school and it was almost as if you'd known them all your life.

But that didn't happen. He tried to look nonchalant as he went through what was to become his daily routine, but he could feel eyes on him everywhere he went, sizing him up, filing his image away for later use.

As he sat in study hall during last period, he began to wonder if he would ever fit in here. All the guys wore basketball or football jerseys with their baggy jeans and enormous white sneakers. He felt over-dressed in his button down shirt and khaki slacks. A lot of the guys had pierced ears and braids in their hair, or the beginnings of dreads, like his uncle Chris, and Ellison knew that his soft, curly hair would never hold those styles even if he wanted it to. He tried not to say much, because he knew he must sound as foreign to them as they did to him. He was often a few beats behind the conversation in class because he was translating the accent in his head. If someone had come to St. Francis with a Southern drawl, using unfamiliar slang words and colloquialisms, Ellison might have made fun of him, called him a country bumpkin. People just didn't talk like that in Chicago. At least, not the people Ellison knew. But now, he felt like he was the one trying to understand a new language, and even though he knew he spoke "proper" English, he was in the minority, and therefore, at a disadvantage.

It was a relief when the final bell rang. Walking outside to catch the bus back home, he passed by a group of boys about his age, their pants hanging off their butts, cigarettes held carelessly between their fingers. They watched him as he approached, so he felt obligated to say something.

"See you guys," he said cheerfully.

They burst into laughter, and he could feel his face redden.

"See you, white boy!" they called after him. He walked right past the bus stop, his ears still burning, and walked until he could no longer hear their guffaws ringing out into the air.

Chapter 9

A couple of weeks after we started school, Ellison was particularly quiet during our drive home and I could tell something was wrong.

"What's up with you?" I asked when we stopped at the first light outside of school. He ignored me and gunned the engine, impatient for the light to change.

I tried again. "How was your day?"

He sighed and rolled his eyes. "It was okay," he said.

I accepted his lie silently. I couldn't force him to talk if he didn't want to. But after a long while, he finally spoke.

"How was your day?" he asked. Our schedules were different and we rarely saw each other during the day.

"Okay. I've met a few new people who seem pretty cool."

He frowned at me. I felt bad, because I knew he didn't like McNeil and hadn't made any friends yet. He had always been the popular one while I was usually left out, and I could tell he didn't like the role reversal.

We rode the rest of the way home in frosty silence. When we walked in the door, our father was sitting in the living room.

"Oh good, I'm glad you two are home. I want to talk to you, Ellison."

I was going to go straight to my room to do homework, but the combination of Ellison's mood and Dad's serious tone made me linger in the doorway.

"What?" Ellison spat.

Our father cleared his throat. "It's about your car."

Ellison took a deep breath, and I could see he was trying

to remain calm. "What about it?"

"Well, it's an expensive car, and we don't have much money, so I thought we'd sell it."

Ellison stood quickly. "You thought you would sell my car? And do what with the money?"

"There are a lot of expenses around here you know, especially with two more people. And there's the future to think of. You'll be going to college next year."

He looked concerned and fatherly, but I knew Ellison would balk. Mom gave him that car, fully paid for, and I knew it was much more important to him than household "expenses." I wished there was something I could say to make things better, but I knew this wasn't my fight.

"Expenses, huh? How much are you paying toward these expenses? Oh, wait, I'm sorry, you don't have a job, right?" Ellison sneered.

I groaned inwardly.

"Don't you talk to me that way," Calvin said, squeezing a red plastic checker piece in his hand. "And I do have a job."

"Oh, right, Calvin, you're a sub. Funny, I haven't seen you doing much work." He paused. "Hey, is that how you know Arnetta? From your 'work?' "

I wondered who this Arnetta person was. And how did Ellison know her? I could see Ellison enjoying the look of fury that came over our father's face. I didn't know what got Dad so angry; the fact that he'd addressed him by his proper name, or the job thing. But our father remained silent, staring out the kitchen window.

"Who's Arnetta?" I asked softly.

Ellison picked up his backpack. "Calvin's girlfriend. Why don't you ask him about her?" He stomped back out the front door down the block to where his car was parked on the street, and I followed him. He dug around in his bag for his keys, and when he turned he saw me standing there.

"Maren, go back inside," he said wearily.

I shook my head. "I'm going with you." Somehow, I knew that there was more going on here than Ellison's "new guy at school" syndrome.

"I'm not going anywhere, just for a drive."

I walked around to the passenger side door and climbed in.

He sighed and shrugged. "Fine." He roared off noisily, never looking back at the house.

We ended up at South Square Mall, even though Ellison hated malls. But it was one of the few places he knew how to get to in Durham, so we'd been there a few times.

"So what's up with you?" I asked between bites of the pizza I'd bought. We sat at a small round table at the center of the food court. Although the mall was filled with the after school crowd, the eating area was nearly deserted.

He sighed and slurped from his cup. "Our father is an asshole."

He meant it to sound malevolent, reflecting his feelings toward Dad, but it came out sounding whiny, making me laugh.

"What happened to going along with everything, not making waves?"

He took the lid off his cup and jabbed at the thick ice cream with a plastic spoon. He seemed to be debating whether to tell me; he must have decided I could handle it, because he took a deep breath and told me about being late for school on his first day, about Arnetta, about the fact that our father had never mentioned his children. He told me about everyone in the office, his lockermate named

Phyllicia, the near-fight with Dad.

"He wouldn't have hit you," I said quietly. I couldn't believe he'd waited weeks to tell me all this.

He shrugged. "Are you asking or telling me? Because I'm not sure."

I looked down at the pizza crusts I'd left behind. "I have to believe he wouldn't do that."

Ellison shrugged. "I know you want to think he's a good guy, and I hope you're right," he said, "but I'm just not as sure as you are."

He didn't tell me about guys at school who called him "white boy," and I didn't tell him that I'd already heard about it from P.J., his lockermate who was quickly becoming my first friend in Durham. I didn't want to make him feel worse than he already did.

I folded my napkin into a tiny square, thinking. "Maybe it will get better," I offered. "I mean, all new kids get stuff like that."

This was a switch—me comforting him. I felt uncomfortable outside of our normal roles, like some protocol had been breached.

He stood up quickly and looked at his watch. "Come on, let's go home. I'm sure they're wondering where we are, and the last thing I need is another run-in with Dad today."

I nodded and followed him away from the food court.

As we pulled up in front of the house, it was already dark and quiet on the street.

I turned to him. "Are you going to call him 'Calvin' from now on? He really seemed like he hated it." I wanted him to agree not to do it, to smooth things over.

"Does a man who would raise his hand to his son deserve to be cut some slack?" he said. "Anyway, that's his name, isn't it? It's not like I called him 'Jackass.' "

I rolled my eyes and pushed past him and walked into the house, where Chris and Grandma Esther sat on the sofa, talking.

I felt a little jump in my stomach when I saw Chris.

"You all were out a little late for a school night," Grandma Esther said. "You missed dinner."

I let my brother do the talking, since she liked him better.

Ellison smiled. "I'm sorry, Grandma Esther. I went for a drive and I dragged Maren with me. We'll call next time."

"Next time, just come home for dinner," she said, the hardness of her words softened by her smile. I wished she would smile at me like that.

He nodded. "Mare, are you coming up?"

Before I could answer, Chris jumped up. "Hey—I think I left something in the closet upstairs. I was waiting for you to get home so I could look for it."

"Sure," I said. "Come on up."

I was happy for the distraction, and even happier that I would get to talk with Chris. We stomped upstairs and he told me stories about how he'd decorated his room as a kid. It was a relief to talk about something that had nothing to do with Ellison or my father or even my mother. It was a relief just being with Chris, and I realized that he was fast becoming an important person in my life.

It was early December before it occurred to me to put something on the walls of my small bedroom. I guess it took me that long to feel slightly at home inside that room, inside that house. Ellison and I had stopped talking as much about how our lives used to be, and Grandma Esther had stopped treating me like an unwelcome visitor. It wasn't that I'd grown on her; I think she just resigned herself to the fact that I wasn't going anywhere and she'd have to live with me somehow.

I woke up one Saturday, looking at the white walls, and decided to make my room look and feel more like a place to be comfortable, to think, to be happy. I wasn't happy yet, but I was optimistic enough to think that someday I might be. I hoped I'd be happy and I hoped that it wouldn't be long in coming.

I kept several boxes full of my stuff in the closet. I'd unpacked clothes and the necessities, but the things that meant the most were still packed away, protected behind sweaters and coats.

The first box I pulled out was filled with childish drawings and paintings on crinkled, yellowing paper, all signed "Maren," many with the "R" written backwards. When I was preparing to leave Evanston, I'd found all of them neatly pressed flat inside an old hatbox in my mother's closet. I'd started to cry when I saw them: the evidence of my childhood. But I couldn't afford to cry, not when there were boxes to label, clothes to sort and phone calls to make—all the practical concerns designed to distract me from the idea of my mother's death. So I'd wiped my face and stuffed the drawings into a box to take with me so I'd never forget how much my mother had loved me.

My cheeks were wet now as I pulled them out carefully and smoothed out the wrinkles. I laid all the papers out on the bed. Pictures I'd drawn of my family, when my family still included a father. Pictures of Ellison made to look like a monster, likely drawn when I was mad at him for one thing or another. Imprints of blue fingers on red construction paper, mine, even though my hand was now nearly twice as large when I held it against the page.

I got up to rummage through my school supplies,

looking for push pins. It briefly occurred to me that I should ask Grandma Esther before making holes in the walls, but I didn't want her to say no, so I didn't ask.

The project quickly consumed me. Rather than carefully considering where each picture should go, I put them up along the wall facing the bed according to feeling. I started with the ones that made me feel like crying the most, the ones that were sweet and somehow sad, even though they hadn't been conceived as such. Then I moved to the ones that made me smile, the ones of Ellison with various stages of horns and missing teeth, the ones that consisted of my name written in block letters and cursive, backwards, upside-down and sideways in different colored magic markers. By the time I got to the ones that were simply splashes of color on the page, with no discernible theme or meaning, I'd covered the entire wall with my artwork. These last pictures were my favorites, because they seemed to offer limitless possibilities, refusing to be categorized and easily defined. I had bits of my innocence and freedom captured in crayon, and I could look at them every day.

Pleased with the results, I went back to the boxes in the closet, suddenly anxious to find more of myself. My back was to the door and I didn't hear Grandma Esther until she cleared her throat and startled me into bumping my head on a shelf.

It was still fairly early, but she was already neatly dressed, her hair curled and fluffed. Grandma Esther never looked mussed or undone. It was as if she slept in her clothes with her head perched ever so lightly on a pillow, so she was ready to go from the moment she awakened. It was a sharp contrast to my mother, who lounged around in her bathrobe, hair tied up in a scarf, for most of the day on Saturdays when she didn't have to work and no one but El and I would see her.

"Good morning, Grandma Esther," I said politely, rubbing my scalp where it had hit the edge of the shelf.

She stared for a long moment at my newly-decorated wall, and I braced myself for a reprimand. But she just blinked a couple of times and turned back to me. "I thought we'd go shopping today."

I was surprised, but I tried not to show it. She hadn't offered to take me anywhere in the months we'd been living in Durham. I think she'd tried to temper her dislike of me, not for my sake, but because there had been a couple of times where she'd made a comment and my father got angry in my defense. Like on Thanksgiving morning— Ellison was still in the bathroom getting ready, so I went downstairs to eat some cereal. We'd had a talk, agreeing that we wouldn't think too much about this being our first holiday without Mom, telling each other that if we could just get through it, things might be easier on the other side.

But I was having trouble holding up my end of the bargain. I couldn't get last Thanksgiving out of my head—it had been the first time we'd had it catered, mostly because my mother didn't have time to cook and I didn't know how. Ellison had said he didn't care who cooked his turkey, as long as it was on the table when he got hungry, but I didn't believe him. He liked the whole tradition of a home-cooked Thanksgiving meal as much as I did, but he was too proud to show our mother how much he wanted it. Maybe he was afraid that if you wanted something too badly, and it didn't come true, it would hurt that much more.

I was thinking about the taste of that catered dinner as I walked into the kitchen (juicy turkey, smooth mashed potatoes, creamy cheesecake—almost too perfect). Grandma Esther was alone, stirring the eggs she scrambled for my fa-

ther every day before she left for work. I wasn't too sure
what she did—it had something to do with her church. I
never really asked, and she never really said, but from the
way she was dressed, whatever her job was would take her
out of the house on Thanksgiving Day. All I knew was that
she paid the bills, since my father worked sporadically and
spent most days writing in his room.

I tried to smile cheerfully as I slid into my seat and
greeted her. She glanced at me, her lips pursed, as if I'd in-
vaded her space.

"If you want breakfast, you're going to have to get it
yourself. We've got a service at church this morning and I
can't be late," she said briskly.

I tried not to stare at the pan filled with eggs and butter,
tried not to sniff at the smell of bread in the toaster. She
had time to make breakfast for my father, but not me.

I said nothing, but Grandma Esther seemed to read my
mind. She whirled around and glared at me. "You
shouldn't prance around here half-dressed," she snapped,
eyeing me up and down.

I wore a long T-shirt I'd stolen from Ellison. It came
down to nearly my knees, and although I wasn't wearing
shorts underneath, it certainly wasn't indecent.

"I just came down for some cereal," I said coldly,
looking her in the eye. I felt like a different person, someone
who wasn't afraid to challenge Grandma Esther. I felt how
Ellison must feel when he called our father Calvin, sneering
and defiant. I was playing the part of someone stronger and
tougher than me, and even though it wasn't real, it was all I
could think to do.

"You're not going to smart talk me in my own house,"
she said. "You're not too grown for a whipping."

I rolled my eyes, thinking that even when I was quiet,

scared Maren, I was smaller and quicker than she was, and she'd never catch me long enough for any whipping.

Realizing her eggs were burning, she turned back to the stove, fussing sotto voce. "Damn smart-mouth girl, don't know how to respect her elders. Just like her mother."

My mouth dropped open and I stood up, ready to do something, although I wasn't sure what. Before I could speak, I saw my father in the doorway, and he looked furious.

"Mama. I can't believe you," he growled.

Grandma Esther turned around in surprise. "Calvin. I didn't see you there. Your breakfast is ready," she said sweetly, throwing a warning glance at me.

He shook his head and came to stand next to me. "Don't talk to my daughter like that," he said.

She scooped eggs onto a plate and set it on the table. She put her hand on her hip. "Now, Calvin, your daughter is the one you need to be talking to. She sassed me, and this is my house—"

My father cut her off. "Maren has been through a lot. How could you say that about her mother?"

Grandma Esther busied herself with removing her apron and smoothing down her long wool skirt.

"Mama?"

She sighed and glanced at me long enough for me to see the remorse in her eyes. "Okay, Calvin. I didn't mean to disrespect Vanessa." She paused. "But you better tell her to watch her mouth."

I looked over at my father. It felt nice to be defended. It was the first time in a long time that I'd had that protected feeling you can only get from a daddy.

He nudged me back toward my chair and sat down across from me. "Get a fork—let's eat these eggs before they get cold," he said, smiling gently at me.

Grandma Esther stalked out of the room, and I couldn't help giggling. None of it was funny, not really, but laughter was the only way I could release the pressure in my chest. It was catching, and pretty soon my father and I were doubled over laughing and couldn't stop.

"What are you two cackling about?" Ellison groused, watching us from the doorway with his arms folded across his chest.

Seeing him there frowning made us laugh even harder, and Ellison just shook his head as he reached into the cabinet for a bowl.

Since then, Grandma Esther had backed off, and we'd settled into a wary truce. I knew I had my father on my side, and I had found a little of the bold sassiness that Ellison and my mother had always possessed. I liked that what had angered Grandma Esther was that I was like my mother. It was like carrying a piece of her inside me, and I cherished it.

But since Thanksgiving, Grandma Esther hadn't said much to me, just the normal, inconsequential conversation that is inevitable when you live together. That's why it was surprising that she was offering to take me shopping.

"Shopping? Well, okay," I said. I didn't think to ask why, or even what we were shopping for. I was mostly just relieved that she wasn't picking a fight with me.

But whatever hopes I had that shopping with Grandma Esther would be a good thing were dashed as soon as we entered the mall. For one thing, she wouldn't let me go in Contempo Casual or Express, or any of the stores with clothes for people under fifty. As it turned out, Grandma Esther had an agenda, and it had nothing to do with grandmother-granddaughter bonding.

"You need church clothes," she declared. We were standing in the section of Dillard's that was filled with long skirts, unconstructed jackets and drab-colored sweaters—all the things designed to cover as much skin and make me look as dowdy as possible.

I'd seen her eyeing me, the T-shirts I'd shrunk to make them fit tighter, the makeup I used to make myself look more grown up, to make myself feel like someone different. But she didn't even know me, not really. That's why I was so aggravated that it took me a minute to fully understand what she'd said.

"Church?"

Grandma Esther nodded and bustled over to the nearest rack. "Yes, church," she snapped, looking at me critically. "You need some structure in your life, some guidance. So I'm taking you to church." She said this as if it were the final word on the subject, daring me to argue.

"So now the whole family's suddenly going to church?"

She turned back toward the rack and began draping clothes I didn't want over her arm. "I didn't say anything about the whole family. I said you."

I could feel tears building in the corners of my eyes, but they were tears of anger, not sadness. I willed myself not to cry. I didn't want to show her any weakness.

"What about Ellison? You're not making him go?"

Grandma Esther sighed impatiently. "Girl, you act like going to church is a bad thing. You went to Catholic school, didn't you? Your mother must have done that for a reason."

Now I felt guilty. It wasn't that I hated church, or that I didn't believe in God. It was simply unfamiliar to me. We'd rarely gone to church in Chicago, except in school. We went to Catholic schools, but it wasn't because we were religious. We went initially because they were cheaper than other private schools, and then, after my mother started making money, Ellison and I already had enough friends to make a change in schools out of the question.

And anyway, Grandma Esther didn't even go to Mass. She was Baptist, and I didn't know anything about Baptist church. One more reason why I didn't want to go.

So I just stood there, watching my grandmother collect a pile of clothes without even asking me my size. When she was finished, she herded me toward the dressing room, where I found that everything she'd picked fit me perfectly.

When we were done, Grandma Esther left me in line at the register while she went off to look for a purse for me to carry to church; I supposed my multi-colored woven backpack wasn't going to cut it.

The girl at the register was rearranging her work area, bent down in concentration. When she looked up, I was surprised to see P.J.

"Hey," I said, trying to smile even though I was still morose at the thought of spending Sundays in church with Grandma Esther. I looked down at the clothes I was holding and immediately became embarrassed. P.J. would think I was so lame.

"Hey Maren." She glanced down at the pile of clothes I'd plopped on the counter, then looked at me.

"These are yours?"

I could hear the incredulity in her voice. "My grandmother picked them out."

She smiled sympathetically. "Going to church, huh?"

"Yeah. How'd you know?"

She raised her eyebrows. "You're, what, 15 or 16, right? No one our age would buy this stuff," she said, holding up a gray blouse by its bow. She rang up the total, and I handed over the money Grandma Esther had left me.

"My grandmother used to make me go to church all the time, too. What is it with them?" she said.

"I wish I knew," I laughed. I grabbed my bag and turned to leave.

"Well, it was nice seeing you," I said.

P.J. nodded and watched me as I turned to leave. "See you in school, Maren," she called after me.

I waved goodbye, feeling better than I had all day. It was nice to have a friend.

Calvary Gardens Baptist Church was unlike any other church I'd been in. The Catholic churches of my childhood were ornate and majestic, and even if the parish wasn't in a particularly wealthy neighborhood, they seemed to rise above their surroundings to tower over mere mortals. Every time I entered one, I felt a sense of calm as people knelt quietly and prayed, or recited the call and response in hushed tones during Mass. The altars were made of expensive wood buffed to a high shine and the pews were spotless. The windows of Catholic churches were covered in stained glass depicting the life of Jesus at various stages leading up to the crucifixion. That was the thing I missed most at Calvary Gardens—there was no crucifix high on the wall like there was at St. Francis. It's funny, I had never really liked the crucifix. It always seemed sad and macabre. But when I sat in the front pews at Calvary Gardens next to Grandma Esther, I missed that familiar image of Jesus on the cross.

Calvary Gardens looked less like a church and more like an old house except for the steeple. The one-story building sat on a small hill, with two sets of steps leading up to the front double doors. On either side of the doors were bay windows with shutters, and dormer windows were set into the roof above them. The church was surrounded by tall pine trees that gave off a mild fragrance in the chill of what passed for winter in Durham. With the whitewashed wood frame and green shutters, it looked unassuming and modest, much more understated than I expected.

Understated, that is, until we walked in the door. Inside there were people crying out "Thank you, Jesus" and "Yes Lord" while the choir sang. There was clapping, both on tempo and off, and the mood was loud and boisterous, not reflective and circumspect like Mass at St. Francis. We were late because I'd spent an hour trying on the different outfits Grandma Esther had bought, trying to choose one that didn't make me look and feel like a senior citizen, to no avail. Ellison, whom I'd begged to come along even though he wasn't being forced to, kept calling out to me to come on, that Grandma Esther was about to have a fit. I thought I might be able to stall until she gave up on me, but Ellison finally just pushed open the bathroom door, took me by the arm and ordered me to come on.

"You talked me into going, and I'm all dressed now, so let's go," he groused as he herded me down the stairs and out to Grandma Esther's car.

Services had already begun when we arrived, but because Grandma Esther was on the church board and worked there, her seats up front were reserved. There wasn't any actual preaching going on yet, but the choir was singing in full force, the sound of their strong, confidant voices sweeping over us as the ushers waved us to our seats. People turned to look as we proceeded down the aisle, and I felt conspicuous and embarrassed. I could feel people sizing me up, and when we got to our pew, I pushed Ellison in front of me so he sat between Grandma Esther and me and

I hugged the end of the bench.

When we walked in, the choir was singing a hymn that seemed familiar, even though I was pretty sure I'd never heard it before. It had a rollicking beat, a mix of funk and R & B, and the only thing that gave it away as gospel were the words. That, and the fact that the preacher punctuated the simple, repeating verses with a disjointed story about how he'd loved going to church as a child.

"Jesus is on the mainline
Tell him what you want
Call him up and
Tell him what you want"

They repeated these words over and over, the clapping and affirmation growing louder with each verse. Each time the reverend declared that "Jesus is on the mainline," the choir enthusiastically responded "Tell him what you want!"

I busied myself with pretending that I was singing, mouthing words that didn't necessarily match the song, while I looked around the church. It was filled with mostly women, women who mostly looked like variations of Grandma Esther. They were older women who held babies in their arms or clasped the hands of fidgeting ten-year-olds. There weren't many people my age at all. I looked around for P.J., hoping to see one familiar face, but I didn't see her anywhere. The few men who attended were ushers or standing up with the choir. I wondered why there weren't more men. There were grandmothers and mothers here, and kids, so there must have been fathers somewhere, but I guessed they weren't regulars at Calvary Gardens.

I assumed that after the first hymn was over they'd launch into the service, but I was wrong. They sang "What a Friend We Have in Jesus" next, and when they began the opening bars to "Amazing Grace," Ellison and I looked at

147

each other. If things kept up like this, we'd be here all day. Grandma Esther always spent most Sundays out of the house, but it never occurred to me that she was in church the entire time.

I leaned over to whisper this in Ellison's ear, but my words trailed off when Grandma Esther shot me a disapproving look. I slumped back and sighed.

"Amazing Grace" was a solo number, and I noticed that one word was different from the way I'd learned it. We used to say "saved a soul like me," but here at Calvary, they sang "saved a wretch like me." It was a small difference, but important, I thought. A soul could be anyone; it was all-inclusive and non-judgmental. But a wretch, well, that was clearly a sinner. It made me uncomfortable to think that at Calvary, you were automatically a wretch before you'd done anything at all. It reminded me of Grandma Esther. She'd already judged me before I even opened my mouth that first day. She saw me as a wretch that certainly needed saving; from what, I wasn't sure.

I became aware of the singer, whose smooth delivery was near professional-quality. When I looked up to see the man whose baritone rang out so clear and strong, I saw Chris. He wore the same black choir robe as everyone else, but he stood a little apart from the rest, singing with his mouth wide open. Toward the end of the song, he spread his arms wide open at a crescendo. Our eyes met at that moment, and as a smile spread over his features, he looked almost angelic. I smiled a little, too, even as I averted my eyes. I was stunned by the sound of his voice, and he made me feel shy.

Chris and I had seen a lot of each other over those months. There was always something that brought him back to Grandma Esther's house, whether it was to wash his clothes, to pick up a book he'd left or to grab a snack. He sometimes called me Mare, just like my brother and my father, but he said it differently. He took his time over it, drawling it out in a way that made me tingle. I knew that an uncle wasn't supposed to make you feel that way, but I couldn't help it. Chris wasn't much like an uncle anyway—he was twenty-one, just six years older than me. It wasn't that much, really. And he liked me. We talked a lot when he came over, sometimes just about silly things like television shows or movies, but sometimes we talked about serious stuff, like college and jobs. He wanted to be a sportscaster, and he was impressed by how much I knew about the television business.

"You're smart," he'd told me. "Not like the girls when I was in high school."

I wondered about Chris while I endured the string of unfamiliar rituals and recitations. Had he been singing in the choir all his life? Who taught him to sing—Grandma Esther? I couldn't really picture her teaching anyone anything in a motherly way. She seemed so stern and dour, and even though she liked Ellison, she wasn't all that affectionate with him. Or our father, for that matter.

But then I remembered that my father had been singing when Ellison and I first arrived in Durham. It must run in the family, although I couldn't carry a tune.

I periodically stole glances at Chris, and many times he was already looking at me, making me blush. My mind wandered, and I heard only bits and pieces of the sermon, which seemed to be about the value of family in times of trouble. Finally, it was over, and Ellison bolted outside. I followed him before Grandma Esther could look up from her conversation with a fellow parishioner.

We stood off to the side of the church, pulling our winter coats around us and blowing on our hands.

Ellison looked at me. "Who the hell goes to church for

four hours?" he grumbled. "At least the Catholics keep it down to an hour."

I shrugged and rolled my eyes. "I'm glad you came with me, though. It was nice having someone there besides Grandma Esther."

He frowned. "I hope you know I'm not coming every Sunday. I can't sit there for that long. I'll go crazy."

I couldn't even get mad at him. "I know," I sighed. "I'm hoping that if I cooperate now, Grandma Esther will get off my case and stop making me go."

He laughed. "I don't think Grandma Esther ever gets off anyone's case." He glanced around the front of the church. "Speaking of which, I don't see her yet, so I'm going to run to the bathroom."

He darted off, and I slouched down on one of the benches set up a little ways away from the church, where I could see the people streaming out but they couldn't see me behind the trees.

"Hey, Maren," Chris said from behind me.

"You have a bad habit of sneaking up on people," I said.

"And you always seem to be staring off into space. What are you thinking about?" he laughed.

He slid onto the bench beside me, and I noticed that he'd taken off his choir robe, leaving his crisp white shirt, blue tie and khaki dress pants exposed. He looked different from when I first saw him, more grown up. His questions seemed to be about more than just my wandering mind, but I wasn't sure exactly what he was asking.

So I changed the subject. "How long have you been singing in the choir?"

"That's what you were thinking about?" he teased.

I blushed. "Do you always answer a question with a question?"

He smiled. "Do you?"

We sat quietly for a while, watching the birds fly from branch to branch in the nearby tree. It was a pleasant silence, not at all awkward, and I enjoyed the feeling of his arm against mine.

He looked down at me. "You went shopping with Mama, huh?"

I grimaced. "Yeah."

"Has she been giving you a hard time?"

There was genuine concern in his eyes, and I was touched. Ellison always played down my complaints about Grandma Esther, saying I was overreacting to her various slights or reading too much into what I took to be barbs directed at me.

"A little," I said cautiously, not wanting to offend him in case he was sensitive about his mother.

He nodded. "She can be hard on people. Can I be totally honest?" He bit his lower lip, as if he too were unsure where the boundaries of this conversation lay.

I nodded.

"She never liked your mom. Mama always felt like Vanessa stole her boy, kept him up in Chicago," he said delicately. "So maybe that's why she's rough on you. You look a lot like your mom."

I didn't believe him, but I treasured Chris's compliment anyway, hoping that maybe there was some truth to it, that maybe I had some of my mother's beauty lurking inside me. "Her boy?"

"Calvin. Your dad."

I was confused. "But they didn't meet until after he moved to Chicago. He went there on his own," I said.

Chris shrugged. "You know how memories are. They don't always have much to do with the truth." He stood up and held out his hand to me. "Try not to let it get you down."

I felt like I was in way over my head with Grandma Esther, but it was nice to have Chris on my side.

"Thanks," I said, taking his hand and rising to my feet. "It's nice to have a friend in the family."

He raised his eyebrows. "I feel the same way. Now let's get you out front before Mama has a fit."

When we got home that afternoon, I changed out of my church clothes and watched part of an old black and white movie with Dad. He fell asleep on the sofa, and I wandered off to find Ellison. As I approached his door, I noticed that it was open just a crack. I could see him sorting through piles of paper and scribbling things onto a yellow legal pad. His brow was furrowed and he looked like he was concentrating, so I didn't want to disturb him. But I did want to know what he was doing, so I craned my neck to try to read one of the large white envelopes on his bed.

I saw "Harvard University" printed in bold letters, and I stepped back quickly. College applications. He was filling out college applications. Which meant he was thinking about leaving.

It wasn't a complete surprise—of course he was going to college after this year. He'd been planning it for years, since he was still a boy. I remembered the first talk he and Mom had about college. Ellison was twelve years old and already plotting his escape from the Emory family.

The three of us were driving home from school one afternoon. Usually, Ellison and I rode the school bus home, but that week, the bus drivers were on strike and Mom had to come from work to pick us up. I sat in the back seat singing along with the radio until Ellison turned it off.

"Can you just shut up?" he snapped at me. I had always bugged him, following him around and teasing him, but during that time things were especially difficult and he could hardly stand to be in the same room with me. I was ten and my main goal in life was to annoy my brother, so I had been singing my off-key rendition of "Isn't She Lovely" just to aggravate him.

He opened his window. It was May, the school year was almost over, and the weather was already warm. I opened my window too; I liked the way the wind swished against my face as we raced through the streets.

I never liked silence, so I started talking again, some nonsense designed to fill the car with noise.

During a break in my chattering, Ellison spoke up. "I'm going to college far away from here," he announced.

Mom glanced at him. "What?"

He rolled his eyes, but facing away from our mother so she wouldn't ground him for being disrespectful. "I said, I'm going to school really far away when I go to college. Really far."

Mom cleared her throat. "El, you're only twelve."

"But it's not too early to start planning, right?"

"That's true. But why do you want to go far away? There are plenty of good schools here—Northwestern, University of Chicago," she said. "I'm sure one of those would be great for you."

I could see Ellison's scowl in the side mirror. "I want to get away from everybody and everything. Be on my own," he said, crossing his arms over his chest.

Mom looked sad even as she smiled. She pulled up to our driveway and turned off the car.

"You're too dumb to go to college," I piped in from the back seat. "You'll have to work at McDonald's."

He sighed and looked at Mom. "See? That's why I want to leave."

We got out of the car and I stuck my tongue out at him. He lunged for me but Mom held him back. "Come on, now. Let's go inside," she said calmly, steering Ellison toward the front door.

He immediately went into the family room and turned on the television, and I followed, readying myself for an argument over what show to watch. But our mother came into the room after a few minutes, already changed into blue jeans and a T-shirt.

"So I thought we were talking about college," she said, stepping in front of the TV and tossing me the remote. "Why don't we make a list of some good schools that are far enough away for you."

Ellison smiled warily. "You mean it?"

"Can I watch whatever I want?" I said eagerly, thinking that I was getting one over on El.

"Sure, as long as it's not on Cinemax," she said, laughing. "El, let's go."

They sat at the kitchen table together all afternoon, looking through the atlas to find good universities that were at least 600 miles from our house. I peeked in periodically and saw him compiling his list happily while Mom looked on, suggesting different names and measuring to make sure the schools were far enough. It wasn't until the sky began to darken that they stopped.

College had always been on my brother's mind, but I just hadn't thought much about it since we'd been in Durham. The thought of Ellison being so far away left a hollow feeling in my stomach. I walked away before he could sense me watching him.

Chapter 10

By Christmas time, Ellison realized that he needed a job. He'd asked his father for an allowance or something, just to help him buy gas money, but that just started Calvin in on his push to get rid of Ellison's car. His father was only willing to give him money for specific purchases, like a new sweater or books, but Ellison hated having to justify wanting ten dollars here or twenty dollars there.

He'd had an allowance in Evanston—a generous one— and his mother had never made him account for the money he spent. As long as he didn't run up the credit card bills too high, she trusted him to figure it out on his own. Maren was used to being more dependent, since she wasn't old enough to drive, but Ellison felt constrained by his father's thrift.

Add that to the list of things that were very different here in Durham, Ellison thought as he circled ads in the Sunday paper. Christmas was just a week away, and lots of places were looking for help. He figured he'd make enough money by New Year's to hold him for a while.

He glanced at the clock. It was 12:30, and the house was still. His father had gone to church with Grandma Esther and Maren, so he had the place to himself. He folded up the paper and stuffed it into his back pocket, then bounded upstairs to check his wallet. He had a little of his own money left, enough to buy a new shirt for job interviews. He picked up his keys and walked down the hallway, but when he passed by his father's room, the door was ajar. Ellison had never been in there. He generally tried to avoid his father, and when Calvin was in his room he was usually writing with the door firmly closed.

Curious, Ellison pushed open the door. The walls were painted a deep blue, unlike the rest of the house. Grandma Esther said she liked white walls. She claimed they made the house look cleaner, which Ellison found ironic since she kept the place spotless anyway. So the rest of the house was painted stark white. Except for this room. The blinds were shut, shadows darkening the room even though the sun was shining outside. The walls were lined with bookcases filled with a different sort of book than the ones downstairs. These were hardcovers, mostly titles Ellison didn't like. He'd tried to read some of them in the ninth grade and hated it—they were too slow and plodding. He'd never gotten past the first chapter of most of them—it was as if they were written in a foreign language. He couldn't understand why so many "classics" were the books that were hardest to understand. Ellison couldn't see what was wrong with a book that just told it like it was, didn't make you search for the answers underneath obscure prose and complicated ideas. Look at Hemingway and Fitzgerald. Or Richard Wright. They wrote about serious stuff, but you could at least understand the words. It was like they wanted their readers to understand. Their writing wasn't an exercise in hiding ideas behind fancy writing.

His father's queen-sized bed took up half of the room, and his desk stood in a corner, covered with torn out sheets of notebook paper and more books. The bed wasn't made, and he stepped over a pile of sheets to the desk.

He'd never asked his father what he was writing. Ellison didn't really believe it was much of anything, anyway, since he never seemed to finish. All he knew was that it was a novel of some kind. Trying not to disturb the papers in case there was some kind of twisted order to the mess, Ellison sifted for evidence that his father was actually writing, rather than sitting up here watching the thirteen-inch television perched on the nightstand.

Most of the notes were indecipherable, the type of disjointed words and half-phrases that people write to remind themselves of things. "Sixteen and a half," one note said. "Borders of grass along a dusty highway," said another. A third note said cryptically: "Peaches." He could see no clear connection between the words, and he wondered whether, in his father's mind, there was something to link them together.

He came across an unlabeled file stuffed thick with papers. He peeked inside, where he found several versions of the same short story. "The Lovers." The title made Ellison want to pick up the papers by their corners, as if they were somehow tainted with his father's sexuality. He began reading the story and was almost immediately sorry, but he found that he couldn't put it down. It was about two lesbian lovers on the beach being watched from afar by a man. The story was filled with too much flowery description, too much cliché. It sounded like a Harlequin romance.

Still, he couldn't help wondering. When had his father written the story? Was the encounter between the women on the beach a fantasy or a memory? Was this the type of thing his father wrote—erotica?

When he'd seen the books on the shelves and the desk, he'd assumed his father was writing a literary novel, the type that critics would love and no one would read. But now Ellison wasn't sure. He wished he had the kind of father he could just come out and ask, about the story he'd just read, about writing, about life. But so far, Calvin didn't seem like that kind of father. It was only when he and Ellison were fighting that Calvin seemed committed to something, even if that something was an argument.

Feeling like he needed a shower, Ellison was about to leave the room when he noticed a brown leather-bound book that had to be a journal. It was tossed underneath a spiral notebook, and he eased it gently from its resting place and held it in his hands.

He looked around, as if someone might sneak up on him and catch him in the act, then examined the cover of the book. The initials "C.J.E." were embossed on the front, and the leather had a worn look, as if his father had owned it for a long time. The journal felt hot in his hands, dangerous, and he suddenly noticed how warm it was in the room. Wiping his forehead, Ellison plopped down in the desk chair and laid the book on his lap.

That small journal could hold the answers to many questions about his father. Maybe there was something in there about his writing. Maybe he wrote about his Grandma Esther, his childhood, his marriage to Ellison's mother. Maybe he wrote about Maren and Ellison.

He took a deep breath put the journal back where he found it. He was afraid of what he might find.

Ellison took his time driving to the mall, impassively looking around at the Christmas decorations. It didn't even feel like Christmas, not really. There was no snow, and it was unseasonably warm, even for Durham, almost sixty degrees. It seemed unnatural to see Christmas trees all lit up when it was still possible to wear shorts. But Ellison preferred it this way. Having a white Christmas, with all the familiar trappings, would have just reminded him even more that his mother wasn't here. This would be their first Christmas without her, and although he and Maren had agreed not to dwell on it, when he was alone, he couldn't help but miss her even more at this time of year.

He shook his head. This Christmas was shaping up to be very different from last Christmas. There wasn't even a tree in the house yet, and he was sure he'd spend most of the day in church with Grandma Esther.

Ellison sighed and switched his thoughts from his mother to his father, thinking about how little he really knew about Calvin, even though they'd lived together for three months and they were connected by blood. And what, really, did his father know about him, about Maren? Ellison had been avoiding Calvin lately, but it wasn't as if his father made an effort to see him, either. Calvin and Maren spent time together playing checkers or watching television, but could he give Maren the kind of guidance a mother would give? What, really, was he bringing to their lives besides a roof over their heads?

It doesn't matter, he thought as he pulled into the parking lot in front of Dillard's. It was December—in a few months, he'd know where he'd got in to college, and then in August, he'd be on his way, far away from Durham and his father.

He thought briefly of Maren, suppressing a pang of guilt. Who would take care of her? But maybe she'd be okay. She was still dressing up and wearing makeup, and she seemed to be making friends, talking a lot about someone named P.J. from school. She'd even become friends with Chris, and Ellison thought it was good for her to be close to someone else in their family, even if Chris didn't seem much like an uncle. More and more, Maren seemed to be taking care of herself just fine these days.

Once he was in the store, he walked in the direction of menswear and spotted a sign. Dillard's was accepting applications. He quickly purchased a blue oxford shirt and headed to customer service for an application.

He handed in the form, and waited in line to see the manager. When he got close to the window, a girl came and eased in front of him.

"Excuse me. I was next," he said politely.

She turned around and looked at him, but didn't move. It was Phyllicia Johnson, his lockermate. She wore a skirt and a blouse, and a nametag that said P.J. on it. P.J.? He had a sinking feeling and hoped this wasn't Maren's new friend.

"Do you know Maren?" he blurted out.

She frowned at him. "Yeah, so?"

"She's my sister."

P.J. rolled her eyes. "No kidding."

He felt dumb—of course Maren had mentioned him to her friend. He blushed, wondering if Maren knew about the "white boy" stuff, too. He supposed she did, even though she hadn't said anything; their paths didn't cross much at school, but she talked to people, unlike Ellison.

He couldn't think of a comeback, so he looked away and pretended P.J. wasn't there. They'd gotten pretty good at ignoring each other whenever they saw one another, which wasn't often since they had different schedules. P.J., Ellison had gathered from her books and notebooks, was a junior, so he counted himself lucky not to have any classes with her.

He saw her around school as he walked through the halls, trying to keep a low profile so as not to draw attention to himself. He hated being called "white boy," so he'd toned down his wardrobe, trying to dress more like everyone else, and he kept his mouth shut so no one could hear his Chicago accent and distinct enunciation.

But one day a couple of weeks before, he'd seen her with

one of the guys who'd first called him "white boy." They were holding hands, and Ellison tried to walk by with his eyes averted. It was seventh period, the end of the day. Ellison was supposed to be in study hall, but he was heading home early. He found McNeil classes much easier than St. Francis so he didn't need much study time at all, and the study hall teacher never took attendance anyway. It had been a long day, and he just wanted to go home.

"Hey, white boy. You don't know how to speak?"

P.J. and her boyfriend, an aggressive guy named Terrell, had stopped in front of Ellison so he couldn't keep walking. He narrowed his eyes and looked at the guy. His head was bald and shining, and he wore hoops in both ears. Trying to think of a way to diffuse the situation, Ellison idly wondered what it was like to fit in, how it felt to be just like everyone else, because even at St. Francis, he'd never been just like everyone else.

Here in Durham, Ellison was surrounded by black people, and yet, he'd never been more self-conscious about his race. At St. Francis, he'd been very aware of his otherness, which permanently separated him from his white classmates. He'd been aware of the subtle slights, the joking comments—all the things that were designed to remind him on a daily basis that he was black. But in a way, racism was easy to deal with. He expected it. He planned for it. He used it to his advantage by allowing people to underestimate him.

But here, he was just one of many black people, and he was beginning to realize that black wasn't simply black. There were shades in between the spectrum of black to white, and his classmates found him decidedly on the wrong end of that spectrum.

It wasn't his skin color—there were black students whose

skin was lighter than his, whose hair was straighter. No, there was something else about him that made him different even among his own. He simply wasn't black enough, and he didn't really know why.

This uncertainty had robbed him of something, he realized as he stood there. Whatever anyone might say about Ellison, he had never been one to stay quiet. He spoke his opinions even when he knew he shouldn't, sometimes because he really thought he was right; many times just to incite or annoy, to elicit some kind of reaction.

But during those first months at McNeil, he'd grown silent and withdrawn, pretending to ignore the snickers and the name-calling. He hated what he had become, and he wished he knew how to get the old Ellison back.

As he considered his reply to P.J.'s boyfriend, the guy's mouth twisted into a cheerfully false smile. All the taunting whispers ran through his mind. White boy. Thinks he's better than us. Oreo.

Ellison felt like fighting, felt like pummeling P.J.'s boyfriend until his hands ached. But he didn't want to make things worse for Maren at school, didn't want her to be an outsider like he was. So he just walked away.

Despite that encounter, at Dillard's, P.J. didn't even acknowledge that he was any more than a pesky stranger. "I work here. I just have to ask a quick question," she said dismissively.

He frowned. He was dismayed to learn that she worked there, and he wished he could take back his application. But it was too late.

"Okay, but I'm next. Then you can ask your question." He hated the way she was always so pushy. It was as if she assumed that she was much more important than the rest of the world. Ellison didn't like being treated as if he didn't count.

"Why are you always such a bitch?" he asked as he nudged her away from his place in line.

She whirled around angrily. "Why do you think you're better than everyone else?"

Ellison raised his eyebrows. "Who's friend called whom 'white boy?' I'm not the one calling other people names."

"Maybe if you didn't act so siddity, no one would call you that," she sneered.

"Siddity?"

She rolled her eyes impatiently. "Stuck up. That's why people call you 'white boy.' You go around talking like you're white, dressing like you're white, like you're too good for us."

"I don't think I'm better than anyone," he protested.

She cocked her head to one side. "Really? You think you're so smart, but people can see you looking down your nose at them. You curl your lip when someone talks, and it's like we can all hear you calling us country bumpkins in your head."

He could feel his cheeks redden in embarrassment. "Bullshit," he said weakly. But what she said was true. He supposed he did think of them as hicks, with their drawling accent and unfamiliar slang. But she was wrong—it wasn't that he simply didn't like other black people. Was it? Did he act white? Did he think he was better than them, because they drawled and went to public high school and didn't have expensive clothes like he did? Did he think he was better than them because he was light-skinned and curly (not nappy) haired?

Just then, the person in front of him moved on and it was his turn.

163

"The manager can see you now, if you want," the middle-aged woman at the window said. She snapped gum between her teeth while shuffling papers.

He agreed and walked into the back room, never looking back at P.J. He couldn't believe Maren liked her, and he was relieved not to have to talk to her anymore.

When he got home later that afternoon, Ellison was surprised to find only his father waiting for him. He looked cautiously around the quiet living room, where his father lounged on the sofa, reading a book. Ellison couldn't read the title, but it reminded him of being in Calvin's room earlier that day, and he felt uneasy.

"Hey," Ellison said. He still didn't know what to call his father. "Dad" still seemed inappropriate, and he reserved "Calvin" as a weapon during an argument. "Where are Maren and Grandma Esther?"

"Still at church. I left a little early." Calvin stood up and smiled uncomfortably. They hadn't found a rhythm in their relationship outside of fighting. "Want to go get a tree with me?"

"A tree?"

"Christmas. It's next weekend, and we always get the tree in time to decorate it on Christmas Eve. I thought maybe you'd want to go."

Ellison fought the feeling that welled in his throat. Maybe it meant nothing, his father asking this. Maybe Calvin hadn't thought about how much Ellison would be missing his mother. Maybe he wasn't trying to change their distant relationship into something more. Maybe this wasn't his father's way of asking for a truce. Maybe he didn't know that Ellison had always gotten the Christmas tree back in Chicago.

Ellison fought his hopes that maybe Calvin had thought of these things, because what if he believed in his father, what if he let his guard down, and he was disappointed yet again? He'd never forgive himself.

So he remained neutral, even smiling back at his father. It was a smile that didn't give away too much. "Sure."

As they stood in the tree lot, Ellison walked over to examine a Douglas fir and inhaled the scent of pine that surrounded him. He thought of his mother that last Christmas in Hawaii, smiling and pretty, and tears rolled down his cheeks. After a few moments, he snapped the tag off the nearest tree, wiped his eyes, and went to find his father.

Chapter 11

P.J.'s room was pink. Very pink. Someone had put a lot of thought into amassing a collection of accessories and decorations in every shade. The bedspread and matching curtains were splashed with large rose-colored carnations. The walls were painted a deep salmon. Even the carpet was pale pink. There were large, framed posters all over the room, depicting ballet dancers in various positions. P.J.'s shelves held knick-knacks instead of books, girlish figurines of kittens and cherubs. The room even smelled pink—the scent of Love's Baby Soft wafted through the air.

P.J. and I had gotten pretty friendly. She'd introduced me to her friends and she took me with her to parties and basketball games. I usually kept quiet, basically acting as P.J.'s sidekick. I didn't mind it, though. Every moment I was distracted from my own life was a moment well spent. So I didn't complain about holding P.J.'s purse while she danced, pretending to like it when guys hit on me. I just smiled and tried to fit in.

This was the first time I'd been in a clique, accepted by the popular kids as one of them. And I did feel a part of something, even if it was only because P.J. dragged me with her everywhere she went. They accepted me and as long as I dressed like they did and didn't say much, everything was fine.

P.J. and I hung out a lot, but I'd never been to her house before today. Her mother wasn't home—never was, according to P.J.—and she'd never mentioned her father so I assumed he was out of the picture. I was surprised when I saw her room. P.J. was pretty and feminine, but she was also tough and worldly, and her decor seemed incongruous.

Maybe her mother had picked the room's theme when P.J. was younger and they'd never gotten around to changing it. I wanted to ask but didn't want to offend, just in case P.J. liked all that pink, so I didn't say anything at all.

P.J. tossed her backpack into a corner and flopped down on the bed. We'd come to her house after school to study; I was a sophomore and she was a junior, but we were in the same biology class. I sat on the (pink) futon underneath the window and rummaged in my bag for my textbook.

"Did you get all that stuff about mitochondria?" I opened to the chapter.

She shrugged and smiled. "Nah. I was too busy passing notes to Terrell." Her smile was conspiratorial, as if she had a secret and couldn't wait to share it.

I raised my eyebrows. "I thought you broke up with Terrell last month."

She nodded. "He went to Shelley's New Year's Eve party with Devonna Wright while I was visiting my sister in Virginia. He thought I wouldn't find out, but I did."

"So, why pass notes to him?"

She shrugged. "Valentine's Day is next week. If we get back together, he'll have to buy me something. I just saw this gold bracelet that I like."

I looked down at the page of my textbook, unsure of what to say. It wasn't the first time P.J. had talked about getting guys to buy her things. I usually changed the subject quickly because I didn't understand how Calvin Klein jeans and Ralph Lauren tops were so closely linked to love for her. To me, love was an abstraction: the smell of autumn leaves burning, the taste of good vanilla ice cream, the feel of velvet under your fingertips. It had nothing to do with jewelry and clothes and CDs.

But I stayed silent and she went on. "Plus, the sex was great."

A nervous giggle escaped my lips before I could stop it. I looked up to see if she was serious. She was.

"You had sex with Terrell?"

She laughed again. "Don't act so shocked. It's no big deal."

But it was a big deal to me. If I'd really thought about it, I might have realized that she was doing more than holding hands with her series of short-term boyfriends. But knowing it for a fact was another matter entirely. I looked out the window, unable to meet P.J.'s eyes. Unconcerned, she turned to the nightstand to fiddle with the boom box, trying to find a good song on the radio. I was glad for the distraction. It gave me a little time to sort things out.

On one level, I was terribly embarrassed. I wasn't sure I wanted to hear about P.J.'s sex life. I'd never really talked about sex with anyone before, not even my mother. Back in Evanston, Jordan and I talked about boys in an abstract way, but never sex. Neither of us was having any, so what was the point? I was fifteen, but sex still seemed too scary to me, too permanent, and I couldn't imagine loving someone enough to let them see me naked.

But my embarrassment was overshadowed by my complete sense of inferiority. Fifteen and sixteen year old girls had sex all the time, I knew that, so P.J.'s admission shouldn't have been so surprising. But it made me feel as if I'd been living in a protective cocoon, distanced from all the things other girls my age were experiencing. It was as if I was masquerading as a teenager rather than actually being one.

I missed Jordan, missed having a friend who was like me, who understood me. I hadn't spoken to her since I left

Evanston. It had seemed too difficult to hold on to any part of my old life, so I'd let her go, not reading her letters, not returning her phone calls. I hoped she understood.

Looking at P.J., I closed my book. I could see we weren't going to get much studying done. She found a station playing Mariah Carey and turned back to me. I could see in her eyes that she wanted to tell me more. So I let her, but I wasn't sure if I did it for her or for me.

"I'm not saying it's a big deal. You just never told me, that's all." I tried to look causal, pulling my legs up under me on the futon. "So, why is he so great?"

To me, Terrell wasn't that attractive. He always made a big show of how tough he was, but he just seemed like a bully to me. He had a bold arrogance that he used as a shield, but I'd watched him enough to know he wasn't nearly as pleased with himself as he pretended to be.

And then there was his thing with Ellison. I knew what people said about my brother, saying he acted white. El never said anything to me about that, so I pretended I knew nothing about it. I felt bad that he hadn't found a place for himself at McNeil. But Ellison had never needed anyone else's approval, and he never complained about school, so I figured he must be okay.

Just the same, I didn't like Terrell and I silently held a grudge against him for taunting my brother. But P.J. liked him. She'd told me more than once that she liked his "thug appeal." They'd known each other since middle school, but hadn't started dating until last year. Then, she found out he cheated on her on New Year's and broke up with him, which was ironic since she'd told me about some guy she kissed while she was up in Virginia for the holidays.

"Well, you know how some guys won't do certain things?"

I didn't know, but I nodded anyway.

"Terrell's not like that. He'll do anything I want him to do."

Anything? Anything like what? I wondered if she was talking about the basics or a whole world of sexual escapades that I knew nothing about. I was disgusted and curious at the same time.

"Other guys don't do . . . anything?" I asked hesitantly.

She shook her head, sat up straight on the bed and proceeded to list, in great detail, who did what to whom and under what circumstances.

I tried not to let my mouth hang open too much as she went on and on. Not only did she cite an astonishing array of sex acts, but the list of guys she'd been with seemed impossibly long and varied.

"And then there was the older guy. He knew what he was doing, but his wife found out about us and we had to stop seeing each other," she said offhandedly.

My breath caught in my throat. "Who?" My voice was squeaky, so I left the question half-finished.

P.J. looked smug. "I can't say his name. I don't want rumors to get out. But let's just say you'd recognize him around school."

"A teacher?" I was horrified.

She smiled and hopped up from the bed. "I'm going to get a Coke. Want one?"

I nodded and watched her hips swing as she left the room. It was too much to take in all at once: the long list of "boyfriends," her insinuation about sleeping with a teacher, my own glaring inexperience.

When she came back with the sodas, she chatted about the Valentine's Day dance as if our whole conversation hadn't happened.

"I was thinking, maybe I should ask someone new to the dance." She paused and looked at me carefully. "Your brother is cute."

I frowned. I didn't like the idea of my brother going anywhere with P.J. First of all, she was my friend, one of the only things I had that was mine and mine alone. And now that I knew she and her dates had a tendency to end up in the bedroom, I didn't want her anywhere near Ellison.

"No, I think he's dating someone."

"Who? I haven't seen him with anyone."

I quickly searched for a suitable lie. "Someone back home. In Chicago."

"Oh." She looked disappointed but snapped out of it quickly. "So who are you going with?"

I shrugged. "No one asked me."

She rolled her eyes. "This isn't the Middle Ages—you can ask a guy out if you want. So who do you like?"

After all that she'd told me, I couldn't admit that I had no experience with guys, that I'd never even been kissed. "There's a guy I like at church," I said, hoping it would satisfy her. I knew she'd never go to church, so I was safe.

But she leaned forward, interested. "Tell me about him."

I sighed. "Well, he's a little older. Tall, dark-skinned. He likes basketball and he sings in the choir," I said, slowly realizing that I wasn't describing a fictitious boyfriend at all—I was describing Chris.

She smiled. "So why not ask him?"

Because he's my uncle. "I'm not sure he likes me." I looked at my watch. "Well, it's getting late. I better get going." I shoved my book back into my bag and walked quickly to the door.

P.J. looked disconcerted. "You have to leave right now?

We're just getting to the good stuff."

I opened the door and stretched my mouth into a smile. "My grandmother's expecting me. See you," I said, waving goodbye. I rushed down the stairs and out the front door before she could convince me to stay.

Valentine's Day was on a Thursday, and I still hadn't decided whether I was going to the dance the next night. P.J. kept bugging me, telling me to ask my "mystery man" from church, but I held her off, saying I hadn't had a chance to talk to him because he'd been sick last Sunday. It wasn't true, of course. Chris had sung another solo that week, "Rock of Ages," which was an unusual choice for Calvary Gardens. He got a standing ovation when it was over and I felt a curious sort of pride when he beamed at me after he hit the final note.

But lying to P.J. seemed both harmless and absolutely necessary. We were friends, but there was no way I was telling her about Chris. We'd never touched or said anything that was inappropriate, but there was this connection that I knew no one would understand. Not even P.J.

And more importantly than the specter of the dance, which I assumed I would spend following P.J. around, I hated Valentine's Day. I'd never had a boyfriend to buy me gold bracelets or chocolates or even a card, so I'd spent every Valentine's Day since boys and girls started to notice each other feeling like an outcast. I knew it was just a marketing holiday designed to get people to spend money, but the marketing was powerful.

Still, I hated the way all the girls wore pink and red on Valentine's Day, acting all cutesy and coy about what their "sweeties" had cooked up for them. I hated the sickening ads selling stuffed animals and diamonds and flowers to the highest bidder. I hated red roses, and carnations made me sneeze.

As far as I was concerned, the only good thing about Valentine's Day was its ironic association with Capone's 1929 massacre of seven fellow gangsters. I liked the bloody tinge those historic killings cast over the whole dumb holiday.

So I was in a dark mood that Thursday. I wore a black skirt and sweater in protest of forced Valentine's Day cheer. Ellison shook his head when I came down for breakfast.

"Why can't you just wear pink like all the other girls," he teased.

I stuck out my tongue. "Pink is not my color."

I figured P.J. would be dressed in pink from head to toes, considering her bedroom decor, but she was wearing a tight orange dress instead. When I saw her that morning, she made a point of emphasizing everything she said with expansive hand movements so no one could miss the new bracelet gleaming on her wrist. Every other time I saw her that day we didn't have a chance to talk because she was glued to Terrell, holding his hand, stroking his cheek, kissing him in full view of teachers.

It wasn't just P.J. who was getting into the Valentine's Day spirit—everywhere I looked there were couples hugging and kissing and giggling. By the end of the day, my mood had darkened considerably.

"Why do you look so sour?" Ellison asked as we walked to his car after school.

"Fucking Valentine's Day. I hate it," I grumbled, slamming the door. I stared out the window, where I could see P.J. walking with Terrell in the distance. They were probably going off to some secret place where they'd do all the things that she'd described to me last week.

"What's the big deal? You never used to get this freaked out about Valentine's Day," my brother said, glancing over at me.

I shrugged. How could I explain the feeling of being fifteen and feeling like a little kid who doesn't know anything? How could I explain that just once, I wanted to be like everyone else, with a boyfriend and a date to the dance? How could I explain that yearning to feel special and wanted?

We stopped at a light and he looked over at me. "You want a boyfriend, is that it?"

I didn't want to talk about my non-existent love life with Ellison. "I don't know."

He shook his head. "You're too young."

I got angry. "In June I'll be sixteen. That's not too young."

He frowned. "Who do you have in mind?"

"For what?"

"Who's the guy you want so badly that you're in this shitty mood?" We pulled up in front of Grandma Esther's house and parked. I moved to open the door, but Ellison grabbed my arm.

"Mare, I'm not trying to grill you. I'm just worried, that's all. Back home, you weren't really interested in guys, and suddenly now you are," he said softly.

I looked away. "A lot of things are different now. Including me," I said.

He let go of my arm. "I don't want you to get hurt."

"Don't worry, okay? I'll be fine."

He looked skeptical, as if he was going to object, but then he simply nodded. I hopped out of the car and jogged up to my room. For some reason, I felt like crying and I didn't want Ellison to see my tears.

I must have dozed off. It was almost dark outside when I

heard a soft knock at my bedroom door. I slowly emerged from sleep and figured it must be Ellison at my door. I wasn't in the mood to talk, so I laid there for a moment before calling out. "Go away, El. I'm sleeping."

The door opened a crack and Chris's head appeared. My room was dark, and he was silhouetted by the bright hall light.

"How can you talk in your sleep?"

"Oh, hi." I quickly sat up and turned on my bedside lamp. I patted down my sleep-tousled hair and tried to look attentive. "I thought you were my brother," I stuttered, now fully awake. He was always catching me off-guard, unprepared. Maybe that's why he made me so nervous.

"Can I come in?" He smiled at me.

I nodded and tried to smooth down my rumpled comforter. But instead of sitting on my bed, he pulled my desk chair over and sat down. He held an envelope in his hand. I wondered what it was, but I didn't ask.

"What time is it?" I said to break the silence. He'd left the door ajar and I could hear voices and footsteps in other parts of the house, but they gave no clue as to the hour.

"Almost dinner time." He stopped and cleared his throat as if he was preparing for a speech. I figured he was about to say something important, so I leaned forward.

"How was your day?" He looked around the room for the first time, noticing my drawings. I felt a little embarrassed at having childish things on my walls, but he didn't mention them.

I didn't think he'd come here for small talk, and I'd never seen him so uncomfortable. Usually, he was cool and confident, not darting his eyes around nervously. Maybe his uncertainty should have made me feel better about mine, but it only exacerbated my own jitters.

I'd forgotten that it was Valentine's Day until Chris asked about my day. Maybe it was a card for Grandma Esther in his hand. Even Ellison, the most notoriously unsentimental member of our family, had always given Mom a card for Valentine's Day. True, it was invariably one of those joke cards that's more an insult than anything else, but still, the thought was there. That's what Valentine's Day should be all about, an unexpected bit of sweetness.

"My day?" I paused, deciding whether to tell him the truth. "Well, I hate Valentine's Day, so it kind of sucked."

He smiled. "You hate Valentine's Day?"

"I hate all the forced affection, all the smarmy advertisements, all the pink and red. All you need are words to tell someone how you feel, right? Or do chocolates speak louder than words?" I was ranting, and Chris laughed.

"Whoa, I don't work for Hallmark. Don't yell at me," he teased. "I was just wondering how you could hate a holiday that's supposed to be all about love."

My cheeks grew hot and I looked down, fiddling with the edge of my comforter. "Well, you asked how my day went."

"True."

I looked up and Chris was still smiling at me. He held out the envelope in his hand.

"What's that?"

He wagged the envelope in the air. "It's for you." He raised his eyebrows. "Just some words to mark the occasion."

I was stunned, with thoughts flying through my mind almost faster than I could register them. This was a Valentine's Day card for me. He'd been thinking of me.

I ripped open the envelope. The card was simple: a purple tulip on a cream-colored background. The paper was heavy, textured like linen. It smelled vaguely floral, as if he'd found it in a store full of womanly things. I opened it and read the inside.

"Maren, thanks for making me smile. Love, Chris," he'd written.

Just as I finished reading, Chris stood up. "Well, I better get going. Got a paper to write." He moved toward the door while I sat there with my mouth open, trying to find the voice to say something.

His hand was on the doorknob when I stood up and walked over to him.

"Chris."

He looked down at me, his eyes hooded so I couldn't tell what he was thinking. I took his hand in mine, and all I could think of was the feeling of his fingers touching mine. I leaned toward him, and I could almost feel his lips on mine as he drew closer.

But he kissed me on the cheek instead, whispering "goodnight" before leaving me standing there, bewildered, ashamed, wanting more.

I didn't go to school the next day. I figured that if I stayed away from P.J. she wouldn't have a chance to pester me about the dance that night.

And anyway, no one cared that I stayed home, not really. I laid in bed until Grandma Esther left the house, and when Ellison popped his head in and asked if I was okay, he didn't press me when I waved him off. My father's bedroom door was still closed when I walked out into the hall to make sure the coast was clear, so I was home free.

I still wore the old gray sweatshirt I slept in every night, and I pulled on the matching pants and padded down the stairs. The morning sun streamed through the windows at the front of the house, and when I opened the door, the weather was mild. I stepped outside onto the front porch and sat on the top step, looking out into the street.

Now that I'd been in Durham a while, I saw the neighborhood through different eyes. When we'd first arrived, I was afraid, afraid of all the dark faces, the old houses, the loud noises that never seemed to subdue. It was all so unlike our old neighborhood in Evanston. No one on Grandma Esther's street seemed concerned about privacy or decorum. Even in the winter, people spent so much of their time outdoors, sitting on porches, playing car stereos, bouncing basketballs or just walking slowly through the streets. In Evanston, you had to imagine what your neighbors' lives were like; here in Durham, you could see for yourself.

Grandma Esther had been right—when I first saw this street, this house, I had thought they were poor. Compared to our old house (which was hardly a palace, especially when compared to some of my friends' homes), these houses looked shabby and worn.

But now, it didn't seem fair to compare Durham to Evanston. I grew to appreciate the old wood frame houses, with their wraparound porches and pine trees all around. I liked saying "hi" to people when I passed by, already knowing their names and their parents' names. I liked seeing so many brown faces around at school and at home. It was a nice change from being the minority everywhere I went.

I had even grown to like the smell of Durham, that faint tobacco smell that mixed with the scent of dandelions and black-eyed Susans, making the air heavy and sweet. I took a deep breath as I watched the kids across the street playing one last game of hide-and-seek before school.

The screen door squeaked behind me. My father, still in his red plaid robe, sat down beside me.

"No school today?" he said amiably, smiling at me.

I wasn't sure whether I needed to make up an excuse or not. Maybe he would understand if I told the truth. "There's a dance tonight. P.J. was trying to get me to go." It wasn't an explanation, but he nodded.

"Just gives us a chance to hang out for the day."

I smiled. "Yeah."

We sat quietly for a while. Finally, my father cleared his throat.

"So why don't you want to go to the dance? Arnetta was talking about it. Sounds like a big deal."

I looked down at my feet. "I didn't have anyone to go with."

"I can't believe you couldn't find a date. Pretty girl like you?"

I sighed. I didn't feel all that pretty, especially next to P.J. Everything about her was loud and engaging. I felt like a mouse next to her.

I wished I could explain it all to him, about P.J. and Chris and the Valentine's Day card that I still hadn't figured out. "I didn't want to go with just anyone," I said, looking up at him.

He nodded again. "Someone special you had in mind?"

"I guess so."

He smiled. "Someone from school? I remember those high school crushes. I never could get up the nerve to talk to girls I liked," he said.

I shrugged, non-committal. Just as well he thought I had a crush on someone from school. I could hardly explain all the feelings swirling around inside me.

He put his arm around me and kissed my forehead. It was the first time he'd done that since I'd been in Durham, the first time since I was a little girl that I felt that fatherly protectiveness. I laid my head on his shoulder.

"Listen, I don't claim to have all the answers," he said gently. "But I know one thing: if you follow your heart, everything will work out."

I sighed, wondering what it meant to have everything work out. "Thanks."

Follow my heart. Now I just had to figure out exactly what my heart was saying.

Chapter 12

Ellison felt as if he'd spent the entire month of March posted at the mailbox, waiting for letters from colleges. One, two, three weeks passed, and he got nothing but class ring advertisements and catalogs from schools he wouldn't even consider. Under different circumstances, he might have laughed at the waste of paper and postage that went into these mass mailings. But he was deadly serious about getting into a good college, and going somewhere far away had become even more important since he and Maren moved to Durham.

Each day, he was acutely aware of the date, and each day that passed could be interpreted as a bad sign. If they wanted him, they'd know right away, right? He grew even more sarcastic and ill-tempered than usual, unable to keep from snapping at Maren, his father, his grandmother, customers at Dillard's—anyone who crossed his path. His family knew enough to ignore his comments and steer clear. He wanted them to keep their distance, but it also made him feel lonely.

After getting home from school on Thursday afternoon, he found the mailbox empty. He stormed into the house, and when he stomped into the kitchen to get a drink, he was surprised to find Grandma Esther. She usually arrived home just before dinnertime and began cooking as soon as she got in the door.

But that day, she was home too early, sitting at the table drinking coffee and wearing her bathrobe. Ellison was alarmed. He'd never seen his grandmother sit around in a bathrobe, especially not at 3:30 in the afternoon. Plus, she barely looked up at him when he stormed in and merely grunted at his greeting. She looked lost, and it occurred to him that he wasn't the only one with a lot on his mind.

"Grandma Esther, are you okay?" he asked, sitting down across from her.

She sighed and looked out the window. "I wasn't feeling well at work, so the pastor told me to come home."

He frowned. "Do you have a cold or something? I can make you some tea." Caring for sick people had never been one of his strong suits; he hated the smell of cough medicines and the sound of sniffling annoyed him. But there was something about the way Grandma Esther sat there, her eyes tired and her shoulders slumped, that touched him. Whether you liked Grandma Esther or not (or, more importantly, whether or not she liked you), there was no denying that she was tough. And that day at the table, Ellison saw no signs of his grandmother's toughness.

"I don't have a cold," she snapped. "I'm just not feeling quite right, that's all."

"Are you sure?"

She glared at him. "Stop fussing over me and mind your own business," she said in a low voice. Any other time, she might have barked this out with venom. But this time the words didn't hold much threat.

But he did as she asked and kept quiet, walking over to get a glass of apple juice. He went back to the table, where they sat in silence for a long while.

Grandma Esther spoke first. "Sorry I snapped at you." She smiled weakly. "I'm just not myself today."

He nodded and took a sip from his glass. "It's okay."

She rubbed her hands over her face, then clapped her hands together lightly as if she was signaling the start of something.

"It's getting late. I better get started on dinner. Meatloaf okay with you?"

He looked at her, worried. She never consulted Ellison or anyone else before deciding what to cook. He agreed that meatloaf was fine and finished off his juice. He watched her back for a moment as she rinsed out the skillet and dug around in the refrigerator for ground beef and pork. He wanted to say something else, but he didn't know what.

Instead, he rose from the table. "Guess I'll go upstairs and do some homework," he said.

She turned around. "Oh, I almost forgot—you got a bunch of mail today."

His stomach recoiled. He'd been watching the mail vigilantly, but he'd also been dreading the day when it would arrive. He desperately wanted to know what his future held and he was desperately afraid to find out. Once he knew where he was going to college, everything would change. He'd have to start thinking about what it meant to live on his own, what it meant to live away from Maren for the first time in his life.

Ellison realized he was still standing in the kitchen doorway, stunned, until Grandma Esther spoke again.

"Go on. It's all out there on the hall table."

He was very methodical about the whole process. He only glanced at the envelopes long enough to grab all the ones that bore his name, superstitiously holding his gaze away from the return addresses. He took the stairs two at a time up to his room and closed the door behind him. He set the envelopes on the bed, face down, and stood in the middle of the room, trying to catch his breath.

This was so important, he wanted to take his time and savor the moment, be it good or bad. College was about more than just getting an education and a good job; it was about a chance to start over. College was the perfect opportunity to be whoever he wanted to be without worrying about his family or anyone else. It was an opportunity to find a new Ellison, maybe one who didn't spend so much time worrying, one who felt more comfortable around other black people, one who didn't care so much about wearing nice clothes and driving a fancy car.

He believed that the only way he could find these things inside himself was to go far away from anyone who'd ever known him. He wanted to leave behind all obligations and history. He wanted to be free.

It wasn't a new thing, this hunger for freedom, but he had put it on the back burner while he tried to adjust to Durham and his new family. But there had always been a part of him that wanted to be on his own. Long ago, he'd made a list of schools with his mother. Now, five years later, she was gone and he was about to see the results of all his plans. His latest list was much shorter, but all five schools he applied to had been on that original list. He only applied to the best schools and didn't bother with a contingency plan. The whole idea of backup schools seemed silly to him. It was like you were courting failure. If Ellison couldn't go to the best schools, well, he guessed he just wasn't going.

Finally, he sat down on his bed and opened the envelopes one by one. Berkeley, Duke, Harvard, Stanford, Dartmouth. They all said the same thing—welcome.

Ellison spread out the letters all round him on the bed. All of them. He'd gotten into all of them. He couldn't believe it. His pulse raced and he didn't know what to feel first, so he felt everything at once. Excited. Nervous. Frightened. Ecstatic. He was still looking from one to another when Maren knocked and walked into his room, and he didn't even bother to yell at her for barging in.

"What are you doing?" she asked, looking at all the papers strewn around the bed.

He leaped up and grabbed her in a huge bear hug. "I got in! I got in!"

"Where?" Her voice was muffled because her face was still smashed into his chest.

He held her at arm's length away from him, grinning. "All of them. Can you believe that? All of them."

She smiled, but he knew what she was thinking: they were going to be apart. But he wasn't ready to think about that, not yet.

"Mare, I know, it's a lot to digest. But just be happy for me, okay?"

She nodded, but her smile was still strained. "I am. You know I am." She took a deep breath. "So what are we waiting for? Let's go celebrate!"

Ellison was still floating when he arrived at Dillard's Saturday morning for his shift. Not even P.J., who was unfortunately working alongside him that day in the shoe department, could bring him down.

He hummed as he arranged rows of leather brogans on the softly lit shelves. He usually hated working in shoes—it required constant straightening and for some reason, people got really angry when you didn't have their size. But today, even shoes couldn't get him down.

P.J. ignored him until just before ten when the store was about to open. He'd progressed from humming to whistling, and he even returned her glare with a smile.

"What are you so cheery about?" She had the groggy look of someone who'd been up much too late the night before.

He held his arms up over his head, a tennis shoe in each hand. "I'm leaving. Outta here. Gone. Goodbye. In just a few months I'll be going to college far away from here," he announced loudly, laughing at P.J.'s exasperated sigh.

"Couldn't you just tell me like a normal person—without the Reeboks in your hands?"

He set down the shoes and walked over to the cash register. "Nope. This isn't just a normal piece of news. This is monumental."

"Lots of people go to college, you know."

He grinned and began pushing the register buttons rhythmically so the beeps echoed through the department. "But lots of people aren't me."

She shook her head and smiled. "So where are you going?"

Ellison hadn't gotten that far yet. He didn't have to notify the schools until late May, so he'd put off the decision-making for a while. "Berkeley, Stanford, Harvard, Dartmouth. Take your pick, I got into them all," he said cheerfully. He didn't mention Duke; he'd wanted to go there when he was younger, but now that he lived in Durham, it was way too close to home.

"Wow—you must be smarter than I thought," she teased, nudging him playfully.

Before he could respond, the first customers of the day came in and they got to work. In between fetching size sevens, Ellison marveled at the change in P.J. today. She was actually civil to him, had even smiled a couple of times. Why had she changed her attitude so suddenly? Or was it he who had changed? He hadn't felt this good in months. He wasn't sure if his good mood was the cause of P.J.'s turn-around, but he didn't really care. She wasn't half-bad when she wasn't scowling. And she really was cute, he thought, watching her walk back and forth across the department. He shook his head. He knew she was still with that Terrell kid who had called him 'white boy'—he saw them draped all over each other all the time lately. And anyway, she was Maren's friend. No good could come of it.

"Do you have these in a six and a half?" a pretty, dark-skinned woman asked, waving a sandal. She looked familiar, but it took him a moment to remember where he'd seen her before. It was Arnetta, who worked at the school's front office and knew his father. Ellison blushed, remembering how she'd seen him and Calvin arguing on his first day at McNeil.

He didn't know whether he should say hello. He saw her in the halls once in a while, and she usually nodded and smiled. But he didn't know if she actually remembered him or just smiled at all the students as some sort of goodwill gesture from the administration.

"I'm sure we have it in your size. Let me go check," he said formally.

Arnetta smiled. "Aren't you even going to say 'hi?' " she teased.

He shrugged. "I wanted to, but I wasn't sure if you knew who I was."

She laughed. "How could I forget you? It's not often that I have a cute new student nearly come to blows with his father right in front of my desk."

Now Ellison laughed. "Yeah, I guess that is kind of memorable."

She just kept looking at him, still smiling, and he didn't know what to say, so he turned the shoe over to look for the stick number. "I'll go get these for you."

He watched Arnetta as she tried on the sandals. He again noticed how young she looked, and he liked the way she still managed to look sexy in blue jeans and a dark red shirt, wearing little makeup with her braided hair up in a ponytail. When she caught him staring, she raised her eyebrows and smiled.

He averted his eyes, pretending to be busy with something on the counter. She made him feel shy, not at all his normal self. And she'd called him "cute." He wondered if she was still seeing Calvin.

"So, how do they fit?" he asked casually.

"I love them—ring me up."

As he handed her the receipt, he took a chance. "Can I ask you a question?" he said hesitantly.

Arnetta waited expectantly and he cleared his throat. "Well, I was just wondering, well, are you still dating my father?"

She looked at him for a long moment. "Calvin and I are friends," she said slowly. "Why do you ask?"

He took a deep breath and spoke before he could talk himself out of it. "I just thought that maybe you'd want to go out for coffee or something sometime," he blurted, keeping his voice low so P.J. and the other customers couldn't hear. All the reasons for her to say no ran through his mind in the few seconds it took her to respond.

"You don't think I'm too old for you?" she asked, looking at him appraisingly. "I'm 22."

Twenty-two was even younger than he'd first suspected. "I'm almost 18," he said hopefully.

She laughed as if he'd told a joke. Ellison smiled, but he didn't think it was all that funny.

"Ellison, I like you, you seem really cool. But I just don't think it would be appropriate, you know?"

He sighed and nodded. If she had said yes it would have

almost been too much—his mood couldn't get much better. "Yeah, I know."

He was grateful that she had at least been nice about the whole thing, so he smiled at her to show that there were no hard feelings. "Enjoy those sandals," he said.

She looked him in the eye and held the gaze for just a beat longer than necessary. "I will."

He watched her walk away until another customer came along and blocked his view.

At four, Ellison's shift was over and he prepared to leave. P.J. was already gone, having whirled off to go hang out somewhere with Terrell. The store was quiet for a moment; Saturday was a busy day overall, but the traffic in shoes died down after lunchtime. Ellison knew from the booklet he'd been given when he started at Dillard's that late afternoon was, in fact, a better time to buy shoes—feet were bigger late in the day and the shoes you bought would fit better overall. But he wasn't complaining. He liked the peace and quiet.

When he was finished counting the money in the drawer and straightening the counter, Ellison unpinned his name tag and rummaged around for his backpack so he could leave. The evening stretched out invitingly before him, and he was still in a celebratory mood. He wished he had a friend to call, someone who would want to celebrate alongside him. But there was no one like that in his life—he'd never hung around with packs of guys anyway, not even back in Evanston. He'd hated the way the big macho sports guys tried too hard to prove just how manly they were. And the computer geeks, well, they didn't have enough style or charisma to hold his interest. He preferred girls as friends, but even close girl friends had always been a rarity for him.

At St. Francis, he'd been a part of the popular crowd, but he couldn't think of one person, guy or girl, that he'd considered a true friend.

Now, at McNeil, he had no friends and he wasn't even popular. He found his keys in his backpack and thought he'd just go for a long drive, maybe spend a few hours just riding with no particular destination in mind.

Ellison turned to leave and he bumped into his father.

"Hey," Ellison said, surprised. "What are you doing here?"

Calvin beamed and waved a letter in his hand. "I have more good news for the family, but no one was home all afternoon and I had no one to tell. Your grandmother's at the church, and Maren is supposed to meet me later for dinner, so I came here to find you."

Ellison smiled warily. "More good news? What is it?"

Calvin pushed the paper into Ellison's hands. "See for yourself."

He read the letter quickly. Someone, a publisher he'd never heard of, wanted to publish Calvin's book. Ellison hadn't even realized his father had finished writing it.

"Wow—this is great," he said. "I can't believe it." Ellison had never seen his father this elated. Calvin was generally mild-mannered (when he wasn't being provoked), but there was pure joy on his face and in his every gesture. Ellison felt an unfamiliar softness toward his father. He could relate to Calvin's pride—it was exactly how he felt about those college letters. "So what's it called?"

"*Jesus Wore Khakis*. Isn't it great?" Calvin gushed.

Ellison tried not to change his expression. *Jesus Wore Khakis*? What kind of name was that? It didn't tell what the novel was about, and it didn't even make sense.

He might have said all this and more on a different kind

of day, but his own good mood made him immune to irritants. "Yeah, it's great."

Ellison made a move to walk toward the entrance, but Calvin stopped him. "There was something else I wanted to ask you."

He shrugged. "Shoot."

"I thought you might want to hang out for a while, you know, maybe get something to eat," Calvin said hopefully.

Ellison smiled and nodded. "Sure. We do have a lot to celebrate."

Chapter 13

That night we ended up at a generic bar and grill, munching on french fries and burgers. My father and brother shared a pitcher of beer Dad had ordered while Ellison sat quietly trying to look older and mysterious. I was surprised when my father suggested the beer, but Ellison pretended that drinking beer was no big deal and poured himself a glass.

Dad hadn't stopped talking since we left Dillard's. He chattered about his novel, which wasn't actually about Jesus, making the title even more nonsensical, but I figured he had his reasons for calling it that so I just smiled and listened.

It wasn't often that my father was in such a garrulous mood, but I supposed that he hadn't often been as happy as he was that night. He talked about Grandma Esther and his childhood. And for the first time since we had moved to Durham, he talked about our mother.

I kept asking questions, because I'd never heard about how they met and I couldn't remember much from when they were together. I'd been six when my parents got divorced and my memories of that time were scattered. Ellison didn't say much, just listened intently and periodically refilled his mug.

In the middle of his story, Dad went to the bathroom and I watched as my brother downed yet another beer.

"Don't you think you'd better take it easy?" I said, looking pointedly at his empty glass.

He laughed, and I could tell he was already beyond tipsy. "Don't be such an old woman."

"I just don't think you should get drunk."

"Why?"

I could see our father walking back from the restroom.

"Just take it easy, okay."

He signaled for another pitcher and waved a hand at me. "Whatever, Mare."

I was uncomfortable with the idea of Ellison and Dad drinking together. They seemed to be getting along okay today, but their relationship was so volatile that I was afraid drinking might upset the delicate balance of civility.

My father slid back into his seat. "Okay, where was I?"

"You were just about to tell us how you and Mom met," Ellison said. I wondered if my father noticed that he slurred his words ever so slightly.

"Well, I was young, you know, and I felt cooped up here in Durham. It was the same people doing the same thing all the time, and I felt that if I didn't get out, I'd end up just like everyone else. So I took a bus to Chicago. I'd never been there, but I'd heard there were a lot of black writers there and I figured I could learn something. Most people were running off to New York back then, but I don't know, something about Chicago called me." He paused to take a sip of his beer, leaving a small bit of foam on his upper lip.

I felt that familiar ache in my chest, the one that came whenever I thought about my mother. Part of me wanted him to stop, because it was so painful to think of her young and alive. It made me want to touch her, to smell her perfume, to feel her arms around me. But I was enthralled and wanted him to keep talking.

"So I got there, and it was late summer, so the weather was still nice. But as soon as I stepped off the bus, I noticed there were police cars everywhere and news cameras filming. There had been a murder near the station and it was big news.

"Well, I'd never seen anything like this back in Durham, so I hung around the edges of the scene, watching the cameramen squat to get just the right angle, listening to the police bark orders at each other. And then I noticed a pretty girl who was holding a pad and pen and pushing her way through the throngs of people to talk to the main cop. She was so petite and beautiful, I couldn't believe the way she forced the cop to talk to her as she scribbled on her pad.

"Something clicked inside me, and I suddenly had to know this lovely, tough, determined woman. So I sneaked underneath the police tape, went up to her and asked her out," he finished, staring off into the air over my head as if he could see that Chicago street corner.

I felt as if I, too, could see my mother as she must have been that day. I was glad to have this new image of my mother to add to the ones already in my head.

"So that was it—love at first sight?" Ellison asked skeptically. I knew he didn't believe in such romantic notions. There had been countless times when he'd made fun of me because I desperately wanted to believe in love at first sight and happily-ever-after.

Dad laughed. "For me, yes. Your mother went out with me, but she didn't like me too much at first. I had to wear her down slowly, but it wasn't long before she fell in love, too. And you know the rest."

Ellison and I nodded. The rest of the story wasn't nearly as romantic and sweet as the beginning.

"Well, what about dessert? I'm going to take a look at the display up front and pick something out for us," my father said.

I looked over at Ellison, who was staring off into space.

"I liked hearing that story," I told him.

He nodded. "It's weird, thinking of our parents like real people."

I sighed and sipped my Coke. I hoped I would find that someday. The good parts, without the divorce and the heartache. There must be some relationships that ended well, I thought, and I was determined to find one.

"Have you ever been in love?" I asked my brother. He never talked much about his girlfriends, other than to tease me about being young and inexperienced. I couldn't remember one that he seemed serious about back in Chicago. I couldn't remember him ever even bringing one of them home to dinner.

Ellison sat back in his chair, looking thoughtful. "I've never known a girl who made me feel the way Calvin felt about Mom," he said. "But I can understand how just the sight of a woman can inspire a man."

I tried not to look surprised. Ellison must really have been drunk; he never opened up this way to me. I thought about pointing this out but I wanted him to keep talking. "Who inspired you?"

He looked around, then leaned toward me with a silly smile on his face.

"Can you keep a secret?"

"Tell me."

He told me what had happened with Arnetta that afternoon, how he'd felt a little of that inspiration looking at her and listening to her laugh.

"Arnetta? But isn't she Dad's girlfriend?" I was worried. The last thing Ellison needed was to get involved in some love triangle with our father. Things were difficult enough already.

Ellison shook his head. "She says she's not."

"But El, you shouldn't—"

"Shh, he's coming back," Ellison whispered. He looked at me. "You promised not to say anything."

I nodded. I didn't know what Ellison had planned, if anything, but I could taste just how wrong it was deep in the back of my throat.

"Cheesecake okay with you two? Anyway, I've never felt the same about any other woman," he went on after ordering the desserts. "The only other woman I've ever really cared about is Arnetta."

Ellison snapped to attention, as if our father's words had sobered him completely. "I thought you were just friends," he said.

I looked at him sharply. If he didn't shut up, it wasn't going to be me who gave away his secret.

Dad shook his head. "It's more than that. I think I love her." He leaned forward conspiratorially. "I mean, she's smart, she's cute, she's great in bed—what more could you want in a woman?"

I frowned. They'd slept together? So Arnetta had lied to Ellison. My brother's shoulders slumped in disappointment, and I was relieved. Well, that was it, then; any dreams he had of him and Arnetta together were impossible now.

Suddenly, Ellison looked sick. I couldn't tell if it was the beer or the news about Arnetta and Dad that made him nauseous.

"Hey, I'm tired, can we go home now?" my brother moaned.

"Yeah, I need to get back to do some homework," I said, hoping Dad didn't notice Ellison's sudden mood swing.

He looked disappointed but nodded. "I'll get the cheesecake to go."

I looked over at Ellison. "We'll wait outside."

I stood a few feet from my brother as he leaned his forehead against the cool stone underneath the neon sign. When my father pulled the car around, Ellison closed his eyes and slept until I shook him awake in front of the house.

The night of the date, the date I dreaded, my first date, I wanted to get ready by myself, but P.J. wouldn't hear of it. She insisted on dragging what seemed like a suitcase full of makeup and several outfits over to Grandma Esther's house and watched me as I tried to prepare.

Aside from my worries about the date, I didn't really want P.J. in my room. It was too close to the real me, where she could see all my childhood drawings on the walls and my books on the shelves. P.J. was my only friend, but it seemed important to keep her at arm's length. That was tough, though, since she and I had been spending most of our time together in the two weeks since Ellison heard from colleges and my father found out his book would be published. I needed relief from all the celebrating, since I had nothing to be all that happy about. Except for Chris, and even that was a secretive pleasure that I had to keep to myself.

P.J. finished slathering makeup on my face and I squinted at myself in the mirror. Even though I wore makeup everyday I wasn't used to quite so much eyeliner and deep red lipstick. Plus, I thought I saw a pimple on my cheek that was growing larger by the minute.

"You look great—much older," P.J. said knowingly. "Randy is going to be so surprised!"

I sighed. I'd been trying to think of a way to tell P.J. that I didn't want to go out with Randy, that I didn't care how surprised he was going to be when he saw me made up like I was in a Broadway show. But there didn't seem an easy way to get out of it, not without lots of explanation and arguing with P.J. It seemed easier to just go on the stupid date.

"What outfits did you bring?" I asked, turning away from the mirror. She hopped up, excited.

"Try this one." She shoved a purple dress at me. I felt the knot in my stomach tighten. I never wore purple. But I grabbed the dress anyway and walked across the hall to the bathroom to change.

Adjusting the spaghetti straps of the tight dress, I cursed P.J.'s name for about the thousandth time since she'd set up this date. She'd been trying to get me to go out with one of Terrell's friends for weeks, but I always made up some excuse about why I couldn't go. But one day last week, she'd caught me in a moment of weakness and I agreed to go out with Randy.

Initially, she'd led me to believe it would be a double date with her and Terrell, but that morning P.J. had called and said that Terrell was sick and we were on our own. I didn't believe for one second that Terrell was sick, but it was too late to get out of it. P.J. knew I was annoyed and bringing over the makeup and the clothes was her way of smoothing things over. But things were anything but smooth, I thought as I pulled on the hem of P.J.'s dress, trying to make it reach below mid-thigh.

I turned in the mirror, trying to see if there was any angle from which I didn't look like slutty. There wasn't, but I didn't know why I even cared. It wasn't as if I was actually interested in Randy. He was nice enough, I supposed, and sort of cute in an Alphonso Ribero sort of way. But he was also friends with Terrell, who was basically a jerk. He was probably dreading this as much as I was, especially if he was expecting someone like P.J. I wasn't sure how he got dragged into P.J.'s campaign to get me to be more like her, but there I was, at six o'clock on a Friday night, trying on this awful purple dress for a date.

I hadn't told P.J. that this was actually my first date. I tried to keep quiet about guys, and she assumed my silence was covering up some wealth of experience. I let her believe that because I was still too embarrassed to admit my thorough inexperience.

I sucked in my stomach and walked back to my room. I was glad no one else was home; I hadn't told anyone I was going on a date and I certainly didn't want Grandma Esther to see me in this dress. My family had all gone out to dinner. They'd invited me to go along, but I bowed out, mumbling something about plans and P.J.

"Wow—you look amazing," she said, spinning me around.

I looked down at myself. "I look like . . . you."

"So what's wrong with that? Terrell loves me in that dress."

I tried to think of a diplomatic way to tell her I had no desire to attract someone like Terrell, but before I could open my mouth, the doorbell rang. P.J. squealed and jumped to her feet.

"That must be Randy. I'll go let him in while you finish getting ready."

She left the room and I wished I could disappear and never have to go downstairs to make small talk. I didn't even know what to say to him—we'd never had a real conversation, only said hi in the halls. And now that he was here, there was no time to find something else to wear, so I was stuck with P.J.'s dress. I looked at myself one last time in the mirror, took a deep breath and went downstairs.

When I walked up to the living room doorway, P.J. was

already gone and Randy had his back to me, inspecting one of the ceramic figurines my grandmother kept on the shelves. I watched him for a moment, looking at his over-sized sweater and baggy jeans, thinking he looked out of place in Grandma Esther's tidy living room. Even from the back he had a casual, almost sloppy look to him, a sharp contrast to the methodical neatness that my grandmother demanded of us and herself. Seeing Randy there among the flowered throw pillows and the gleaming wood end tables was odd, and I was acutely aware of the tightness of my dress. I wasn't ready for this, I didn't want to go out with him, and I fleetingly considered running back upstairs to hide. But I must have made a sound, because Randy turned around.

"Hey, girl. How long have you been there?" Randy was short and stocky, with neat, close cropped hair and a thin mustache that looked like he spent way too much time grooming it.

Something about him made me uneasy, and I didn't like being called "girl" in that overly familiar way by someone I didn't even know. I still thought I might just claim I was ill, but I realized that sick people don't typically sit around in tight purple sheaths.

"Hi Randy."

He looked at me appraisingly, making me fidget.

"Do you want something to drink?" I asked, trying to draw his eyes away from my breasts.

He shook his head. "I'm alright."

I didn't know how to fill the silence. I sat down on the sofa and tried to smile. If I had to be here with him, I might as well try to keep things pleasant. As I was considering various small-talk intros in my head, he spoke.

"I've been wanting to take you out for a long time," he

said, sitting too close to me on the couch. His cologne was sweet and pungent as he put his arm up on the back of the sofa behind me. I wished I'd chosen to sit in the chair instead.

"Oh?"

"Yeah, I thought you were one of those church girls, but I can see I was wrong," he murmured, looking down approvingly at the purple dress. He slipped his arm down off the couch and onto my shoulder, and I tried not to show my discomfort. I had no idea what the protocol was for dating. Was I supposed to grin and bear this unwanted touching? Maybe this wasn't that big a deal in the dating world. Would I be overreacting to tell him to move his arm? Could I do what I wanted to do, which was kick him out of Grandma Esther's house immediately, and still save face with P.J.?

Before I could decide on a plan of action, I heard a key in the front door and Chris walked in. I jumped up, relieved for the distraction.

"Hey Chris!" I walked over and hugged him quickly.

He smiled. "Hey, Mare." Chris looked over at Randy with raised eyebrows.

I turned back to Randy. "This is Chris. Chris, this is Randy."

Randy nodded but did not look happy to see Chris, and it occurred to me that this was my way out. I turned back to Chris and gave him a look, begging him with my eyes to play along.

"Chris, I completely forgot that you were coming over. I guess you want to go run those errands for church on Sunday, huh?"

Chris looked at me for an extra beat. "Yeah, I guess we need to do that now."

Randy stood, frowning. "Wait, I thought we were going out. P.J. said everything was all set up." He folded his arms across his chest and looked suspiciously from Chris to me.

I tried to look apologetic while wondering exactly what all P.J. had "set up" for this evening. It sounded like Randy had been expecting something more than a simple dinner and movie outing. "Randy, I'm really sorry. I totally forgot that I had to do this family thing tonight."

He stepped toward me in what might have been a threatening way if Chris hadn't towered over him by several inches.

"Family, huh? What does this guy have to do with it?" Randy spat.

Chris smiled, but it wasn't his normal smile. It was a smile that stopped before it reached his eyes, a smile that said he wasn't going to tolerate Randy for much longer.

"Oh, didn't you know? I'm her uncle," he said mildly.

Randy scowled. "You act more like her boyfriend."

Chris's smile disappeared. "You act like you know me well enough to get an attitude in my mother's house."

They stared at each other, and I decided I'd better say something before things got out of hand.

"Randy, maybe we can reschedule for some other time, but I think you'd better go," I said sweetly.

He looked at Chris as if he wanted to say something more, but he just shook his head, walked to the door and slammed it behind him.

I couldn't help giggling when he was gone.

Chris smiled. "So what was that about?"

"Come with me to get a soda and I'll tell you all about it."

We sat at the kitchen table, and it suddenly occurred to me that Chris might have plans that I was keeping him from. He was a little more dressed up than normal, wearing black slacks and a light blue sweater, and I hadn't expected to see him that night.

"Were you going somewhere? I'm so sorry I dragged you into that whole Randy thing," I said quickly.

He held up his hand to stop me from babbling. "Actually, I came over to see what you were up to," he said. "I thought you might want to go to a movie or something." He paused, looking away. "And then I saw that guy was here," he added, his voice trailing off.

His voice changed when he mentioned Randy. He sounded annoyed, but I couldn't tell if it was because of Randy's attitude or because I had a guy over.

"That whole Randy thing, it was all P.J.'s idea. She's always trying to get me to go out with guys she knows, and then she came over with this dress, which I hate." I spoke rapidly, using a lot of words trying to say what I meant: I'd rather be with Chris than with anyone else.

He smiled. "The dress isn't so bad," he said, looking me up and down quickly.

I pulled nervously at the bodice. "It's too tight. It's too purple."

"Well, you fill it out nicely," he laughed.

I blushed, feeling pleased and embarrassed at the same time. I didn't know what to say next.

"What movie?" I asked.

"Huh?"

"What movie are you taking me to see?"

He shrugged playfully. "Well, I don't know now—got anymore boyfriends lurking around?" He stood and pretended to look under the table.

I got to my feet, looking up at him. He'd been teasing, but suddenly things seemed very serious. I took a step closer, and our bodies were almost touching.

"I don't want to be with anyone else. Just you." I said it softly, in a voice I didn't even recognize. It was as if I was across the room, watching myself put my arms around his neck, watching myself kiss him. I kissed him like I knew what I was doing. I kissed him like I'd kissed a million times before. I kissed him like he wasn't my uncle.

When it was over, I opened my eyes and pulled away slightly. He had an unreadable expression on his face, and I couldn't decide whether he was happy or angry that I had kissed him.

"You better get changed so we can catch the late movie," he said gently, turning to look out the window at the darkened street.

"Okay." All the reasons why I should regret kissing Chris flitted through my mind, but I pushed those thoughts away.

This was my first date, and I was determined to enjoy it.

He let me pick the movie, and I chose *Bad Boys*. I didn't want to choose some sappy romance that would make him think I was just some silly little girl, and I thought a horror movie might be too obvious—me curled up against him, jumping at every sound. I wouldn't have minded the excuse to sit closer to him, but I thought he might see through that. *Bad Boys* seemed to have the right balance of action and comedy, and I'd loved Will Smith since I was a little girl.

I was glad we'd gone to a movie instead of dinner; in a movie, we could sit close and be together without talking. I was afraid that talking might ruin everything. Talking might make him think that kissing me had been wrong. If we talked, he might say something like "we can never be together" or "this is so wrong." Thinking those things was one thing, but saying them aloud would make the words real.

So we sat in the darkened theater as if we were a normal couple, blending as if this were a date like any other, surrounded by the whispers of other couples and the pungent buttery scent of overpriced popcorn. When I reached over and took his hand, he held onto mine as if it were the most natural thing in the world.

Chris didn't say much on the ride home. I sat in the passenger seat of his old Cavalier, watching my breath make steam on the window and breathing in the floral air freshener that permeated the air. I sneaked a glance at him every few minutes, but he just stared ahead, watching the road as if he was concentrating even though he must have known the route from South Square by heart.

I thought about a lot of things during the car ride, but what I thought about most was how we'd say goodbye. Would we kiss this time? Would I be pressing my luck if I kissed him again? He rolled to a stop in front of Grandma Esther's house, and I tried to think of a way to tell him how much this night meant to me. I tried to find words that were true, words that wouldn't make things weird between us.

"So I'll see you in church tomorrow?" I asked lamely.

He nodded, looking thoughtful. I opened the car door. I wished I were older, more experienced, so I would know what to say or do. But I was still only fifteen, just a girl who liked a boy.

"Maren?"

I turned to him, my stomach in knots. Please don't say it, I thought. Please don't ruin it.

He looked at me for a long moment, then sighed. "See you tomorrow."

I got out of the car quickly before he had a chance to call me back to say whatever was really on his mind. I didn't know exactly what he couldn't or wouldn't say, but I had a feeling

I wouldn't like it. I waved goodbye at the front door before going inside.

Ellison sat on the sofa watching when I came in.

"Hey," I said, plopping down next to him. I was still buzzing from my date with Chris and I knew I wouldn't be able to sleep. Plus, Ellison and I hadn't spent much time together since he found out he'd gotten into college. He'd been floating around in an uncharacteristic good mood, while I had been pretending to be happy for him, trying to figure out what I would do without him.

In a way, I resented Ellison for being able to escape and being so eager to do so. So I'd kept my distance for a couple of weeks, and when I saw him sitting there chuckling at the television, I realized that I missed him.

He offered me a bag of Doritos and I grabbed a couple of chips.

"Where have you been?" he asked.

I shrugged, trying to look casual. "Out with P.J." I figured Ellison and P.J. would never compare notes about me since they could barely speak for five minutes without arguing.

Ellison eyed me critically. "What did you do? It must have been fun, because you're practically glowing."

I waved a hand at him, trying not to show my alarm at his perceptiveness. "Glowing?" I scoffed. "We just hung out, that's all."

"Where?"

"Why are you interrogating me? Since when do you care where I am every minute of the day?" I said, keeping my eyes on the television and reaching for more chips.

When I glanced up at my brother, he was staring at me with narrowed eyes.

"Since when are you so secretive?"

I ignored him, laughing loudly at a Chris Farley skit that brought only a smattering of titters from the studio audience. Finally, I could feel Ellison look away from me back toward the television. Neither of us spoke for a long while, and then the program was over.

He switched off the TV and I stood up.

"Well, goodnight," I said.

He grabbed my arm lightly. "Maren, wait, okay? Can I just say something?"

"What?" I just wanted to go upstairs to bed and dream about Chris—I didn't feel like listening to a lecture.

He sighed. "Look, I know you've been kind of upset about the whole college thing," he said gently.

I was surprised. I didn't think he'd noticed.

Ellison smiled a little as if he could hear my thoughts. "I've been on cloud nine, but I'm not blind."

I laughed and relaxed.

"Anyway, all I wanted you to know is that it's not you I need to get away from."

He left the rest of the sentence unspoken, but I understood. Things were okay with Dad and Grandma Esther, but this still didn't feel like home. If it weren't for Chris, I would want to leave too.

"I'm still here for you," he continued. "I mean, with Mom gone and Calvin . . . well, we need each other. And that won't change no matter how far apart we are."

I nodded, trying not to cry. I hated thinking of Ellison and I being apart, and then he had to go and mention Mom. Here I was, fresh from my first date, and I had no mother to share it with. She'd always talked about dating and boys, and even though I resisted, I'd always imagined us sharing a bowl of ice cream as we discussed my dates.

"I guess all I'm saying is, I worry about you, and if

there's something going on you can tell me about it."

For a split second, I believed him, and I opened my mouth to tell him everything, about feeling inexperienced next to P.J., about Randy and the stupid purple dress, about Chris. But before the words would come, I realized that my brother was sincere, but even he couldn't understand how I felt.

"El, there's nothing going on."

He frowned. "Are you sure?"

"I'm sure. You worry too much." I could tell from the look in his eyes that he didn't believe me, but he let it go.

He just put his arm around me and said, "Love you, Mare."

I managed to hold back my tears until I was lying in bed, thinking about Mom and Chris but mostly about Ellison, wishing I hadn't been too stunned to tell him that I loved him, too.

Chapter 14

Calvin had given Ellison and Maren copies of *Jesus Wore Khakis*. He'd handed them over as if he were passing on an ancient and delicate heirloom, holding the manuscript copies with both hands, careful not to smudge or bend the pages.

Ellison had tried to hand his back, saying he wanted to read the finished product with a hard cover and a book jacket with a photo of Calvin on the back. But his father had pushed it back into his hands, insisting that his kids should be among the first to see what he'd been working on all this time.

Now, a month had passed, and the manuscript still sat unopened on Ellison's night table. Tonight his father was having a big party to officially celebrate the book, and whether or not Ellison had read it was bound to come up.

In a way, he felt guilty that he hadn't read the book, especially since Calvin had been on his best fatherly behavior lately. And he knew Maren had read it already. They'd talked about it late one night.

"So what did you think?" he asked. They were sitting on his bed cross-legged. Maren was in her pajamas, looking sleepy and young.

She thought a long while before she answered. "Well, it's cool that he finished a whole book," she said diplomatically.

He laughed. "So that means you hated it, right?"

She smiled. "Hate is sort of strong. It was just kind of weird. There were all these sex scenes in it. Made me feel gross."

Ellison remembered reading the story about the lesbian lovers the morning he'd snooped through Calvin's room. It still made him uncomfortable to think about it.

"I know what you mean."

She shifted on the bed. "I wondered if some of them were about Arnetta."

Ellison tensed up at the mention of her name. Ever since the night they'd celebrated Calvin's book, he'd regretted telling Maren anything about Arnetta. He'd been grateful that she never brought it up, but he cursed the beer for making him reveal so much of himself.

He yawned and stretched. "It's late. We should get some sleep."

"Don't want to talk about her, huh?" Maren's eyes bore into his, trying to read his thoughts.

"You never talk to me about your love life," he shot back.

She blushed. "That's different."

"Is it?"

She stood up and straightened her pajama top. "I'm going to bed." She walked to the door.

"Now who doesn't want to talk."

"Goodnight," she called over her shoulder.

" 'Night."

He picked up the book off the nightstand, thinking he might give it another try. But he couldn't bring himself to read even the first page. Nothing about it appealed to Ellison—not the title, not the length, which approached 500 typed pages, and not even the fact that his father had written it. So it sat, unread.

Ellison took extra care getting dressed for the party, which meant that he spent even longer combing his hair, ironing his shirt and making sure he looked flawless. Maren liked to call him vain, but as he took one last look at himself in the bathroom mirror, he thought it was more attention to detail than anything else. He was the type of person who cared about the little things, and so what? Was caring about how you looked such a bad thing? If you spent time on the minutiae of life, there was wasn't much time left over for the big stuff, which was how he liked it.

Maren pounded on the bathroom door. "Are you done yet, pretty boy? I have to finish my makeup," she said.

Ellison opened the door and rolled his eyes at Maren. He considered pointing out that, lately, she was spending just as much time primping as he was, but she rushed past him and slammed the door before he could formulate the words.

He shrugged and went downstairs to join his grand-mother and father in waiting for the guests to arrive. He could hear Grandma Esther moving around in the kitchen, humming a gospel tune. Calvin stood alone in the living room, pacing back and forth underneath the "Congratula-tions" banner hanging from the ceiling.

The rooms downstairs in the house were decorated with festive streamers and balloons taped to the walls. There was confetti sprinkled all over, and a bright red tablecloth cov-ered the dining room table, where snacks were set out for the guests. The windows were all opened, letting in the warm spring air, and Ellison could smell the roses that grew underneath the front bay windows. Grandma Esther's home was usually neat and somber, but earlier in the day, she and Maren had transformed it into a warm, festive place.

Calvin fit right in, with his bright yellow polo shirt and wide smile. He reminded Ellison of a kid before his own birthday party, expectant of what the evening will bring, ex-cited to be the center of attention. At one point, he and his father found themselves standing near each other in the living room. They searched silently for something to talk about.

"So. How did you like it?" Calvin asked.

"Like what?" Ellison wished he could disappear so he wouldn't have to admit he hadn't read the book.

Ellison considered telling the truth, but he didn't want to get into an argument in front of all these people.

"I've had a bunch of homework this month, so I'm only halfway through," Ellison said apologetically, sitting down on the sofa and taking one of the hors d'oeuvres from a dish on the coffee table.

Calvin hurried over to sit beside him. "So what do you think of the main character? It was tough writing him, because he's so young, but I tried to capture that whole adolescent angst thing."

Ellison nodded and tried to think of a neutral response. "Umm, yeah, he's pretty believable."

"How about the plot? I know you haven't finished it, but does the set up of the bank robbery work well against the Methodist preacher's subplot?" Calvin went on.

Ellison was flabbergasted. Bank robbery? Methodist preacher? It sounded absurd. "It's hard to tell how plots will come together until you've seen the end, you know?"

Calvin nodded knowingly. "Well, you know, I can always tell you how it ends so we can talk more about the plot."

Ellison held up his palm and tried to smile. "No, you'll spoil it for me," he said.

"So just tell me your overall impressions, then," Calvin said eagerly.

Ellison cleared his throat and looked away. The longer the silence stretched, the more certain he was that he couldn't pretend any longer.

He met Calvin's gaze and sighed. "Okay, you know what, I haven't read it. I'm sorry."

His father frowned. "You haven't even read any of it?"

Ellison shook his head.

"Why not?"

How could he tell his father that he'd already seen some of his writing and hadn't been that impressed? How could he tell him that he hated the title? How could he tell him that he was afraid it would suck? Ellison just shrugged.

Calvin's pale face turned a deep red and Ellison could see a vein throbbing in his neck.

"You are so selfish. When was the last time you thought about someone other than yourself?" his father snapped.

"What?" Ellison had expected him to be mad, but there was no need to launch a personal attack.

Calvin stood up. "You heard me. All you ever think about is yourself and what you want. Maybe you should try thinking about your family for a change, like Maren. She read it," he said, gesturing angrily.

Ellison stood, too, but walked over to the window, where he looked out into the night. He knew his father was wrong. He did care about his family. He'd cared about his mother. And he cared about Maren. That was his real family, the only family he could count on.

"You've got a lot of nerve. Where have you been the past five or six years? Did you care about family—your own children? Talk about selfish," Ellison spat.

"I took you in when you had no one else."

Ellison laughed sarcastically, turning toward Calvin. "My mother died. You're my father. Did you really have a choice?"

Calvin continued as if Ellison hadn't spoken. "And how do you repay me? Walking around here with an attitude problem, acting like you're better than everyone else. Is that what they taught you up in that white school?" The words hit Ellison

213

like a punch in the stomach. Now, he was being called white boy at home, too. He clenched his fists, glad he and Calvin stood across the room from each other. "*Repay* you?"

He wanted to hit something, someone. And he wanted a father who was interested in him, not as a reader for his novel, but as a person. He wanted a father who would understand that changing his whole life around wasn't easy. He wanted a normal life, in Chicago, with everything that felt familiar and right. He wanted his mother back.

"You are an asshole. I can't wait to get away from you," Ellison said quietly.

"And I can't wait for you to leave," Calvin replied. They stared at each other for a full minute before Grandma Esther called for Calvin to come help her in the kitchen. He stalked out of the room, and Ellison began making plans in his head. He would go to college as far away as possible. Berkeley.

The party had two distinct phases. While Grandma Esther was there, about fifteen people, many of them from the church, milled around, making small talk, listening to jazz play quietly in the background, politely commenting on the food. During this time, Ellison sat in a corner, glaring at his father and wondering how long he had to endure this before he could go upstairs to be alone. He'd considered skipping the party altogether, but Maren had complained.

"You're going to leave me here all alone?" she whispered to him as the first guests arrived.

He'd shrugged. "You'll be fine."

She looked at him pleadingly. "Please, just stay for a while. For me."

He sighed. "And what's in it for me?"

"You'll make your little sister really happy?" she said hopefully.

He laughed. "I was hoping for something a bit more concrete than that, but I suppose I can hang out for a while. For you."

"Thanks, El," she said, kissing him quickly on the cheek.

So he was here, counting the minutes until he could escape.

But then the whole tone of the evening changed. Grandma Esther began to look worn out and apologized before going to her room. As if on cue, her church friends left and more people arrived. The new guests were younger and brought beer and liquor instead of flowers and cookies. The house filled up quickly and the noise level rose as the lights dimmed. The laughter was louder, the smell of smoke filled the air, and Ellison thought he might just hang around a little while longer.

He slipped into the kitchen, lit a cigarette of his own, and grabbed a bottle of Heineken. When he turned to leave the kitchen, he bumped into Chris, who had just arrived.

"Hey, man," Chris said cheerfully. He nodded his head toward Ellison's beer. "Got any more of those?"

Ellison pointed toward one of the coolers on the floor and took a long drag of his Newport.

"So how's the party so far? Did I miss anything?" Chris asked as he opened his bottle.

Ellison laughed. "Just a bunch of old church people." He looked around the kitchen as the growing crowd milled in and out. "This group is a lot more interesting."

"I can see that," Chris said, eyeing an attractive young woman in tight blue jeans.

They walked back to the living room and carved out a place near the back where they could see the entire room.

215

Ellison finished his cigarette, watching his father with a martini in one hand and gesticulating wildly with the other as he talked to a man with a beard and an unfashionable Afro. Just the sight of Calvin annoyed him, and he took a long gulp of his beer to erase the nasty sound of his father's words. Selfish, spoiled. His father wanted repayment? Repayment for what?

Maren caught his eye from across the room, raising her eyebrows at the beer in his hand. He smiled and shrugged at her, and she laughed.

He turned to Chris, who was looking across the room at Maren, too. "I'm glad you're here. It's good to have someone to hang out with."

Chris nodded, still looking at Maren. "Yeah, this type of thing can be deadly dull without a partner."

Ellison smiled and followed Chris's gaze. "She's so different from the way she was back home," he said.

Chris started and glanced at him. "Who?"

"Maren. That's who you were looking at, right?"

Chris cleared his throat. "Oh. Right."

"She's a lot more into makeup and hair and things now. But she's almost sixteen, so I guess it's normal," Ellison said, taking a long gulp from his beer. "I even think she's seeing someone."

Chris looked alarmed. "You do? Who?"

Ellison looked at him, his eyes narrowed. Something was weird. Maybe Chris knew who Maren was dating? They had gotten pretty chummy—maybe she'd confided in him.

"She won't tell me," he said slowly. "Why are you acting so strange? Do you know something?"

Chris shook his head and finished his beer. "I'm going to get another. Want one?"

Ellison nodded. He was just about to go over to Maren

to ask her about Chris when someone tapped him on the shoulder.

"Hey, stranger." It was Arnetta. She wore a long black sundress with spaghetti straps. It was made of some kind of jersey so it skimmed her curves without being too tight, and she wore the sandals Ellison had sold her in Dillard's. She wasn't wearing much makeup and her hair was swept up on top of her head. She held a glass of white wine in one hand, and Ellison noticed that her fingernails were painted the same bright red as her toes.

When she tapped him, it was a long moment before he spoke. He hadn't even thought about the fact that she, as a friend of his father's, would be here, and she looked amazing. He wondered if he'd ever stop feeling out of sorts around her. Maybe if he saw her more often, her face would grow commonplace and ordinary, but now, her prettiness still tied his tongue.

She laughed. "Either I look that good, or that bad to have put you at a loss for words," she joked.

He finally found his voice. "That good."

"What a relief," she joked.

Chris came up with Ellison's beer. "Hi—it's Arnetta, right? I don't know if you remember me. I'm Chris, Calvin's brother."

She nodded. "We met once a while back. It's good to see you."

The three of them stood there quietly sipping their drinks. Ellison cursed the fact that he never knew what to say to Arnetta while wishing Chris would go away.

Chris seemed to have read his mind. "I should go talk to my brother for a minute. Excuse me," he said, making his way through the crowd.

Ellison sighed inwardly with relief and turned to Arnetta.

"Nice sandals," he said, remembering the day he'd sold them to her at Dillard's.

She held out her leg as if she were admiring her feet. "You like them? A really cute sales guy sold them to me."

He blushed. There she went again, calling him cute. But the conversation he'd had with Calvin that night at the bar flashed through his mind. According to his father, he and Arnetta were much more than just friends. She was here, and she looked gorgeous. Ellison didn't think women dressed like that for their friends.

But then again, Ellison wasn't sure whether to believe his father. It wasn't like they had a great, honest relationship or anything. And tonight, especially, Ellison wasn't all that interested in how much his father supposedly loved Arnetta. She was standing here, looking up at him with those limpid brown eyes, not Calvin.

He smiled down at Arnetta and held up his empty bottle. "I'm going to get another drink. Do you want one?"

She looked at her glass, which was half-full, and downed the rest of her drink. "Sure," she said when she finished.

He laughed. "Be right back."

When he returned, she was talking to a group of women who looked about her same age. He didn't recognize any of them, so he hung back, waiting for a lull in their raucous conversation. Ellison watched the way Arnetta seemed to be at the center of the group, the way her girlfriends laughed at everything she said, the way she threw her head back when something was particularly funny. He was charmed by the way she unconsciously patted her hair to make sure it was in place, the way she stood with her weight on one leg, hand on her hip.

Ellison would have been content to watch her for hours, but it wasn't too long before Arnetta caught his gaze. She broke through the circle of women, holding out her hand. He took it shyly, embarrassed and pleased.

"Girls, I'd like you to meet a friend of mine. Ellison."

He smiled and said hello, pretending he didn't see the surprised glances the women gave him.

"You haven't told us about this new *friend* of yours," a tall, dark-skinned woman said slyly, addressing Arnetta while staring at Ellison. "Where did you two meet?"

Ellison cleared his throat. He suddenly felt like a child and he wished more than anything he didn't have to say he and Arnetta had met at school.

"Oh, we have mutual friends," Arnetta said breezily, winking at Ellison.

The women chuckled, their eyebrows raised. He knew they were wondering what was really going on, and he wondered the same thing. Were he and Arnetta truly "friends?" And what motivation did she have to protect him by saying they'd met through mutual friends? He was happy she'd saved him from embarrassment, but was there more to it than that? Was it possible that she had changed her mind, that she was interested in more than just an occasional flirtation?

Ellison spent a considerable amount of time questioning Arnetta's motives, but he chose not to examine his own too closely. He would rather just think about his attraction to Arnetta, the way she made him feel, and forget about the fact that flirting with the woman his father wanted was a convenient way of getting back at Calvin.

"Arnetta, we're going to get a refill," the tall woman said, herding her friends toward the kitchen. "It was nice to meet you, Ellison."

Arnetta turned to him. "Don't worry, they don't know Calvin, so they probably don't know you're his son. I just invited them to make sure I'd have someone to talk to."

He tried to look nonchalant. "I wasn't worried," he said calmly, considering her words. "I would have thought you wouldn't have been lacking for conversation here, though."

She looked curious. "What does that mean?"

He shrugged and drank from his bottle. "It means, you and my father are pretty close—I would have thought you'd talk to him."

They both glanced over at Calvin, who was loudly telling the story of how he'd found out he was getting published.

Arnetta looked up at him. "What do you mean, pretty close?"

He finished off another beer and realized he had already had too much to drink. The beer, which had tasted slightly acrid at the beginning of the evening, was now going down smoothly. He hadn't had anything to eat since breakfast, and the alcohol had gone right to his head.

Maybe that was why he felt bold and confident, standing there with Arnetta. Maybe that's why he just blurted out, "I'd say sleeping with someone is pretty close."

After he said it, he immediately regretted it. He thought she might be mad, that he'd crossed some invisible line. But after a short pause in which they stared at each other, she just laughed.

"You think I'm sleeping with your father?"

"That's what he said."

She rolled her eyes. "Do you believe everything you hear?"

"Shouldn't I?"

She smiled and glanced around at the crowd, which was still thick and loud. "You know what?" she said, leaning in close enough for him to see the tops of her breasts and smell her floral perfume. "We should talk about this in private. Why don't you meet me out back?"

Ellison nodded. He knew there were a million reasons not to go outside with Arnetta. But he didn't feel like heeding any of them.

Chapter 15

I didn't enjoy my father's party. I had never felt comfortable around a bunch of people I didn't know. I always had this innate shyness that kept me from knowing what to say, how to start small talk, how to be confident and witty at parties. Ellison had a way of seeming comfortable in any situation, even when I knew he wasn't. But my shyness was a badge, a scarlet letter that revealed the parts of me I wished no one would ever see.

That's why I was pleased at the beginning of the party, when all of Grandma Esther's church friends were there. I'd met them all one Sunday or another, but Dad took me around and we greeted them all, and they fawned over me, enveloping me in big bear hugs, exclaiming about how much I looked like my father even though I couldn't see much resemblance. They made me feel safe and warm, and I didn't need to struggle to find something to say because they filled every silence with church gossip, compliments on Grandma Esther's décor and offers to get me another plate of food.

Even Grandma Esther had been nicer than usual, and she looked happy as my father and I shuffled between the small clusters of guests. Even though this was a party for my father, Grandma Esther presided over it like royalty, dressed better than the rest of us in her silk blouse and long straight skirt, sitting in the most comfortable corner chair and waiting for guests to come to her. She was smiling – a rare and welcome sight.

But soon, the mood of the party had changed. My father was quickly swept away into a crowd of people, younger people who were smoking and drinking freely. Grandma Esther and her friends disappeared, and I felt out of place. Dad didn't introduce me to any of these people, so I slipped into a corner, looking around in vain for Ellison and wishing I had someone closer to my own age to talk to.

"Hey." Chris seemed to appear from nowhere. We hadn't seen each other since the night of our date. I'd thought about calling him, even had my hand on the receiver a few times, but I didn't know what to say. What I had to say was probably best said in person, anyway. I wanted to tell him how I really felt. I wanted to tell him that I was falling in love with him.

"Hey," I replied, searching his face for any signs of his feelings about the kiss we'd shared. But there was nothing, just his dark eyes staring back at me.

Chris and I had shared many comfortable silences, but this wasn't one of them. I stood awkwardly, looking around the room for a distraction.

Chris and I watched Ellison and my father arguing from across the room. They weren't loud, but I could tell from the expressions on their faces that they were butting heads yet again. My own shoulders tensed as I tried to read their lips to figure out what it was this time that had them red-faced and angry.

Chris nodded at them. "They just can't get along, huh?"

I shrugged. There was no real way to describe Ellison's anger and my father's inflexibility. I was beginning to think they might never be able to coexist peacefully.

"It's complicated," I said. "Ellison is still hurting, a lot. We both are."

"You manage to get along with Cal."

I looked up at him and brushed his hand off my shoulder. I didn't like him blaming Ellison for everything; it wasn't his fault that Dad hadn't been much of a father to him.

"That kind of thing isn't as easy for Ellison. And it's not like Dad is making things easier for him," I said defensively.

Chris put up both hands. "Whoa, I know that. I wasn't blaming Ellison. I was just pointing out how different you and he are."

I took a deep breath. "I'm going to get something to drink."

I spotted Ellison surrounded by a group of women. One of them was Arnetta. I watched the group of women around Ellison giggle as he stood too close to Arnetta. I could see even from across the room that he was looking at her breasts.

Chris appeared at my side, his smile a silent apology. "What do you think Ellison and Cal were arguing about this time?"

"Who knows?"

He followed my gaze and laughed knowingly. "Maybe it has something to do with Arnetta," he said.

"You think there's something going on between them?" I asked nervously.

Chris shrugged. "She's gorgeous."

I felt uncomfortable hearing him say that about Arnetta. Would he like me better if I were wearing a slinky black dress instead of this T-shirt and black jeans? I looked down at my feet.

"But she's not my type, though," he said softly in my ear.

I turned to look at him and our faces were close, close enough to kiss. "Who is your type?"

He looked away and stepped back, for the first time seeming unsure of himself. "Guess."

As soon as he said it, he looked away. "I'd better go," he said quickly, moving through the crowd and out the front door before I could answer.

I wanted to think about Chris, what he'd said, but I was too worried about my brother. After Chris left, I stood alone in a corner while Ellison talked to Arnetta. I didn't like the way they laughed, the way she put her hand on his arm possessively. I suddenly wished I'd done something about this situation, maybe convinced El that it was a bad idea. Or told my father, or even talked to Arnetta. I would have done anything to keep her from whispering in his ear just before she slipped away. Anything to keep him from waiting a few minutes before he too crept toward the back door. I looked around to make sure my father wasn't nearby before I followed.

Once I saw that Ellison was headed out to the backyard, I quickly went out the front door and sneaked around to the side of the house, where I could watch him without being seen. When I stepped outside, I was startled by the quiet. I could still hear the voices from inside the house, but they sounded muted and far away. I breathed in deeply, freeing my lungs from cigarette smoke, which permeated the house even though I couldn't imagine that Grandma Esther would approve.

The leaves had only recently returned to the trees that dotted the yard, and I was unused to the deep shadows they created. The yard was large and fragrant, smelling of the sweet red roses Grandma Esther had planted near the fence and damp grass that was still moist from an early afternoon rainstorm.

I settled into a shadowed nook where I watched Ellison's movements. He was clearly waiting for something, or someone, and I prayed it wasn't Arnetta even though I knew better. He looked around, then sat on a wooden bench in the far corner of the rectangular yard underneath an old oak tree whose gnarled branches hung low to the ground.

I was hidden, but close enough to see Ellison's face. He leaned back against the bench and closed his eyes. But it wasn't long before I heard the back screen door close and the sound of footsteps on the damp grass near him. Holding my breath, I watched Arnetta walk toward him, her heels sinking slightly into the soft ground. Ellison opened his eyes to see Arnetta standing there, holding out a beer.

"Thought you might want another."

He sat up and accepted it. "Thanks." He moved over to make room for her on the bench, and she sat down next to him, close, closer than was necessary, I thought.

"I wasn't sure you were coming," he added so softly that I had to strain to hear.

She took a sip of her own drink, now a tall glass full of dark liquid.

"Well, I'm here," she said. She was facing Ellison, her back to me so I couldn't see her face in the darkness, but I could hear the smile in her voice.

"I just want to make one thing clear: I'm not your father's girlfriend," she said sweetly, putting her head on his shoulder.

I worried they could hear my heart beating. Was she lying? Or was Dad the one who had been less than truthful?

"He said he loves you," Ellison said.

Arnetta pulled away and stood up. My eyes had adjusted to the low light and I could see the outline of her body underneath her dress.

"He might think he loves me, but he doesn't," she said slowly, looking down at Ellison. I wished she were wearing something looser; I wished my brother wasn't looking at her in that hungry way.

He stood up and pulled her into his arms, kissing her deeply and holding her tightly around the waist. Her glass dropped into the grass, and the next thing I knew, his back was against the tree and she was pulling at his clothes.

I felt like an intruder. I knew I shouldn't be seeing this, that Ellison would hate me for watching, that I would be better off than if I had stayed in the house and simply wondered about what was going on out here. I was embarrassed by the raw sexuality of their embrace; I couldn't believe that my brother would go this far to spite our father.

They rolled around in that soft grass for what seemed like hours, making almost no noise at all. And then it was over and she lay next to him, her head nestled in the crook of his arm. I considered sneaking back into the house, but El sat up, glancing around.

"We'd better get back inside," he said. I could hear the sounds of people leaving, car doors slamming, giggles fading away in the distance.

Arnetta nodded. He pulled on his pants and watched her smooth down her dress.

"Arnetta."

She turned to him. "Hmm?"

He cleared his throat. "You know, you never answered my question earlier."

"What question?"

"Did you have sex with my father?"

"What difference does it make?" she asked.

It made all the difference, I thought.

He narrowed his eyes. "Yes or no?"

She sighed and took his hand. "Ellison, the sex was nice. Don't ruin it."

Ellison frowned. "What's that supposed to mean?"

She shook her head. "It means it was sex, that's it—don't make it into a big deal. You don't get to question me about my past. It's none of your business."

Her flip answer reminded me of P.J. and how she saw sex as a big game. I didn't see it that way at all, and from the look on Ellison's face, I didn't think he did, either.

My brother's laugh was low and humorless. "We're talking about my father. It is my business."

Arnetta put her hands on her hips. "Funny, you weren't all that concerned about this when you were pulling my clothes off right here in your backyard," she spat. "But to answer your question, yes, I slept with your father a few times. So what?"

For the first time, it occurred to me that she might have another agenda, one that had nothing to do with Ellison and everything to do with my father. I didn't know what was going on between Dad and Arnetta, but judging from the casual way she was treating Ellison, the way she didn't seem to care one way or another, she was getting back at my father for something.

Ellison quickly turned away and hunted around for his shirt so I couldn't see his face. I couldn't see if he was hurt or surprised or angry.

"So you fucked two generations of Emorys. That's a first, huh?" he said over his shoulder.

Arnetta stared at him, but he refused to look at her while he slowly fastened his shirt buttons.

Finally, she spoke. "Ellison, grow up."

He ran his fingers through his hair and glanced at her. "Whatever, Arnetta."

As I watched her walk back into the house, I could hear my father's voice, bidding one of the guests goodbye. I watched Ellison pick up Arnetta's discarded glass and his beer bottle and sit on the bench.

My head ached, and I had no desire to go back inside. I didn't feel like facing Arnetta, my father, Ellison or anyone else. But I didn't want my brother to know that I'd seen and heard everything, so I tiptoed away silently, leaving him sitting there with his head in his hands.

Inside the house, I headed toward the hallway and the stairs as the last few guests left the house. My father waved goodbye and shouted out something to their disappearing backs, and he turned just in time to see me heading to my room.

"So how did you like the book?" he asked.

I'd been wondering when he would ask me about his novel. I'd read it in just a couple of days after he gave it to us. It wasn't the kind of book I usually liked—his book focused on the plot, and it was the characters who interested me most in fiction. But I'd wanted to like it because I knew it was important to him.

"It was good, Dad. Really good."

His smile lit up his face. "Thanks honey. That really means a lot to me."

I wondered if he was talking about my opinion of the book, or my calling him "Dad." In my mind, he'd been Dad for some time, but today was the first time I'd said it aloud to his face. It had just seemed like it was time.

"See, you're such a good kid. I wish Ellison were more like you," he added, his smile fading.

I was getting tired of having to defend my brother. "What do you mean? Ellison's a good person."

Dad frowned. "You know he didn't even read my book? He's just selfish. And he's always got that bad attitude. He's hard to love."

I looked away. This must be what they'd fought about earlier. Ellison and I hadn't talked much about the novel, but it didn't surprise me that he hadn't read it. But I knew my brother, and I knew his reasons for not reading it were likely more complicated than my father knew.

I'd spent the last eight months wishing Ellison and my father could get along, if only to make life at home less tense, but every time I thought things were getting better, they fell back into their old patterns again.

"It's not all his fault," I said softly, not meeting my father's eyes.

He nodded. "I know. I've made mistakes. But I just wish things were different with Ellison."

"Things will be okay, I'm sure," I lied. "He'll come around." I made a move to go up to my room. I figured Ellison would be coming in soon and I didn't want to face him, not after watching the ugly dance between him and Arnetta.

"Maren, hold on a minute," he said.

I suppressed my sigh. I didn't want to talk, not to him, not to anyone unless it was Chris. And Chris was gone.

Dad walked over to me. "Where's Ellison? I haven't seen him in a while."

I shrugged. "I thought you were mad at him."

He nodded. "I just wanted to try to clear the air with him. I think we both said some things we regret."

What else is new, I thought, but I didn't say it. "Maybe he's out back. I'm going to bed," I added.

He put his hand on my arm. "Maren, I was hoping you would come talk to Ellison with me."

I couldn't think of anything less appealing. "Why?"

My father cleared his throat. "Well, I thought it might be easier for us to talk if we have someone else there."

Now I couldn't hold back my sigh. "A referee."

"A *mediator*," he corrected. "Please?"

I couldn't think of a way to get out of this without making my father suspicious.

"Okay, okay." I followed him out to the backyard where Ellison still sat on the bench underneath the tree.

I hadn't seen him look this bleak in months, not since right after Mom died. I wanted to comfort him, to tell him that Arnetta was a bitch, to tell him that I loved him, but I couldn't. I sat next to him, but he didn't look up.

"Are you okay," I said softly.

He nodded, then noticed Dad standing there silently.

"What do you want? Did you come out here to call me a selfish brat again?"

Dad frowned. "Can't we have one pleasant conversation?"

Ellison looked incredulous. "You acted like I owed you something for being my father. Now you want to be *pleasant?*"

Even though my brother looked angry, I could also see something else in his eyes, something I didn't think Dad could or would see. Hurt. No matter how much Ellison pretended that he didn't care what our father did, he had been hurt by whatever our father had said to him earlier. And then he'd gone and gotten back at him, only I hoped he wouldn't say anything about that part of it all.

"El, you didn't even bother to read my book. How was I supposed to react?" My father's voice rose angrily.

I closed my eyes, wishing I'd made it upstairs before my father caught me.

"Dad, I thought you came out here to talk," I said, figuring he would be easier to calm than Ellison, who was now glaring at me as if I had betrayed him.

"Talk?" Ellison spat nastily. "You want to talk, then

let's talk about Arnetta."

Chris's words floated through my head. He'd said she was gorgeous, implying that no man could or would try to resist her, especially not a seventeen-year-old-almost-a-man who was hurting. And he'd been right.

My father looked confused. "Arnetta? What about her?"

Ellison stood up and smiled, a dark smile that was so unlike his real smile that it was frightening. I stood up too, although I didn't know why. I guess I just didn't want to be sitting down for what I knew was coming.

"You were right, Dad," Ellison said sweetly. My stomach fluttered. Ellison never called our father Dad, not ever. He either referred to him as Calvin or not at all. I looked at my father to see if he noticed, but his puzzled expression never changed.

"I was right about what?"

Ellison stepped closer to Dad, looking him right in the eye. "She's good in bed," he said slowly, enunciating each word. "Or, should I say, in the grass," he added, looking pointedly at the ground underneath my father's feet.

In the stunned silence that followed, I silently prayed to be transported far, far away from that backyard. It was eerie, the way the muscles in my father's face froze. I couldn't even breathe as I waited. I couldn't move as my father's hand slowly rose, then seemed to move in double time as he slapped Ellison across the face.

And then they were fighting, and I was screaming, screaming for them to stop, trying to get in between them but getting pushed aside time and again.

And then Grandma Esther was in the back doorway, awakened by the commotion.

"Calvin! Ellison! Stop it!" she shouted. "Calvin . . ." her words were cut off by a strangling sound in her throat, and then she fell. I ran to her, and soon Ellison and Dad were next to me. She was lying there, quieter than I'd ever seen her. Her skin had a gray, ashy tone; her chest rose and fell only slightly.

No one said a word. Ellison and Dad both kneeled next to her, my father touching her forehead and Ellison looking helpless and stricken. I ran inside and called the paramedics then stayed near the front window, waiting for the flashing red lights. I couldn't bear to go back outside.

When I went into Ellison's room while we waited to hear from my father at the hospital, I thought I could be calm. I was scared about what would happen in the wake of his liaison with Arnetta and Grandma Esther's collapse, frightened of how our lives could change for the worse. How would my father and Ellison live in the same house together after what happened?

His door was just pulled shut, not closed completely, and I looked in. Ellison was lying on his back in the darkened room, his arm thrown across his eyes.

"El. Can we talk?"

He didn't move. "I don't feel like talking."

I walked in and sat on the edge of his neatly made bed.

"But I need to," I said quietly.

He sighed and put his arms behind his head. I could see him glance at me in the grayish light coming through the curtains.

"Look, I don't want to hear it, okay? I know you want to talk about Arnetta and Calvin and Grandma Esther and all that, but I don't. It's been a long night."

I waited a long while to answer him, listening to his breathing grow more regular, slower, as if he was falling asleep.

"Do you think Grandma Esther is going to be alright?" I

felt guilty about her collapse, as if I had some part in bringing bad karma to her home. Maybe she wouldn't have been so stressed if Ellison and I weren't around. Maybe if we all hadn't been in the yard, arguing, she wouldn't have gotten sick.

"I don't know, Maren. I hope so." He didn't say it but I knew he was thinking the same thing I was. We couldn't take another death in our family. Not now. Not yet.

"I saw you," I blurted before I even realized what I was doing. I hadn't planned to tell Ellison that I'd seen and heard everything between him and Arnetta—it just slipped out before I could stop myself.

He sat up quickly. "You saw me what?" He stared at me intently until I looked away.

"I saw you and Arnetta. Together," I whispered, afraid that he would blow up, shout that I had no business spying on him, afraid that he would tell me all the things I already knew.

Ellison jaw tightened and his eyes blazed, but he said nothing. Finally, he stood up and began pacing around the room.

"You shouldn't have watched, Mare."

"I know."

"So why did you?"

I considered the question. "I followed you because I was worried that something was going on between you and Arnetta, something that would be bad."

He stopped pacing and stood in front of me. "So why did you stay?"

I shrugged. "I don't know."

And I didn't. I could have sneaked away at any time, but I stayed until the end.

Ellison suddenly sat on the floor crossed-legged in front

of me, so I was looking down at him as he spoke.

"So you heard the whole thing, about how it meant nothing to her, right?"

I nodded. "Were you hurt?"

"Please," he scoffed. "It was just sex." But he looked away when he said it and I didn't believe him.

There was a long silence. It was weird, being in the house when it was so quiet. Usually there were small noises, even at night. The sounds of Grandma Esther washing dishes in the kitchen, or the sound of our father typing in his room. Tonight there was nothing but the nearly imperceptible swoosh of our breathing.

"Why did you do it?" I thought that if I understood why he did it I could forgive him for making our home life unbearable.

Ellison looked up angrily. "Why should I explain anything to you? You won't even tell me about this boyfriend of yours."

I felt my cheeks burning. "I don't have a boyfriend."

"Yeah right," he spat. "Did you tell Chris?"

I looked away quickly so he wouldn't read the panic in my eyes. "What do you mean? Why would I tell Chris anything? I mean, there's nothing to tell anyway," I stammered.

Ellison leaned forward. "What is going on with you?"

I got up from the bed and practically ran to the door. I had seen him and Chris talking at the party, but it never occurred to me that they might be talking about me. What had Chris told him?

"Why are you changing the subject? You're the one who slept with our father's girlfriend. You're the one who ruined everything. All you ever think about is you, you, you!" I cried as I burst out of the room and down the hall. I slammed my door and stood with my back against it. I hoped my brother wouldn't follow me. He didn't.

It was raining steadily the May afternoon Ellison graduated from McNeil High School, the downpour interrupted occasionally by crackling thunderstorms. He looked so pleased sitting in that huge auditorium with hundreds of other seniors, all on their way to one adventure or another. They all wore the same thing, some with honors sashes, most without. I knew that most of the graduates and the families who'd crowded in to watch were thinking about new beginnings, but as I listened to the rain pounding the roof of the building, all I could think about were endings.

It was the end of our childhood together, the end of an era when, particularly since Mom died, I turned to Ellison whenever I needed something familiar, even if that something was a sarcastic comment or even the comfortable silence that only a brother and a sister can share.

He'd been busily making plans to leave for California, buying his plane ticket with money left over from our old life, bringing home boxes, making plans to drive across country alone. We hadn't talked about it much; I couldn't think of him leaving without crying and he couldn't think of leaving without smiling. I knew he wasn't trying to make me feel bad, but it marked a change in our relationship just the same. Illogically, I'd always thought he'd be there to protect me, to take care of me, but soon he would be gone.

I hated that I could only think of myself, especially when I'd accused him of the same kind of selfishness. How could I begrudge my brother the one thing he'd wanted since he was a little kid—to go far away, to be on his own, to be free? I just wished his happiness wasn't dependent on distance. I wished he could find a way to be happy and near me at the same time.

But since Dad's party, it had become absolutely clear that Ellison and my father would never see eye to eye on anything. In the three weeks since that night, Ellison and I had maintained an uneasy truce and he and Dad had studiously avoided each other. I never knew what happened with Arnetta and my father; no one ever mentioned her name again.

Grandma Esther was okay. She had a stroke, and the doctors said that eventually, she'd be able to talk and walk again. Unbeknownst to any of us, she'd been having a series of tiny strokes leading up to the big stroke. Looking back, we could all see that she'd been acting differently—quiet, tired, not her normal self. But we'd all been so involved in our own lives that we hadn't paid much attention to her.

They kept her in the hospital for a while to adjust her medication and start physical therapy. Ellison and I went to visit her, but she was usually sleeping, or if she was awake, she couldn't really move the right side of her face, so talking wasn't an option. Plus, my father rarely left her side, and the air thickened uncomfortably whenever he and Ellison were in the same room.

So it had been just Ellison and me at Grandma Esther's house in the days leading up to graduation. The seniors got out of school two weeks early, so Ellison spent his days packing or driving around; as my last days as a sophomore wound down, I avoided P.J. and her friends and counted down the days until summer vacation.

I didn't even see Chris during those days. He called, and we bumped into each other at the hospital, but I kept our conversations short. I didn't want anything that reminded me of the night Grandma Esther had the stroke. Ellison and

I studiously avoided talking about the night of the party. My father was busy by my grandmother's bedside, and even though I missed Chris, I couldn't even face him. I regretted not trying harder to get close to Grandma Esther. I thought that was the reason I felt nothing but numbness when she collapsed. I wished I could grieve for her lost motor skills, but all I felt was a distant sympathy, the kind you'd feel for someone you hardly knew. Maybe my numbness was because of our troubled relationship. Or maybe I didn't have any more grief to spare.

Now, I was the only one here to see Ellison graduate. Near the end of the ceremony, when all the seniors stood, he turned and searched the crowd until he saw me. I wore a red summer sheath so he could spot me easily. My brother smiled at me, a sad smile that said so much. We're survivors, that smile said. We can handle anything that comes our way. We made it. I smiled back, but I didn't believe it. *He* had made it. I still didn't know what would happen to me.

After graduation, I met him in front of the auditorium, where I took some pictures before we walked to the car, stepping around all the families who looked happy and normal. When we got to the car, Ellison paused to take off his robe. He wore a suit underneath, and it occurred to me that I hadn't seen him in a suit since Mom's funeral.

"You're dressed up," I said superfluously.

He nodded. "It's a big day." We were both painfully aware that it was just the two of us here, when it should have been a big family celebration, with dinner and gifts. He should have had friends surrounding him, dragging him off to all-night parties to celebrate the start of the next phase of his life. He'd probably imagined that was how it would be, before our whole lives changed.

"I'm proud of you," I offered gently. And I meant it. Despite all my fears about him leaving me, I meant it.

He smiled and hugged me. "Thanks, Mare."

We separated and climbed into the car. "Want to go out to dinner? We should celebrate," I said. I wanted to make him feel loved, because I could see in his eyes that he felt alone.

He maneuvered out of the parking lot before answering. "I know what you're doing."

"Yeah, I'm trying to get something to eat."

He glanced at me. "You're trying to make me feel good because I wasn't exactly surrounded by family at graduation."

I looked out the window at the trees lining the highway. There were so many places in North Carolina where it seemed you were in the middle of nowhere, surrounded by pines, and then, suddenly, you were back in the city again.

"Is that so bad?"

"Nope. But I feel like being alone, to think."

I laughed. "One of your famous drives, huh?"

"You know me," he smiled, making the turns toward Grandma Esther's house.

He dropped me off in front and made sure I got into the house safely before taking off. I closed the door behind me and stood in the living room, marveling at how still the house was. It had a different feel to it now that Grandma Esther wasn't here and my dad was gone most of the time. The emptiness wasn't peaceful. It was simply lonely, and I hoped Ellison would come home soon.

I walked into the kitchen and nearly screamed. Chris was sitting at the kitchen table, his head in his hands.

"Sorry I scared you," he said when he saw me in the doorway.

I felt shy around him, that same shyness I felt when we first met. "Hi."

"I didn't think you'd be here. I thought you were out at Ellison's graduation."

"He wanted to be alone, so I came home."

He nodded, looking almost sick.

"What's wrong? Is Grandma Esther okay?" I said, sitting at the table.

"No, she's okay. I just needed to get out of the dorm, so I went to see Mama and then I came here."

He looked at me, intensely, and for the first time I could read his eyes. He looked at me the same way that Randy had looked at me, the same way other men looked at me after I started wearing skirts and makeup. It was the look of desire, laced with something else. Love?

"I was hoping you'd be here," he whispered.

We were alone in the house, but I whispered, too. "Why?"

"I missed you."

I stared at him, not thinking of anything except the two of us and the sound of our breathing. Suddenly nothing else mattered, not my brother's graduation, not my grandmother's stroke, not the fact that he was my uncle. There was just this moment, where we gazed at each other and the only thing to say was the truth.

"I love you," I said. I repeated it, more loudly. "I love you."

And then he was taking me into his arms, and this time he was kissing me. All I remember about going upstairs is that he carried me, and our lips never separated.

I didn't know what to do or what to expect, so I imitated his actions. When he took off his shirt, I removed mine. When he kissed my neck, I kissed his. When he closed his eyes at the moment when he entered me, I did the same. Neither of us spoke nor made a sound outside our ragged panting. There was an initial jab of pain, then nothing much, just the unfamiliar feel of his weight on top of me, the unfamiliar musky smell of his skin.

I didn't let myself think or wonder, I just lay there, my eyes firmly shut, my mind firmly blank. Maybe that's why I didn't hear Ellison come in the house. Maybe that's why I didn't see him in the doorway of my room. I imagine that he must have stood there for a moment, shocked to see his uncle lying naked on top of his sister. I imagine it took him only a moment to move across the room and snatch Chris's body off of mine, throwing him to the floor in a heap.

I screamed, worried that Ellison would pummel Chris to a pulp, embarrassed that I was lying there naked and exposed, ashamed at Chris's nudity as well.

Ellison towered over Chris, who was frozen in shame, but he didn't touch him. He simply looked at me with hooded eyes.

"Get up and get dressed," he said. Then he turned to Chris. "Get out."

Ellison left the room abruptly, and we obeyed his orders, careful not to look at each other. I grabbed my clothes and ran into the bathroom, and I didn't come out until I heard the front door slam.

Chapter 16

There are times in life, especially when you're a kid, when you do something that you know is wrong, ignoring the voices in your head that tell you stop, no, you'll be sorry. Even as the deed is done, you feel the wrongness of it deep in your bones, knowing that the sickness of regret will soon follow. And yet, you cannot stop yourself. You cannot choose another path, because you have been led to this point, by God or fate or karma, and there is no undoing it.

During these times, the knowledge of your mistake precedes the act. But in other instances, you don't realize just how wrong you've been until you see it through the eyes of someone you love.

That is how it was for me. I didn't acknowledge the impossibility of my relationship with Chris until I saw it through Ellison's eyes, turned into angry slits at the sight of his sister and uncle entwined. It wasn't until that moment that I saw that all the things leading up to it—the late-night talks with Chris, the way I'd kept us a secret from everyone —these things were all signals to show me how wrong it was.

But it was shame that finally made me see. Shame made me shut myself in my room for days on end, ignoring my father's pleas to tell him what was wrong. Shame made me stop eating, stop caring about how I looked. Shame made me take shower after shower, as if the hot water would wash away what I had done.

I was ashamed because I knew better. I was ashamed because I had read the question in my brother's eyes: what would Mom think?

And yet, I couldn't stop thinking about Chris, wondering how he was feeling. Was he thinking of me? How would it be to see each other again? The fact was, no matter how wrong it was to fall in love with my uncle, I had done just that, and I didn't know how to make the feelings go away.

A week went by before Ellison spoke to me. I figured he was angry with me and I didn't blame him. I couldn't look him in the eye; I'd judged him for sleeping with Arnetta, but I had done worse. I had slept with my own uncle; I had fallen in love with my own uncle.

"I feel like this is all my fault," he told me. He'd waited until I went down for breakfast early one morning and followed me. We stood in the kitchen alone, although we could hear our father's whistling from the other room.

"What?" I was startled by his words. I felt like I should be the one apologizing.

"If I'd paid more attention to you, you wouldn't have turned to Chris, and he wouldn't have taken advantage of you," Ellison said. "I hate myself for not seeing what was going on. He was always hanging around, looking at you. And you wouldn't talk about that 'guy' you liked. I should have known."

I turned away to the refrigerator, where I poured a glass of orange juice. Sipping from my glass, I spoke slowly. "I don't know that you could have done anything, El." I paused, afraid to say the words aloud. "I love him."

Ellison looked dismayed. "Love? How can you be in love with your own uncle?"

I shrugged and sat at the table, and he followed.

"I don't know how it happened. I just know that it happened," I said softly. "But now it feels all wrong."

"I can see how my finding out would change things."

I looked up at him sharply, then managed a weak smile when I realized he was joking. "You know what I mean."

He nodded. "I felt the same way with Arnetta. Once the moment was broken, it seemed really tawdry."

We sat there, looking at each other.

"Maren, I promised Mom that I'd watch out for you, and I didn't. And now you're in this mess . . . if I'd been a better big brother, none of this would have happened. And I am so, so sorry for that."

I reached over and hugged him. "I'm sorry, too."

"You can't be sorry for being fifteen, for needing someone," he said. "You can't be sorry for being human."

"Neither can you."

Ellison sighed, then pulled away gently, still holding on to my shoulders with both hands. "Have you talked to Chris?"

"He hasn't called." I was uncomfortable talking about it with Ellison, and I wished it would all just go away. But he was all I had. What I needed wasn't an older brother; I needed a mother. But he was doing the best he could.

"Was that your first time? I mean, with Chris?"

I started to cry. He pulled me to him and I buried my face in his shirt, wetting it with my tears.

"I'm sorry, Mare. I'm so sorry."

I sobbed harder and he squeezed my shoulders, kissing the top of my head and repeating the words in a soft voice.

"What are you sorry about?" our father said from the doorway. He looked at Ellison warily. "What did you do to Maren?"

As far as I knew, this was the first time either of them had addressed the other directly since the night of the party. But the tension was still there and I wasn't sure what kept Ellison from making a snide remark when Dad came upon us in the kitchen.

"It's nothing. Just brother and sister stuff. She'll be fine," Ellison said.

"Yeah, Dad. I'm okay," I said, wiping my cheeks and trying to control my breathing to help stop the tears. Neither of us wanted to get into the whole Chris thing with him. It was between us, and Chris, and we wanted to keep it that way.

"My daughter is crying, so it's not okay," Dad said, crossing his arms over his chest.

Before Ellison could respond, I spoke.

"I'm fine, Dad. Really. Don't worry."

"Are you sure?"

I nodded. My father looked uncertain, but he let it go.

"Your grandmother is feeling a little better—I'm sure she'd love to see you," he said to me. "You, too," he added, glancing at Ellison.

Ellison rolled his eyes. We both had a hard time believing she'd "love" to see me. I doubted that her stroke had given her a complete change of heart where I was concerned. Plus, how would Dad know what Grandma Esther wanted—she couldn't talk.

I was grateful that Ellison didn't say any of this. I didn't think I could handle another argument.

"We'll go see her later," he said.

Our father nodded and left the room.

Ellison turned to me. "Are you really okay?"

I sighed. "Not really."

"But you will be," he said, hugging me.

"How do you know?" I whispered.

"I just know, that's all."

He was a lot more confident than I was. I wasn't sure I'd

ever feel like my old self, and I couldn't remember what being "okay" felt like.

Later, Ellison went out and I sat in my room, wondering how I would fill the long days of summer vacation. I was too old for camp, too poor to travel. I wasn't sure when Ellison would leave for school, but I didn't think he'd want to hang around with his little sister all summer. And I wasn't sure I wanted to spend my days with him, either. Neither one of us was very happy, and we reminded each other of everything that was wrong in our lives.

I looked around at the drawings on my walls, at the evidence of the girl I once was. I'd loved bright colors, happy colors. My childhood wasn't perfect, but at that moment, I missed it terribly. I missed my innocence. I missed the Maren I'd been before my mother died, before Durham, before Chris.

Right then was the first time I'd considered calling him since the night Ellison caught us together. I just wanted to talk, to figure out where we could go from here. I knew that he would tell me what I already knew, that we couldn't be together, that what we'd done was wrong. I knew he'd tell me that it was a good thing that Ellison caught us because who knows how much worse things might have gotten. I knew that he would remind me that he was my uncle. But I needed to hear him say it. I needed to hear his voice.

Before I could change my mind, I went into my grandmother's room and picked up the receiver. The room smelled strongly of Grandma Esther's perfume and something else, a dusty old lady smell that lurked quietly underneath. I dialed the number, and as I waited for Chris to answer, I realized that I had never been in this room in the entire eight months we'd lived here. Its neatness was no surprise, and the upholstered chair matched the sofa downstairs. What I didn't expect were the walls, which were crowded with family photos that must have dated back to her own childhood. The framed images told the story of her life, from Grandma Esther as a little girl to my father's high school graduation to a picture of Chris that must have been taken recently. He had the earrings in his ears and he smiled sweetly into the camera. I couldn't stop staring at that photo.

"Hello?" he answered after many rings.

"Hi."

He exhaled into the phone. "Maren."

I couldn't tell from the tone of his voice whether he was happy to hear from me or not, and I suddenly wished I hadn't called. I didn't know what to say, or how to say it, and I was afraid of what he would say to me.

So I said nothing, listening to the sound of his breathing at the other end.

"Are you still there?" he asked after about ten seconds.

I nodded, then realized he couldn't see me. "Yes."

He cleared his throat nervously. "I've been wanting to call you."

"Why didn't you?"

He sighed. "I thought Ellison might kill me if he heard my voice."

The weight of what we had done hung heavily between us. I wanted to tell him how sorry I was, but I wasn't quite sure what part of things I regretted. Was I sorry that Chris and I had gotten so close? Was I sorry I had fallen in love with him? Or was I just sorry that we'd gotten caught?

"Mare, none of this changes how I feel. I love you."

I was taken aback. This wasn't what I had expected, and his words made my hands shake.

"What do you mean?"

"I mean I love you and I want to be with you. We can figure out a way, I know we can," he said, excitement creeping into his voice. "We can't let your brother stand in our way."

I sat down hard on the bed, wondering if he could hear my heart beating. He was willing to risk everything to be with me. He still loved me. And deep inside, I knew that I loved him, too.

And yet, I also knew that what he was saying was insane. I knew that there was no way for us to be together, and I knew my brother wasn't the problem. Even though I didn't want to admit it, I knew that our love was the worst kind—a love that had grown in secrecy and darkness, a love that had brought shame instead of happiness.

But I didn't know how to tell him this. I didn't know how to break up with someone—I had never done it before. I didn't know how to tell my uncle that we couldn't see each other anymore. So I hung up.

He called back, many times that night and over the next few days, but I wouldn't take his calls. I didn't know when I would see him, or how it would feel to be near him, or how I would get past this. But I realized that I had to figure it all out without him.

Ellison was quiet during the plane ride back to Chicago. Both he and I had talked enough to last us a long while, so we sat next to each other in first class, sharing a mimosa that Ellison had ordered even though the flight attendant looked at him suspiciously.

Champagne was called for, he said, because going back home was something to celebrate, even if the occasion wasn't exactly a happy one. Our mother's old television show, *The Daily Dish* was doing a tribute to Vanessa Emory on her birthday, June first. It was just two days away, and the show's producers had paid all the expenses to have Ellison and me back for live interviews. And my sixteenth birthday was the next day, so that was something else to celebrate.

Going home was a welcome relief from the way things had been in Durham lately.

In mid-May, we got the call from the producers. We were surprised to hear they were doing a special show on Mom; the story of her untimely death was old news, and television (especially gossip shows) aren't known for their loyalty or long memories. After the initial blanket coverage, it had seemed that people had quickly forgotten about Vanessa Emory.

And now we were on our way to Chicago, where we'd do a day of taped interviews, a live broadcast on the day of the show, then stay for a couple of days before flying back to Durham. Ellison and I had agreed that we wouldn't go back to see our old house in Evanston. Neither of us wanted to see some other family living in our home.

But we would go to our mother's gravesite. I had never been, since I skipped the funeral, and I looked forward to the chance to feel a little closer to my mother. These had been the hardest months of my life, and I'd missed my mother in more ways than I thought possible. I missed the day-to-day contact and the parental protection that even a mother who worked too much provided. I missed having a woman to talk to about love and sex and life. I missed having my mother there to help me become the person that I wanted to be. I missed feeling like a family.

There was about an hour until landing, so I dozed beside my brother, my head on his shoulder.

"Mare, are you awake?"

I yawned. "No."

"I'm going to Duke," he said.

I sat up, rubbing my eyes. "You're going to Berkeley."

He smiled. "I'm going to Duke."

I'd tried to get used to the idea of not having Ellison around. I'd even tried to come up with a way that I could go with him to California, a way that we could escape Durham together. But I'd never imagined that he might not go at all. All he'd ever wanted was to get away, to start a new life in a new city. And now he was giving that up. For me.

"I can't let you do that. Not just for me."

He shook his head. "I have to do it. For *us*. I called Duke to see if I could still accept their offer, so it's done."

"What about Dad?" I couldn't imagine them living together for one second longer than was necessary.

He rolled his eyes. "I'll live on campus—far enough away from him, but close enough to you."

I stared at him for a long time. "Are you sure?"

He nodded. "Now go back to sleep. Another hour, and we'll be landing."

I had never been to Brookline Cemetery, or any cemetery, for that matter, so I was surprised by the eerie feeling of all the tombstones rising from the ground at identical heights, the coldness of the elaborate mausoleums, the sickeningly sweet smell of flowers left by well-meaning relatives. Ellison put his arm around me and I know he felt me shivering.

We walked over the manicured lawn, and I couldn't help thinking about all the bodies underneath my feet. I knew I wasn't supposed to think of it that way, that this was supposed to be a place where you honor the dearly departed, but it just seemed morbid. That's why I didn't come to the funeral or the burial; I didn't want to watch as my mother was treated like a body, something to bury and hide away. I wanted to remember her full of life, not silent in death.

It had been months and months, but Ellison could still remember exactly where Mom lay without looking at the headstones surrounding hers and he led me there by the hand.

There it was. The headstone was made of a pinkish marble, slim and rounded at the edges. I knew my mother would have liked it—it was simple and elegant, but it stood out among the rest, as if she were making her mark in death the way she'd made her mark in life. There was no inscription, no Bible verse or proverb. It simply read: "Vanessa Garnett Emory. June 1, 1957–September 15, 1994." There was a stone bench right in front of the headstone, so we sat down. I couldn't take my eyes off the dates. So much had happened, and September seemed so long ago. And then again, the last words my mother had said to me still rang sharply in my head. I'd heard of people forgetting what their loved ones looked like after they were dead, as if memories were only good for so long before they started to disappear like smoke. They faded, faded, until the end product hardly resembled what you had once known. But it wasn't like that for me. My mother's face was still clear to me; it was almost as if I saw her yesterday, coming home from work with bags of take-out food and a smile on her face. I would have given anything to have things back the way they were.

"The headstone, it makes it seem so real," I whispered. "Sometimes, when I can't sleep, I pretend that everything that's happened since was just a bad dream. But here, looking at her grave . . . there's no pretending."

Ellison sighed. "I've done the same thing about a million times."

"Do you think it'll ever hurt less? Will I ever be able to think of Mom without crying?" I asked.

He leaned forward, putting his head in his hands. "God, I hope so, Mare."

I put my hand on his shoulder, rubbing until he sat back up. And then we sat quietly, not saying anything for the better part of an hour. We listened to the birds that dotted the nearby telephone lines and watched the fluffy white clouds roll in to mar the cerulean blue sky.

Eventually, Ellison reached into his pocket and pulled out a small, rectangular package wrapped in bright yellow paper, sealed with a green bow. He handed it to me.

"Happy birthday."

I smiled. "I didn't think you'd remember," I said, taking the package and looking at it. "What is it?"

He rolled his eyes with mock impatience. "Open it, dork."

I laughed as I tore the paper neatly and folded it before opening the box. I slowly pulled out a carved wooden picture frame that held a snap shot of the three of us, my mother, my brother and me. It was a photo that I hadn't seen in years, taken when Ellison was twelve years old and I was just ten.

"Do you remember where that was taken?" he asked.

I nodded, my fingers tracing the outlines of our bodies and the ripples of the lake behind us. "We went to Milwaukee that summer, just for the weekend. She took us to the lake on Saturday, and we splashed around all day. We asked an old man walking by if he'd take a picture of us."

He continued the story. "And even though we'd seen

Lake Michigan a hundred times, there was something spe-cial about that weekend."

I nodded, tears in my eyes. "No one was arguing. No one was sad. We were just . . . a family."

Now I was crying, and Ellison reached out to touch my cheek. "I didn't mean to make you cry, Mare. I just thought you'd want a picture of us all, maybe to put by your bed."

I wiped my eyes and looked up at him. "Thank you."

I looked away, over the cemetery into the skyline in the distance. I took a deep breath and glanced back at the grave. Turning, my brother kissed me on the forehead and took my hand as we walked away.

About the Author

Africa Fine has published a novel, *Katrina,* along with short stories in various magazines. She earned her master's degree from Florida Atlantic University and her bachelor's degree from Duke University. She teaches college English and lives in South Florida with her husband and son.